THE GUILTY ONES

DI Jackman & DS Evans Book 4

JOY ELLIS

JOFFE
BOOKS

Published in paperback 2020
by Joffe Books, London
www.joffebooks.com

ISBN 978-1-78931-277-5

Dedicated to Yvonne Bark. Thank you for keeping Jacqueline occupied on the badminton court while I write books! This one is for you, and in memory of your lovely mum, Margaret Bark.

PROLOGUE

The boy sat on his sister's bed. He gazed at her reflection.

'Dad will kill you if you go out after dark.' He wasn't being angry or reproving, he was simply full of concern.

'He won't know, will he?' In the mirror, his sister's eyes narrowed and her accusatory stare seemed to penetrate his very being.

His eyes were wide. 'I won't tell him, honest.'

'I don't trust you. You've snitched on me before.' She twisted her long blonde hair into a complicated plait and pinned it up. It made her look much older than she really was.

'I only told because he hit me. He hurt me, you know.' He felt tears well up at the memory and tried to blink them away. 'He really did.'

'You need to toughen up, little brother. You're a wimp. You'd do well to remember that I'm all you have. Father doesn't give a damn about either of us.'

It was true, and even if his sister was hateful to him, it was only with words. She never touched him, unlike his father. By now he was used to her sudden mood swings, though he didn't understand how she could go from caring to mean in a nanosecond. It was just how she was, he supposed.

'Where are you going?'

'That's my business, so keep your nose out of it.' She tapped the end of her nose. 'It's that boy again, isn't it?' She'd never mentioned his name, but he knew exactly who she was seeing. He'd followed her several times and once he'd seen her kiss him. Anyway, he knew by her behaviour that something was going on — sometimes she was almost nice to him. Lately, he'd been seeing another side to her, a much softer one.

'You're wasting your breath, little brother, and don't go prying because I'm not telling you anything.' She picked up her schoolbag, took out some books and pens and then produced a small pouch. Her makeup.

The boy leaned forward. He loved this bit. A few brightly coloured sticks and powders would soon turn this ordinary girl, the one that prepared his packed lunch every day, into an exotic stranger. It seemed like magic. Sometimes, when she was out, he would sneak the pouch from her bag, twist the lipstick open, and stare at it. Maybe it was because she kept it hidden — their dad had forbidden her to wear makeup. It made it seem extra-secretive, like the cloak-and-dagger stuff in the comics he read.

'Go back to your room. If he checks on you, pretend to be asleep, okay? I'll see you in the morning.'

She leaned towards him, and for one impossible moment he thought she was going to kiss him. Instead, she drew him close and said, 'You have to be brave. Just hold on a little longer. We are going to get you away from here.'

He went to speak, but the expression on her face had suddenly altered. She seemed to believe that he could only really understand something if it was couched in violent threats.

She gripped his shoulder hard and whispered in his ear, 'What is going to happen tonight is very important to me, little brother. I want it more than anything else in the whole world. One word to Father, just one word, in fact, if you *ever* tell *anyone* — this is what will happen . . .'

She dropped her voice to a murmur, but her message was crystal clear. She said, 'Swear! Swear you'll never tell.'

He swallowed hard, swore, and ran from the room, this time allowing the tears to cascade down his cheeks.

Huddled in his bed, he wondered why she was so horrible to him. She didn't have to threaten him. If only she could see! He understood love just as much as anyone else.

* * *

He couldn't sleep. Her words haunted him. She would do what she said, he had no doubt of that. And what did she mean by "we" will get you away from here? He curled up under the covers and shivered with fear at what she had threatened. He heard a click — the window closing. He slipped out of his bed and without turning on the light, tiptoed to where the curtains were slightly parted.

He peered through the gap. His sister, carrying a pair of high heels and a sparkly handbag, crept silently across the flat roof of the garden room and out of sight.

He stood motionless, still considering her terrible threats. Then the urge to know became too much for him. He grabbed his jeans and a zip-up top and pulled them on over his pyjamas. He slipped his feet into his trainers, took a deep breath and followed her out.

CHAPTER ONE

DS Marie Evans dismounted from her gleaming new Suzuki Hayabusa. DI Rowan Jackman's parking space was empty. She thought for a moment, but couldn't recall him saying he would be away from work today.

Hoping that he wasn't unwell, she pulled off her helmet and marched up to the entrance of Saltern-le-Fen police station.

The desk sergeant was shuffling papers.

'Morning, Sarge,' she called out to him. 'No DI Jackman this morning?'

'Haven't seen him, but the super was around earlier, and she looked pretty bothered about something.'

Marie began to worry. Superintendent Ruth Crooke was rarely seen on the shop floor at this early hour. Sensing that something serious had happened, Marie hurried up to the CID room.

She was the first one in, so there was no one to ask. But moments after she got to her desk, she saw the superintendent's stick-thin frame approaching her, tight-lipped and frowning.

'Ma'am? Is something wrong?' Marie asked.

Ruth Crooke nodded and beckoned for Marie to follow her.

Inside her office, with the door firmly closed, Ruth gestured to a chair and Marie sat down, wondering what on earth was going on.

'I heard from Rowan very early this morning. He has a family emergency to attend to. Would you be able to cover the cases he was dealing with for a while?'

Marie thought Ruth looked more than mildly concerned about this "family emergency."

Desperate to know what had happened, she said, 'Of course, ma'am.'

'He said that he would contact you himself later today.'

'Do you know what's happened?' Marie knew that Jackman's mother was only in her early sixties and as far as she knew, was a fit, healthy woman who rode several times a day and had her own stables. A riding accident, maybe? She also knew that Jackman had one married brother with two young sons, and hoped that the children were not involved in whatever was keeping Jackman away.

There was a moment of silence, then Ruth leaned forward and whispered, 'Rowan's sister-in-law has disappeared. She left for work yesterday morning and hasn't been seen since.'

Marie gasped. 'Oh Lord!'

'She didn't come home last night, and her business said that she hadn't shown up for work. Rowan's brother is understandably distraught, so Rowan is doing what he can to help.'

'And the children?'

'He says that his mother has them at the moment. They are not aware of the problem. They just think they are being allowed a couple of days' fun at Granny's. It's a beautiful house with a livery stable attached, and understandably the boys love it.' Ruth gave a little shrug. 'And that is all I know, I'm afraid.'

Marie's brain went into overdrive trying to recall everything she knew about Jackman's family. She realised that she knew precious little. Jackman was a very private man, and although she counted him as a dear friend, as well as her boss, he rarely discussed his personal life. 'I'll take care of the workload here, ma'am. We're pretty well up to date with the drugs case, and I'm au fait with the fraud job that we are working on with DI Pete Lawrence, so no problems there.'

'Good, just keep the ship on a steady course, and let's pray that there is some kind of domestic situation that the sister-in-law couldn't deal with, and she's taken off for a few days to sort herself out.'

'Leaving her kids?'

Ruth pulled a face. 'We've seen worse when women feel like they can't cope anymore.'

Marie nodded. That was true, but she didn't believe it was the case this time. One thing she did remember Jackman saying was that he sometimes envied his brother's wonderful family life with his loving wife and two beautiful sons. Jackman's mother was always trying to marry him off. She kept saying that he should be more like his brother — settle down and enjoy a family of his own.

Ruth looked at a towering pile of paperwork on her desk. 'I'd better get on. But let me know if you need any assistance with your cases, and also if you hear from Rowan.' She paused and drew in a long breath. 'He sounded wrung out, Marie. I got the feeling that his brother is practically out of it, and no good to man nor beast. Rowan seems to be trying to hold everything together.'

'I'll do anything I can to help.' Marie meant it. And right now, she just wanted to talk to him.

* * *

With all the additional work, the day had flown by. Marie had decided not to give the rest of the team any details until after she had spoken to Jackman. For now they just knew it was a family matter, and had all pitched in to keep on top of the workload. Only PC Gary Pritchard seemed to realise that it was something rather more serious. As the day drew to a close, he took Marie aside and asked if there was anything he could help with. Before she could answer, her phone rang.

'Jackman?' She gestured to Gary to sit and wait, and listened intently to what her boss was saying.

He asked if she could possibly drive over and meet him at his brother's house when she finished work. His tone was stilted. 'Things are pretty bad here, Marie.'

'No word of her?'

There was a telling silence. Then finally he said, 'I can't explain on the phone. Please come. It's Rainham Lodge, Water Lane, Amberly Fen. It's about a mile and a half down the long lane, over a narrow bridge on the left-hand side.'

'I'll be there within the hour.'

'Thank you, Marie.' The line went dead.

Gary was staring at her. 'It sounds bad.'

'It is. And I suspect it's even worse than I feared. I didn't like Jackman's tone one bit.'

'Can you tell me anything? You know that it will go no further.'

Marie nodded. 'Let's use his office and I'll fill you in, although I imagine I'll be able to explain better after I've spoken to him.'

She told Gary what she knew.

He shook his head. 'He's a dark horse, our DI. He hardly ever speaks about his family, does he? Are both parents still alive?'

'Yes. I get the impression his father is wrapped up in business from morning till night, and Jackman's closer to his mother. And, of course, he shares her love of horses.'

'Now horses are something he does talk about. He told me they're his first priority when he's finished with the force.' Gary smiled.

'He's got the outdoor space at the mill where he lives, so I'm sure they will be.' Marie sighed. 'I don't like to hear him so anxious. It's just not Jackman.'

'Ring me tonight, when you get home. Doesn't matter what time. Just keep me updated, and if you need a hand with anything at all, just ask. I like the DI very much, he's been good to me, and I'd like to help if I can.'

Marie smiled at Gary. 'I will, I promise. Now I really need to go.'

Fifteen minutes later, Marie was driving past the long flat stretches of fen farmland, wondering what she was going to find at Rainham Lodge.

CHAPTER TWO

Marie rode across the bridge over a deep, reed-lined watercourse and into a wide parking area. Alongside Jackman's Land Rover were three other vehicles. Two were marked police cars, the other a BMW.

The house stood on its own, the nearest neighbour was about a quarter of a mile down the lane. Rainham Lodge was a solid looking, three-storey Georgian former farmhouse, and it reminded Marie of how different her background was to Jackman's. The Jackman family came from money, and clearly the eldest son was pretty well-heeled.

She looked around. Although it was an expensive residence, it also looked welcoming. Autumn was almost upon them, yet bright flowers still cascaded out of hanging baskets and troughs, and children's bikes leaned haphazardly against a wall. It looked lived in, and well loved.

'This is no domestic,' she whispered to herself. And if it wasn't, that left some very dark options.

Jackman appeared in the open doorway. 'Marie! Thank you so much for coming.'

She hurried over to him and grasped his arm. 'Are you alright?'

For a moment, she thought he was going to cry. Then he leaned forward and gave her a quick hug. 'I'm not sure, Marie. Frankly, I don't think I am. This is just horrible.' He looked back over his shoulder. 'James is with a family liaison officer at the moment, and there are several other people with them. Let's go around to the garden, so I can tell you what's happened in private.'

At the back of the property was a wide expanse of lawn, and at the bottom, a summerhouse.

Jackman held open the door and they went inside.

Inside, more evidence of a happy family life. A well-used croquet set, cricket stumps and bats, old-fashioned deck-chairs with names printed on the backs, piles of board games and in one corner, an artist's easel with wooden boxes beside it that probably contained paints and brushes.

The place smelled of wood, and made Marie feel quite nostalgic. Her parents didn't have the money that Jackman's did. They were divorced, but that meant she'd had two homes, one in Wales with her mother, and one here in Lincolnshire with Dad, and both were filled with love.

Jackman sank into one of the larger deckchairs and Marie followed suit. For a while they just sat in silence. Jackman was clearly unsure how or where to begin.

'Sarah is dead,' he said.

The words hung in the air.

'Dead?'

Jackman let out a painful sigh. 'She drowned herself.'

'What?'

'I know.' He lifted his hands, palms up. 'I said it was horrible, didn't I?'

'But I thought they were so happy.'

'They *were* so happy. She loved James and she adored the boys.' He swallowed. 'It doesn't make sense. She wouldn't leave them.'

Marie frowned. 'They are sure it was suicide? Not an accident or even foul play?'

Jackman shook his head. 'Suicide. Indisputably.'

10

He rubbed at his eyes. Marie thought she had never seen the immaculate Jackman look so dishevelled. He had obviously been up all night.

'Let me explain it — well, as much as I have gleaned from my wreck of a brother and the local police officers. Yesterday morning, Sarah made breakfast for everyone, made sure that the boys were washed and dressed, then got ready for work.'

'Where did she work?' asked Marie.

'Just outside Lincoln, although her work as a rep took her to various locations. She job-shared with another woman, to give her more time with the boys. That day it should've been Lincoln. But she never arrived. She left her car in a shopping precinct car park in Greenborough and took a train to Peterborough, and then on to London. She was caught on CCTV coming out of King's Cross Station.'

'Did she have some kind of appointment that she didn't want anyone to know about?' Marie was thinking of hospitals.

'No, she was caught several times en route to East London, then nothing, until a short time ago.'

'They found her?'

Jackman nodded. 'I'm going to have to identify her. James is in no fit state, and both of Sarah's parents are dead.'

'Would you like me to go with you?' Marie asked immediately.

'Bless you, but a car is coming for me in about an hour. I'll be okay — hell, we've done enough of them, haven't we?'

'But not your own family, Jackman.' She felt a tug of grief, suddenly reminded of her husband's tragic death.

'Honestly, I'll be okay. In fact, I know it sounds awful, but I need to get away from my brother for a while. His anguish is tearing me apart. At least I'll be doing something practical, something that I *can* do, and it will take the burden off James.'

'Those poor boys,' whispered Marie.

'I know. Mother is being amazing, and Dad is motoring home from some business deal in Belgium, but I have no idea what's going to happen in the long term.'

'How old are your nephews?'

'Ryan is eight, and Miles is seven. They are both sharp as tacks, so it won't be long before they catch on that something has happened.'

Marie felt overwhelmed by the sadness of the situation. She could imagine the terrible aftershocks. 'Jackman? How come they are so sure it was deliberate?'

'More CCTV. There was a camera at the rear entrance to a club down by the river.' He bit his lip. 'She was all alone, Marie, and she jumped. It was suicide, no question.'

Marie didn't agree. She had many questions. The biggest one was *why?*

CHAPTER THREE

Instead of going straight home, Marie drove across her village to the small bungalow where Gary Pritchard now lived.

She parked her bike next to his Nissan Juke, and pulled off her helmet.

By the time she turned around, Gary was at the door. 'Come on in. I've already eaten, but I've saved you something.' He left her to make her own way in. From the kitchen she smelled the delicious aroma of beef stew and herb dumplings and immediately her spirits lifted. 'Oh yes! Just what I need right now.'

She took off her leather jacket and hung it in the hall, then hurried through to where Gary was placing a bowl of food on the table. 'I guessed you wouldn't have eaten,' he said.

'My hero. I'm starving.'

'You dig in, I'm thinking, by the look of you that you've had a harrowing time.'

'Not nearly as harrowing as Jackman. I've never seen him so upset.'

While she ate, Marie told him what had happened. 'He's asked me to tell the team first thing tomorrow. He wants them to know before it hits the media.'

'And he's identifying her tonight?'

'Yes, the car came for him just as I was leaving. It's too weird for words. What on earth made her do such a thing?'

'You know what they say, you never know what goes on behind closed doors. People are very good at putting on an act. Maybe they had hidden problems and the poor woman couldn't see a way out.'

'You didn't see that house, Gary. Everywhere screamed Happy Families, from the pictures and notes stuck on the fridge to the framed photos in the lounge, and you could tell they must have almost lived in the family room, it was full of kids' and adults' things all jumbled up together. It was so . . . so cheerful. I don't think you can easily fake that.'

'What if she was ill, like terminally ill?'

'I wondered that.' Marie stared thoughtfully at her plate. 'Maybe the inquest will tell. Oh, and Jackman has requested that Professor Rory Wilkinson carries out the PM in person.'

'I'm not surprised. That man doesn't miss a thing, no matter how obscure.'

Gary sat back and crossed his arms. 'There is another explanation, although it seems a bit unlikely. What about a serious mental health issue? Although, I'd have thought Jackman would have known about that.'

Marie screwed up her face. 'If that were the case, I don't think her husband would be quite so totally shocked and grief-stricken.'

'Maybe we'll never know. Although for the family's sake, I hope they get some answers.' He pointed to Marie's empty bowl. 'Want some more?'

'Phew, no thanks, Gary. That was wonderful, and very thoughtful.' She glanced at her watch. 'I'd better make a move.'

'You go careful on that great brute of a motorbike.'

'Harvey? He's not a brute. He's a pussycat.'

'You call your bike *Harvey*?'

'So?'

Gary laughed again. 'Nothing. It just looks more like Satan or Godzilla to me.'

'Nonsense. That bike purrs like a kitten. I bet I leave here and don't disturb a single neighbour.'

'I'd be grateful for that. Most of the guys around here are in bed by half eight.'

She stood up and pushed her chair under the table. 'Thanks for the supper, Gary. I do appreciate it. See you at work tomorrow.'

'Bright and early. And if you speak to the boss, give him my best, won't you?'

Marie nodded. 'Of course I will.'

* * *

Back home, her house seemed empty, and even though she put the lights on it still felt dark, like her mood. Her cheerfulness in Gary's company had evaporated, and she was left with a dreadful sadness at how suddenly lives can turn around, devastated by a single act.

Jackman rang at eleven p.m. He sounded exhausted and said how relieved he was that the business of identifying Sarah's body was now over.

'I'm staying with James again tonight. We have to go to Mother's first thing in the morning and tell the children. We cannot risk them seeing or hearing something before we've had a chance to talk to them.'

'Have you got a professional going along too?' Marie knew the value of specialist help in cases involving the traumatic death of a parent.

'Laura Archer has offered to go with us.'

Laura was the force psychologist, and after a particularly difficult case concerning an officer who had been close to Marie, they had all become friends. 'That's really good, she's brilliant. How is your brother?'

'The doc's given him something to help him sleep, although I doubt it will work. I would have never believed that he would react like this. He's a strong, direct man, stoic and self-assured, but now . . .'

'The shock must be horrific for him. I know when I witnessed Bill die, it was unimaginable. You are completely consumed by the simple awfulness of what's happened. You just cannot function properly.'

Jackman gave a little groan. 'I'm so sorry. I shouldn't lay all this on you, it's not fair.'

'Sod that, Jackman! I'm your friend. You lay all you like on me, you know what a tough old dragon I am. I can simply empathise, that's all.'

'Tough, yes. Old and dragon do *not* apply.'

There was a hint of the old Jackman in those words, and it gave her heart.

'That's better.' She told him she had talked to Gary and that he had sent his best. 'The team are keeping everything ticking over until you get back, so no worries there. They will appreciate you putting them fully in the picture.'

'No other way, they are my friends as well as my work colleagues.'

'Jackman, you sound out on your feet. Go get some rest, if you can, and keep me up to date with how it goes tomorrow.'

* * *

At the same time, in a different part of the county, a family and a few close friends were gathered together in the sitting room of a small farm cottage.

Dale, who had guided the family since their father's death, had just returned from the hospital. 'They have given Mum three months to live.'

The words caused a stirring of murmured sighs and groans.

'And I think we've finally come to a watershed moment.' His tone was serious and everyone looked at him in silence. 'We need to decide. Do we fight on and hopefully bring her some kind of justice before she dies, or do we call it a day and allow her last days to be peaceful, with no more talk of retribution?'

'How can we give up now? After all these years of trying!' Liam exclaimed. 'This family is not, and never has been, about conceding defeat.'

'You said it yourself though, all these years of trying, and where has it got us? Our dad is dead, our mum not long for this world, and all we've achieved is more heartbreak. I think it's time to let go.' Yvette, the younger of the two women, was near to tears.

'We can't give up on Brendan!' Liam spat back.

'*He* gave up, didn't he?' said Kenny sadly.

'Because he was a good-looking young lad incarcerated in a prison full of psychopaths! God knows what happened to him! You'd have given up too! But *we* don't have to do the same.'

'Liam! Brendan is dead! What are we fighting for? Justice for our brother? Or to make you feel better?' Susie echoed her sister's sentiments. 'Let's make Mum's last days happy. Let's treat her to the things she loves, spoil her rotten and enjoy our time with her.'

The argument went on for over an hour, then someone asked Dale why he was so quiet.

'Because I've been waiting for one of you to make the most obvious statement, but as yet I'm still waiting.' He threw them a look of sadness, tinged with contempt. 'I know I asked the question, but the answer should have been, "We'll do whatever our mother wants."'

For a while there was silence. Then Yvette ventured, 'So has she told you?'

'She has. Although she doesn't want us to do anything that we are not happy about, I expect this family to act as one in respecting her wishes. Is that clear?'

There were murmurs of assent.

'She wants justice for Brendan. She wants us to fight on, even after she dies. She cannot bear to think of her beautiful boy in his grave with the label "murderer" hanging over his head. She wants a posthumous pardon and says we must never rest until that happens.'

No one spoke, then Liam jumped up and punched the air. 'Justice for Brendan! Let's make our mother proud!'

CHAPTER FOUR

It was late afternoon when Marie left DI Pete Lawrence's office after an hour-long discussion about the fraud case they were working on. As she walked back to the CID room, she noticed that Jackman's door was ajar. She frowned and went to check who was inside.

'Jackman? What on earth are you doing here?' Marie asked.

Her boss was leaning forward, peering at his computer screen, the printer disgorging reams of paper. 'Oh, hi, Marie.' He gave her a weak grin. 'I know, I'm not supposed to be here, but I needed a few minutes away from all the trauma. My office was the only place I could think of where I could gather my thoughts in peace.'

'And gather a whole lot of other stuff too,' she said, pointing at the growing mountain of paper.

'Just something that's bothering me.'

Marie thought he looked much better than the night before, but he still had that awful haunted look in his eyes. She wasn't sure how to ask, so she simply said, 'How did it go with the boys?'

'As bad as you'd imagine, I guess. Probably the worst thing I've ever had to do. You have to be so careful how you explain the concept of death. I'm so glad that Laura was there to guide us. I'm sure James and I would have made a terrible mess of it between us.'

'I doubt that very much. I've seen you talking to children. You have a very gentle manner, and you don't talk down to them either.'

'Not too sure about that.' He puffed out his cheeks and exhaled. 'The worst is yet to come. Nothing has sunk in yet. They seemed to accept it rather too well. When we'd finished they asked if they could go back to the horses. Laura said they grieve in a more sporadic way than adults, sad one moment, then excited and happy the next. It's quite disturbing.'

'So where is James now?' Marie asked.

'He's staying at Mother's tonight, with Ryan and Miles. Father is home as well. We agreed it's best for the children to have adults around them all the time in case they need to talk or ask questions.' He ran a hand through his hair. 'I'm going back too, just for this evening. Laura has given me a whole heap of things to watch out for, and told me ways of answering their questions so that they don't blame themselves for what's happened.'

'Why would they do that?'

'Children often do, apparently. They take some insignificant thing that they've done wrong, and decide that's the reason their mummy died, ergo, it's their fault.'

Marie's heart went out to Jackman and his family, yet lurking in the background was the suspicion that something was terribly wrong about this carefully planned suicide. But now wasn't the time to discuss her fears. 'You know where I am if you need me. Day or night. Just don't take on more than you can handle, and do use the support that is offered to you.'

'Yes, Mother.' He threw her a rueful smile. 'Of course I will. The whole family needs to talk about how we manage in the short term. It's too soon for future plans, but we need to do what is best for the boys, and get James back down to planet earth. We're meeting tonight.'

'Good luck. I'll be thinking of you.' She stared at the pile of paper. 'What *is* all that?'

'I'm not sure.' He stared hard at her. 'It could simply be because I'm a detective, but I don't like the feel of this at all. In fact, it stinks.'

Marie nodded. 'Then we need to talk, just as soon as you've sorted out your family. Because I feel exactly the same.'

A look of relief spread over Jackman's face. 'Thank heavens for that! At least I know I'm not being paranoid.'

'That remains to be seen. I'm a detective too, don't forget, and we both distrust every situation until we've seen the evidence, so let's not make assumptions. Maybe we're *both* being paranoid.'

Jackman gathered up the printouts and pushed them into a folder. 'Bedtime reading.'

'About Sarah?'

He nodded. 'And suicide. If you had known her, Marie, you'd understand why I believe this suicide is not what it seems. It can't be.'

Marie needed no explanation. 'Okay, then we'd better do what we do best, and find the truth.'

'I'll see you sometime tomorrow, and thanks again, Marie. It's good to know we are on the same wavelength.'

She smiled. 'Aren't we always?'

* * *

That night, dinner was an acutely painful affair. The children were uncharacteristically badly behaved, but none of the adults had the heart to tell them off. Apart from a few desultory words, James hardly seemed to notice them, and it was almost impossible to drag more than half a sentence from him about anything.

Jackman felt he should try to keep the whole thing afloat, but realising he was failing miserably, whispered in his mother's ear that maybe they should allow the boys to go up to their room and watch a film before bed.

She readily agreed and ushered the two boys upstairs.

'I don't know what to say.' Jackman's father took a long swallow from his wine glass. 'It's not their fault, those poor little children are a mess.'

As is their dad, thought Jackman. He caught his father's eye and nodded towards James.

The older man looked helplessly back at him, and Jackman knew that James wasn't the only one out of his depth.

'Uh, come on, son. Why not talk to us? We are all here for you, you know,' their father awkwardly waded in.

James responded with a silent shrug. 'I don't understand. I just don't understand. How could she? And why? In heaven's name, why?'

Jackman had never seen his big brother so helpless. It was more than shock and disbelief; it was as if James' whole world had tilted on its axis and sent him into freefall.

'We don't know why she did it, James.' Jackman placed his hand on his brother's arm, 'But I'll do everything in my power to find out. I promise you that.'

James looked up, his eyes full of tears. 'The worst thing is that I know that no matter what I do, I'll never see her again.'

Their father stood up and stiffly went over to his son. He cradled James to his chest like a child. He didn't speak, he clearly had no words, but instead he made a soothing noise.

Jackman couldn't remember their Dad ever cuddling him, not even as a toddler.

After a while, James' sobs died down to a soft snuffle, and their mother returned and sank back down into her chair.

'I've got them ready for bed and they're watching a cartoon, but I don't think they'll stay awake too long. They're so tired.' She looked at James, and then up to her husband. 'I've lit the fire in your study, darling. Why don't you take James there, give him a little brandy and have a chat? Rowan and I will clear these things away.'

Jackman nodded in agreement, then watched as his zombie of a brother followed his father from the room.

It didn't take long to clear the table and stack the dishwasher, then after tidying up the dining room and checking that the boys were finally asleep, he and his mum went into the kitchen. They both looked and felt exhausted after such a traumatic evening trying to understand the inexplicable.

Harriet Jackman poured each of them some more red wine and shook her head. 'This is a living nightmare.'

His mother looked like she'd aged ten years overnight. She was a strong, resilient woman, but this was enough to knock anyone sideways. 'I think James is worrying me even more than the boys.'

His mother nodded. 'And I always thought *you* were the sensitive one.' She reached across the table and touched his hand. 'Actually, I still believe that's true. James is completely out of his depth. He has no idea how to deal with what's happened to him.'

'Deep emotional issues were never his strong point. Bit like Dad. Although I have to admit he's doing his best for James; he even hugged him while you were up with the boys.' Jackman held his mother's hand for a moment. 'Even so, I get the feeling that the basic, common-sense decisions regarding this family are going to have to be handled by us, don't you?'

His mother released her hand and picked up her glass. 'Oh yes. But it's always been that way, hasn't it? Where feelings are concerned, your father is about as much use as a lead parachute!' She snorted. 'Give him a balance sheet, or ask him to predict the stock market, and he's your man, but as for domestic problems, well . . .' She shook her head.

'So, short term? How do we tackle this?'

'I've made a list of people to contact — about Sarah's death, I mean, but then there are the children to think about. I'll ring their school tomorrow and explain what's happened. I think it's important not to disrupt their normal schedules too much.'

Jackman nodded. 'I agree. They need normality, or as much as we can emulate, and the school teachers will know the best way to handle this.' He took a gulp of wine. 'But we have to keep them on an even keel at home as well. We need James on side for that, and I'm not sure it's going to happen.'

His mother leaned forward. 'Rowan? I've been thinking. Last week I met Ella Jarvis in the supermarket car park. She told me she's given up her job.'

Jackman nodded. 'I heard about that. It was very sad.'

Ella had been Ryan and Miles's nanny when they were small. After she left the family, she'd trained as a scene-of-crime officer. A few months ago she had been called out to a tragic case of child abuse, and it had proved too much for her. That same day she handed in her notice.

'She was very close to Sarah. They kept in touch regularly, I know. The boys adored her.'

Jackman saw at once where this was going. 'Do you think she would help?'

'Can you think of anyone better? That would give them back just a tiny bit of their old life. What do you think?'

He smiled. 'Mum, you're a genius.' He glanced at his watch. Nine o'clock. 'Do you have her number?'

'It's probably still in my address book.' She pushed back her chair, went into the sitting room and a minute later called back, 'Got it!'

After the initial shock of hearing about Sarah's death, Ella Jarvis wasted no time on considering Harriet's request. She simply said, 'Yes, of course I'll help. I have no ties here at present, and frankly I'd have been hurt if you'd asked anyone else. I'll come to you tomorrow morning and we'll decide exactly what you want me to do.'

Harriet replaced the receiver and let out a long sigh of relief. 'She'll do it.'

Jackman smiled. 'Stage one, complete. And it might help Ella too. I heard on the grapevine that she's been at rock bottom. She was a damned good crime scene officer, and I know Rory misses her. She was a particularly good photographer and he valued the work she did on difficult cases.' Jackman also considered that it would be good to have

Ella on hand because, as his mother had said, she knew Sarah very well. Maybe she could shed some light on his sister-in-law's tragic death.

'You look pensive, son.'

'Mum? Did Sarah seem okay to you over the last few weeks? Was she,' he shrugged, 'herself?'

His mother made a huffing noise. 'Now you come to mention it, I'm not sure that she was.' She rubbed her hands together. 'She brought the boys over for a riding lesson a week or so ago, and I thought she looked anxious. She denied it when I asked, but she looked drawn and preoccupied.' She stared at him. 'It was bad enough to worry me, but she said that she just felt a bit under the weather, that was all.'

'People don't just end their lives without a very good reason, Mum, and being a bit under the weather certainly doesn't qualify. I haven't seen a single thing in Sarah's life that would lead her to do such a devastating thing — to herself, to James, or to her darling children. Do you think she was ill?'

'Not physically, no.' His mother was quite emphatic. 'She said that she'd recently had a health MOT and she was fighting fit. Mentally? Of course I'm no expert, but she had times when she was,' Harriet frowned, 'overly concerned by things, especially when they involved Miles and Ryan. All mothers are protective, or they should be, but sometimes I thought there was an underlying, and slightly out-of-proportion, anxiety about the children's wellbeing.'

'You never said anything.'

'It wasn't something I could explain really, and I thought that maybe I was just being over sensitive. But now this has happened, I keep thinking there were other things that I should have paid more attention to.'

'We're all experts after the event, Mum. I don't think anyone would have been able to predict what happened.' He pulled his mother's notepad towards him and read through the list. 'You've been very thorough.'

'I know there's not a lot we can do until we have the death certificate, but I need to make plans. At least there is the Tell Us Once system in place now, and that makes notifying official bodies much easier.' She took another sip of wine. 'Poor James. Sarah was his lifeline to the real world. He's so like your father, I'm not sure how he'll cope.'

'That's where Ella could be a blessing. She'll make sure the kids have their school kit washed and their lunches paid for.' He tilted his head to one side. 'Talking about people being alike, she's very much like Sarah, isn't she? Not in looks, but in character and the way she behaves.'

'Could have been sisters. I always thought that. And without Ella, Sarah would have struggled after Miles was born.' His mother bit her lip and looked at him anxiously. 'Do you think it's connected? The postnatal depression?'

'I doubt it, Mum. She made a full recovery, and it's a common problem. I don't spend a lot of time with them as a family, although I love taking the boys out for treats every now and again, but I never witnessed anything to suggest she was depressed.'

Harriet emptied her glass. 'I suppose going over and over all this is quite natural, but it isn't getting us anywhere, is it?'

'We need to talk it out.'

She sighed. 'And James most of all.'

Jackman knew she was right. James existed in parallel universes. In one, he revelled in his business ventures and was totally in command, and in the other, with his family, Sarah ruled. Even though she worked part time, she had run the home, organised the children. She planned their holidays, found great days out, parties and surprises. James had just been willingly swept along, almost like a third child, enjoying every minute. Now he had no navigator. His children needed him, but Jackman had a feeling that James would not, or could not, be there for them.

'Rowan?' His mother was smiling at him rather sadly. 'I do appreciate you helping out right now, but don't let your work suffer, will you? I know what it means to you.'

'Family comes first,' he said quickly.

'I know, but I just wanted you to know that although your father never quite understood why you wanted to be a policeman, I did. And I know why you are happy as you are, not treading on people to get up the ladder.'

'Do you really know why I wanted to be a policeman, Mum?'

'Of course, I do. I'm your mother!'

Jackman looked at her with undisguised surprise. 'I never said anything, did I?'

'You didn't have to.' She sat back. 'Correct me if I'm wrong. It was winter and you must have been, oh, eight or nine, and you were helping out in the stables. Something happened and you heard shouting coming from the exercise barn. Something had spooked one of the bigger horses and he had lashed out, catching one of the grooms and knocking her unconscious. Before you could raise the alarm you saw a man come out of nowhere, and leap in front of the horse before it could trample the girl. Somehow he managed to calm the beast, and then carry the groom to safety. He knew exactly what to do to help her until the ambulance arrived.' Harriet grinned at him. 'Right so far?'

Jackman nodded. 'I found out later he was an off-duty policeman waiting to collect his daughter who was one of your stable hands. He was so brave, and so in control. And that's what I wanted to do, to help people. After that, I never wanted to be anything else.'

'You changed that day, boy. You had a different appreciation for people and for how they behaved.'

'Sad that even if I made chief constable, Dad would probably only be mildly accepting.' He grinned ruefully at her. 'As a mere DI, I'm a terrible disappointment.'

'Actually, he's very proud of what you do. Just don't ask him to admit it. If he did, he'd have nothing to complain about.'

'What, you mean all that waste of a university education? No drive to attain that gold braid? No incentive to get wealthy? And so on and so on.'

26

'That's the kind of thing.' Her smile faded. 'Rowan, please find out what happened to Sarah! You are an excellent detective, the best. So please get us some answers.'

'Actually, Mum, that's exactly what I intend to do. I *know* something isn't right, so yes, I'll get you answers, even if they aren't what we want to hear. I'll find the truth.'

CHAPTER FIVE

DC Robbie Melton hurried across to Marie's desk. 'Morning, Sarge. I've just seen the desk sergeant on my way in, and he says there's a suspicious death down near the river. He's asked for a CID presence. Can we attend?'

'Great! Just what we need when the boss is out of action.' Marie stood up. 'Any more info than that?'

Robbie shook his head. 'Sorry, Sarge, not much. He said that there's this old guy who's dead, but although it looks like suicide, he's not convinced.'

The mention of another suicide made Marie stiffen. 'Sure, go tell him we're on our way. And grab Max if he's free. Three heads might be better than two. If Sergeant Conway is feeling iffy over this, ten-to-one he has good reason. I'll go and get the keys to a pool car. See you in the parking area.'

He nodded and trotted over to the door. Robbie was the latest addition to the CID team. He hadn't been with them for long, but already fitted in well.

As Marie made her way downstairs, she wondered what had roused the sergeant's suspicions. The sad reality was that it wasn't uncommon to find vagrants and street people dead.

* * *

As soon as they arrived at the scene, they pulled on all-in-one overalls and shoe-protectors and went to examine the body.

A single uniformed police officer stood by the blue-and-white cordoning, and another kept watch a few feet away.

Without contaminating anything, Marie got as close as she dared and stood silently, appraising the scene.

The man had a craggy face and stubble. He was dressed in torn, dirty clothes and lay curled up in a pool of blood. His body was close to the edge of a rather overgrown and rarely used footpath that ran along the margin of the river. Close to his right hand lay a bloody Stanley knife, and on closer inspection Marie could see that the blood had come from a deep wound in his left wrist. It certainly appeared to be a suicide, but she was beginning to understand the uniformed officer's concerns.

'The doc is on his way, ma'am,' said PC Kevin Stoner. 'I haven't requested any forensics yet. I thought we should wait for your opinion.'

'We're definitely going to need them, Kev.'

'You have the same reservations as the sarge?'

'Probably.' She stared at the body. 'How many street deaths have you seen where the victim slit their wrists?'

'None, ma'am. They usually drink themselves into the grave with dodgy alcohol, or else they overdose, starve, get mugged, or get hypothermia.'

'Mmm.' She turned to Max and Robbie. 'Your thoughts?'

'His hands are dirty, Sarge, but not ingrained with filth like most rough sleepers,' Robbie observed. 'And he's got neatly trimmed fingernails.'

'This bloke is no homeless tramp,' Max asserted.

'Explain.'

'His hair, Sarge. Sure it's dirty, like the rest of him, but you can't fake an expensive haircut.'

Marie looked closer. 'How do you know that?'

Max threw her a mocking look. One of the coolest and smartest young detectives in Saltern, he could easily have passed for a GQ model. 'This man uses a top stylist, trust

29

me on that one. It's been roughed up a bit, but the cut is awesome, for an old geezer.'

'Beautifully put, Max.' Marie tried not to smile. 'But I agree. We need a pathologist, and a SOCO or two.'

'I'll arrange that.' Robbie already had his phone out.

She turned to PC Stoner. 'Kevin? I want either a tent or some tarpaulins erected, and get this area sealed off. This is now a crime scene, so if you would establish a security log?'

Kevin nodded and started talking into his radio.

'Are we looking at murder, Sarge?' Robbie and Max stared down at the unfortunate man.

'To be honest, guys, I have no idea what we are looking at, but it certainly isn't a vagrant with a death wish.'

* * *

Marie arrived back in the CID office to hear her phone ringing.

'Marie, I need your help. If I come over now, can you spare an hour?' Jackman's voice was urgent.

She explained what had just occurred, then added, 'But I've already got uniform out talking to locals and street people, and Charlie and Rosie are tracking down CCTV cameras in the area, so frankly I've done all I can until the forensic guys have something for us. Come as soon as you like.'

When Jackman walked in, the first thing Marie noticed was that his air of shocked numbness had gone. His step was brisk and his expression animated. He pointed to his office, and after checking that the team was fully occupied, she followed him in.

Jackman's eyes glittered. He threw himself into his chair, and said, 'We were right.'

Marie sat opposite him. 'You've found something?'

'I went to Rainham Lodge early this morning to get some things for the boys, and I found her work bag pushed right into the back of Ryan's wardrobe. She used that bag for work every day, but she left it behind on the day she disappeared.'

Marie frowned. 'And that tells us what?'

'Her laptop wasn't in it. Apparently she used it as an appointments diary and a memo pad, and kept a ton of work stuff on it. It was practically glued to her, and she always kept it in her work bag.'

'So where is it?'

'She tried to destroy it.'

'What? Why?'

'I'm hoping IT can tell us that.' He produced a smashed and dented laptop from a carrier bag and laid it on his desk. 'I found it at the bottom of the rubbish collection bin last night. Bit of luck really, as the bin men call today.'

'I'm seeing the bigger picture.'

He gave her a grim smile. 'Also, my mother said that Sarah was anxious and preoccupied a few weeks back. A close friend of Sarah's rang mother and said she hadn't been returning her calls, which was very unusual.'

'But James never noticed anything odd about her behaviour?' asked Marie. 'It's usually the husband or the wife who takes the brunt of mood changes.'

Jackman shook his head. 'He swears she was absolutely normal.'

'Then she was either a damned good actress, or it had nothing at all to do with her family and she didn't want to worry them with what *was* bothering her.'

Jackman shuffled through some papers. 'Ryan gave me her Facebook password, and I've been trawling through the posts. There's a few weirdos who want to be "friends," but so far nothing too sinister.' He stared at the battered laptop. 'It's what's on *this* that I want to see.'

Marie looked at the cracked and broken device and wondered what on earth Sarah had hit it with. If IT could salvage that, they'd be miracle workers. Then again they were, weren't they? Or their boss, Orac, certainly was. Marie tried hard not to laugh. So that was why the laptop was still here and not already down in the basement department. Jackman couldn't face Orla Cracken, the techno-wizard in charge of the IT unit. She was certainly off-putting, with her white blonde hair styled in a Mohican cut and her mirror contact lenses, but she was incredibly smart. She loved to tease Jackman.

'Want me to run it downstairs for you?'

Jackman beamed at her. 'Oh please, Marie, only I really should go and have a word with Ruth Crooke, and . . .'

'Relax. I'll take it, okay?' She looked at him. 'If that was her work computer, surely she backed all her files up? Maybe there's an external hard drive somewhere, a memory stick. Or if she used something like Dropbox and you had her email address and password, you could access all her information from any computer.'

Jackman drew in a breath. 'Good point!'

Marie stood and gathered up the carrier bag and laptop. 'But first, let's ask Orac to work some magic, shall we? If she fails, and she never has before, we'll go the backup route.'

Jackman nodded. 'Thanks. I'll have a word with my brother and search the house thoroughly. This screams out that something is wrong with the whole situation.' He paused. 'Oh, I forgot to tell you the most important thing. Ryan and Miles's old nanny, Ella Jarvis, has agreed to come back to live in for a while.'

'Ella the scene-of-crime officer?'

'That's right. She was a really close friend to Sarah, so just maybe she knows something that we don't.'

'I tell you what,' said Marie, 'she could help you look for anything suspicious. She was hot shit with crime scenes, wasn't she?'

'She certainly had an eye for detail, and she has a logical, enquiring mind, so yes, you're right, Marie. I'll speak to her as soon as I get home.'

She hesitated. 'Hate to ask, but when do you think you'll be back?'

Jackman puffed out his cheeks. 'Not too long, I hope. I need to talk it over with Ruth Crooke. Now that we know the children will be cared for, some of the pressure is off.

Mum and Dad are doing their best with James, so as long as I'm on call for any emergencies, I guess we're looking at early next week.'

'Well, don't worry about it, we are keeping our heads above water. It will just be nice to have you back. It doesn't seem right here without you.'

Jackman shivered. 'And I'm like a fish out of water with all this high-emotion stuff. It's like a bad dream you can't wake up from. Other people's problems I can handle, but this is horrible. My own brother in meltdown and those two poor little lads.' He shook his head and looked around the book-lined walls of his office. 'I belong here, Marie. Doing my job.'

'I know you do,' said Marie softly. 'But right now you need to do your job by finding out what happened to your sister-in-law.' She paused in the doorway. 'Do you really believe that someone drove her to kill herself?'

'Without a doubt, Marie. I have no idea why, but I'm certain there was something very dark going on in Sarah's life.'

'Then just tell me what you want me to do, and I'll do it, okay?'

'Wilco, Sergeant.' Jackman smiled. 'I'll be in touch.'

CHAPTER SIX

The church was empty. He stepped down the central aisle, careful to avoid treading on the memorial stones set into the ornately tiled floor. His footsteps echoed in the silence. He always felt calm in the company of saints and martyrs, even if they were just statues. He looked at each one of the fourteen Stations of the Cross and considered Christ's last day on earth as a man. The Way of Sorrows. Via Crucis. Via Dolorosa. He liked the words. He understood suffering.

At the bottom of the nave he sat down in one of the carved wooden pews and stared through the sanctuary to the altar. This was the only area of the church that was heavily ornate. A central golden crucifix hung high on the wall and below it three exquisite paintings, a triptych showing Mary and the infant Jesus, with angels either side. It soothed him to look at them, and this intrigued him, as he wasn't a Catholic. In fact, he wasn't religious at all, but something in the utter certainty of the belief he saw all around him resonated deep inside. The pictures, the stained-glass windows, the ornate statues and soaring, vaulted ceiling embossed with gold and painted plaques, were all evidence of lofty principles and unshakable faith.

He sighed. He felt safe in here, as if the moment he dipped his finger into the Holy Water in the stoup, his mind was cleansed of all fear. The smell of incense filled the church, stilling his thoughts and slowing his pounding heart. It was sad to think that outside, beyond the heavy wooden door, lay chaos and lawlessness. He longed to carry this peace with him when he left, but he knew it wasn't possible. He could, however, right some wrongs. He could redress a few terrible mistakes that had been made in the name of so-called justice. After all, the guilty should never go unpunished, and if the system wasn't able to do the job, then it was up to those that were to show them the error of their ways. Irreligious as he was, he recalled a verse from Proverbs that had somehow lodged in a corner of his memory:

Who so diggeth a pit will fall into it, and whoever rolls a stone . . . it will come back on him.

He appreciated the Old Testament doctrine of retribution. He too believed in an eye for an eye. Sometimes God, if indeed he existed, needed a little help.

He closed his eyes and breathed in the silence. It was time to arrange for another pit to be dug.

* * *

'Professor Wilkinson is in London today. I'm Lisa Forbes. I was called out to look at your vagrant.' She sounded young for a forensic pathologist, but Marie noticed that was happening a lot recently. Expert witnesses, CEOs of big organisations, professors and consultants were all starting to look like school leavers to her.

'Thank you so much. Can you give me a preliminary briefing over the phone, or should I come and see you?' Marie hoped that the latter wouldn't be the case.

'I can't tell you much yet, but it's not exactly an open and shut case, Sergeant Evans, if you'll pardon the pun. You were right to suspect foul play — that's what I really wanted you to know. And contrary to appearances, he is certainly not a rough sleeper.'

Nice one, Max. 'Any idea of time of death?' Marie asked.

'Preliminary guess only, around two hours prior to your finding him. Rigor mortis had hardly set in, although it was detectable in the small muscles in the face and neck. Lividity had just started to appear, so yes, a couple of hours, which would make it around 7 a.m., give or take.'

Marie quite missed Rory's usual quirky reluctance to yield up the time of death, but on this occasion it did speed things up.

'Thank you, that's much appreciated. Was the slash on his wrist the cause of death?'

Lisa Forbes hesitated. 'I need to do a full examination before I comment. I'll send my preliminary report through as soon as I've completed the autopsy.'

And that was all she was going to get. No veiled suggestions of evil doings, no cryptic hints about medical enigmas. Yes, she certainly missed Rory Wilkinson's take on post-mortem news. Still, she now knew they were right to be suspicious, which meant they had a murder on their hands, and the timing wasn't perfect considering Jackman's personal investigation. With a grunt, she went off to find DI Pete Lawrence. With a bit of grovelling, there was a good chance that Pete would shoulder the rest of the fraud case, and that would make life considerably more manageable. Whatever happened, no way was she going to let Jackman down when he needed her, and apart from that, Sarah Jackman's death was occupying a lot of her waking thoughts, and a good few of her sleeping ones too. For some reason she had a really bad feeling about what had happened to Jackman's sister-in-law, and she was becoming as obsessed with it as Jackman himself.

* * *

When Jackman arrived at Rainham Lodge, he saw his mother's car parked there, and a white Honda Jazz that he was pretty sure belonged to Ella Jarvis.

He found them in the lounge, deciding on the strategy for the coming days.

'Rowan! Come in, darling.' His mother greeted him with a tired smile and patted the sofa next to her. 'Ella's moving in first thing tomorrow. She's going to have the guest bedroom nearest to the boys' room.'

Jackman went up to Ella with his hand outstretched. 'I can't tell you how grateful we all are for what you are doing.'

Ella shook his hand and shrugged. 'It's no big deal, honestly. I want to help. Sarah would have done the same for me.'

Ella was tall with long pale blonde hair, and Jackman was pretty sure it wasn't dyed. She had blue-grey eyes and well-defined features. It made a change not to see her in a forensic protective suit and mask. He guessed that, like him, she was in her mid-thirties. She exuded a sporty kind of strength.

'I was wondering,' said Jackman, 'if you would like to talk to our force psychologist — about handling bereaved children, that is. She's really approachable and I'm very aware that you are taking on a tough assignment here.'

Ella smiled but then sighed. 'No need, sir. Sadly I've been there before, with my half-brother when he was young. I think the most important thing to remember is to be honest. Talk to them in simple language and make sure they really understand what you are saying.'

'Ah, it sounds like you know what you're doing.' He looked apologetically at her. 'I didn't mean to suggest you aren't competent, I just know this isn't going to be easy. And I'm not "sir" anymore, Ella, everyone calls me Jackman, except my mother.'

'Okay.' She smiled at him, and he could see why the boys liked her so much. Her open face radiated honesty, and that was a very good thing in Jackman's book.

His mother looked up at him. 'We're going over to the boys' school in a few minutes, Rowan. We have an appointment with the school counsellor. The boys miss their friends and are anxious to get back,' she tilted her head slightly, 'and James isn't up to it, but Ella has kindly offered to come along.'

'Want me to come too?'

'No, we are just going to let them know exactly what's happened and how much we have told the boys. Then they are going to tell us how to prepare Ryan and Miles for the kind of comments they might encounter from their friends.'

Ella nodded. 'They need to have a few stock responses ready. Other kids can be hurtful when they don't understand properly. Their form teachers have said that they will have a quiet chat with their closest friends and classmates and stress the importance of being kind at a time like this.'

'Looks like you two have everything in hand. I'll use the time while you're away to make a thorough search of the house, just in case there's something here that might explain things more clearly.'

Ella's fleeting glance was full of curiosity, and he knew Marie had been right. She had a keen nose for things not being as they should.

'Can you give me a couple of moments, dear?' his mother said to Ella, 'I have a phone call to make and I need to check with my husband that James is okay. I won't be long.' She left the room.

'Do you understand any of this?' Ella pre-empted Jackman's words.

'Absolutely not.' He threw up his hands. 'Nothing makes sense. What about you?'

'The last time I saw her I knew something was wrong, but she refused to say what it was.' Ella nibbled on her bottom lip. 'I thought it might be a problem between her and James, but she laughed at the idea, and I could see she meant it. She said she was happier with James and her sons than she had ever dreamed she could be.' Ella exhaled. 'She really did mean it, I know she did.'

'And then she killed herself?'

Ella looked at him. 'Was that really the case?'

'She was recorded on CCTV. I've seen the footage, Ella. She threw herself into the river. I couldn't quite believe what I was seeing, but there is no doubt at all that it was a deliberate action.' Jackman leaned forward. 'Will you help me, Ella? I have to find the truth. We cannot allow this to be passed off as some mental aberration. We need to know why Sarah died.'

Ella pursed her lips. 'Children see things. They notice things, even if they don't understand them. I'll be talking to them a lot over the coming weeks. I'll tell you if anything sets off alarm bells.'

He nodded. 'Thank you, and keep your eyes open too. Apart from her work, she lived for Rainham Lodge and her family. Something might draw your attention, or someone might mention something, if you know what I mean?'

'I want to know what happened too, so of course I'll stay vigilant. And I'll contact you if anything worries me.'

Jackman reached into his pocket and took out his personal card. 'Day or night, Ella, okay?'

'Ready when you are.' Harriet Jackman stood in the doorway.

Ella stood up. 'Nice to see you again, si— er, Jackman. I just wish the circumstances were different.'

'Ring me if you need a hand with Miles and Ryan. I'm not sure that you will get too much support from my brother, but just shout if you need a man's assistance with anything.'

After the door closed behind them, Jackman looked around the big house and wondered where on earth to begin.

It was on his mind that her smartphone hadn't been recovered. There was a strong possibility that it was somewhere on the bottom of the Thames, but the clothes she had been wearing had no deep pockets, so maybe the phone was somewhere around the house, like her bag and her laptop.

'Right,' he said aloud. 'Come on, Jackman, use police search procedure and don't waste precious time.'

He ran up the stairs and into James and Sarah's bedroom. He had his brother's permission to look for whatever he wanted. And what he wanted was to know why his brother was a widower and his young nephews were facing a future without their mother.

CHAPTER SEVEN

Marie yawned. It was time to go home, but she felt restless, as if she hadn't done enough to warrant shutting up shop for the night.

'Something bothering you, Sarge?' Robbie called over to her.

'Dead men dressed as vagrants for a start,' she said. 'Why does nothing make sense these days?'

'Mmm. Considering what happened with the boss's sister-in-law, I'll agree with you there.'

'I was just wondering if we might hear any more from forensics tonight. We need to identify our faux tramp.' While she was speaking, the phone rang and Marie snatched it up. She was surprised to hear Orac, the IT boss.

'Marie? You can tell that gorgeous DI of yours that I've indeed worked miracles on that massacred laptop he so kindly sent me. But I don't think he's going to like the contents of her inbox.'

Marie took a breath. 'There's something incriminating on it?'

'Someone didn't like Sarah Jackman, not one little bit.'

Marie jumped up. 'Thanks, Orac. I'm on my way down.' She put down the receiver. 'You get off home, Robbie. I could be a while. I'll see you tomorrow.'

'Can't I come with you? That woman fascinates me.' He grinned broadly.

'Not tonight. She might not have eaten, and she has a voracious appetite. You'd be the perfect snack.'

'She eats detectives?'

'Regularly.' She hurried out of the office, calling back, 'And *never* go down there after dark!'

Orac was sitting in front of a bank of screens. 'Come in, Marie. Have a seat.' She indicated an office chair close to hers. 'This isn't very nice, I'm afraid. I'm just sorry that you have to pass it on to Jackman when he must be feeling pretty shitty already.'

Marie sat down. 'He'll be relieved I think. He swears she would never have acted as she did without provocation.'

'I think he's right.' Marie looked into those strange metallic-looking eyes. She knew that Orac had been blinded in one eye in an attempt on her life, and she wore the contact lenses to hide the damage.

'I've printed off all the stuff from this person, and I've also looked through a whole load of deleted files and found a few drafts that might be connected in some way.'

'I don't suppose there's a contact name or address on these emails?' Marie didn't hold out too much hope on that one, but had to ask.

'No, he moved around. I might be able to trace it, but there are some pretty sophisticated methods in use these days. Not that I'll give up on it. You know me.'

Marie smiled. 'Oh, I do. If anyone can find the sender, it's the woman right beside me.'

Orac smiled. 'How is Jackman taking it all?'

Marie sighed. 'It's the children. That's what hurts him the most.'

'Oh, it's always the children,' Orac said softly.

Marie had never heard the person she privately thought of as cyber-woman speak with so much feeling.

Orac gazed into her screen. 'One night, my sister was stolen from her bed. She was three years old, and we never saw her again. It devastated the village where my family lived. Nothing was ever the same, not for us, nor anyone else. Men looked with suspicion at men they had lived and worked with since they were bairns. Brothers suspected brothers. And we never had an answer. A blight entered our home that night and destroyed everything good for miles around.'

Marie was silent, so shocked she could find nothing to say. For a fleeting moment she wondered why this intensely private woman chose to open up to her. What was it about her that brought forth these deeply personal revelations? She shivered.

'Sorry. I don't know why I told you all that. Ancient history now, but it still hurts, as you can tell.'

'I'm *so* sorry. I'm not sure how you live through something like that.'

'It's what we humans do. Survive. Like you when you lost your Bill, we find ways of dealing with things. Well, most of us do, but some don't. Like Sarah Jackman.' She passed Marie a sheaf of printouts. 'Something happened in Sarah's past, something terrible. And whatever it was, this anonymous person wanted Sarah to account for it in some way. Read them, see what you make of it, but I'm pretty sure this man, and I'm certain it is a man, wanted retribution for something.'

Marie stared at the paperwork thoughtfully. 'So, we need to find out all we can about Sarah's past. The thing is, is it something she told her husband about, or did she keep it to herself?'

'I'd go with the latter. Our self-styled judge and executioner seems to have been forcing her to revisit a very dark time in her life.' Orac sat back. 'Or he could be a messed up screwball and all these accusations are a complete fabrication, and sweet Sarah could neither understand nor cope with them.'

42

Marie glanced down at the messages. Some seemed to be almost biblical in their wording, others were just accusations. All of them seemed to be demanding justice. But for what?

'Good luck, and I'll try to track your sender.' Orac looked at her. 'I don't like people who threaten others, do you?'

'Especially not one who has the power to make a woman abandon her children.' Marie set her jaw. She was glad that she had something definite to give to Jackman, something that would confirm his theories, but she was afraid too. Exactly what was lurking out there? Just what had crept back from the murky depths of Sarah's secret past?

* * *

Marie arrived back in the empty CID room to find a note on her desk. *Ring pathologist before you leave. She has something for you. Rob.*

Marie picked up the phone, and was surprised to hear Rory's voice.

'Ah, the very woman! My dear Marie, how are you? Personally, as I *know* you were about to ask, I'm recovering from a ghastly day in the capital! All that traffic! And the noise! Give me my lovely homely mortuary here in the damp and dreary fens any day. *So* much better.'

Marie smiled to herself. This was more like it! He'd only been away a day but she had missed him. 'Sorry to hear that, Rory, but I'd expect nothing less from you. Now, I was asked to ring Lisa Forbes?'

'The lovely Lisa! Actually the dear girl hung on to get my opinion on the deceased gentleman that you so kindly provided her with earlier. And he *was* a gentleman by the way — well, up until recently that is. He's new to the streets, that's for sure.'

'Max guessed that from his trendy haircut. Robbie looked at his manicured hands and corroborated it.'

'Astute young men, our Max and Robbie. But listen, it's not his history that interested Lisa, it's the deep laceration at

43

his wrist. I've looked at it with her and we both agree, you will find the dead man's prints on that Stanley knife.'

'He killed himself? But I thought—'

'Patience, woman! Rory hasn't finished his tale.' He paused for dramatic effect. 'But. The laceration is a strange one. There are several what we call hesitation wounds visible. Small nicks and cuts inflicted prior to finding the courage to make the fatal incision. These, from close examination, were made by a shaking hand. Then we get to the main cut. It too was inflicted *to begin with*, rather hesitantly. Then there is the slightest change of direction of the blade, and a deep killing wound is administered. We suggest that although our man began the deed, another, gloved, hand exerted extreme pressure over his, and "helped" him on his way.'

'A deliberately assisted suicide?' Marie exhaled.

'Forensics is *so* exciting, is it not?' Rory was almost purring. 'The tiniest deviation from what you expect to find and a whole new scenario opens up before you!'

Marie shook her head. 'Doesn't it just!'

'Well. Now the interesting bit is over, I should tell you the rather sadder news about my trip to London.'

'Sarah?'

'Poor girl. Drowning is a particularly unpleasant way to take your life. It takes almost two agonising minutes to lose consciousness, after an automatic struggle for survival as the air supply is shut off.' Rory made a tutting noise. 'Thing is, without a reliable eyewitness to the whole event, it is difficult to determine the *manner* of death. She drowned, no question, but did she fall into the water as the result of a slip, a trip or a dizzy spell, or did she actually jump?'

'CCTV shows she jumped.'

'Have you seen it yourself?'

Marie frowned. 'Jackman saw it.'

'Not the same thing. He is personally involved. You should look too. Impartially.'

She would, first thing tomorrow. 'So what next?'

'I've performed a complete toxicology analysis, just to determine whether there were any drugs in her system that could account for her actions, but the tests will take a little time, I'm afraid. And to be honest, I saw nothing physical to indicate that she had taken anything.' He sounded unnaturally sombre. 'I hate to say it, but in this case I think you may deduce more from the circumstances surrounding her death than from my lab reports.'

'Will you be ringing Jackman, Rory? Or shall I tell him?'

'I'll phone him immediately, but I suggest you check on him later. I hope he didn't expect more of me, only drownings are such a complicated business.'

'Don't worry. He'll know that no one could have done more. And I'll check that CCTV and talk to you tomorrow, okay?'

'Nighty-night, sleep well. If you can.'

Marie wasn't too sure about that. But whatever, she'd probably sleep better than Jackman, after he'd received both Orac and Rory's news. She gathered up her things and was about to go when she saw Annie, the cleaner, waving to her. Part of a private cleaning company, Annie had been working at the station for years and was on first name terms with most of the officers.

'Are you finished in here, Sarge? Only it's just Stefan and me tonight, and we need to get on.'

'Sure, I'm just off. There's only one duty officer on tonight and he's had to go out.' She grinned at Annie. 'Eric sick again?'

Annie's face darkened. 'That man! If I didn't have my lovely Stefan on my rota, heaven knows what I'd do. He never takes a day off, not like bloody Eric!'

Stefan waved at her from across the room. 'Evening, Sarge. You okay?'

She waved back, wondering vaguely what part of Eastern Europe Stefan came from. His accent was very slight. One day she'd ask him, but not tonight. 'Gotta go. I'll let you guys get on.'

She rode home, deep in thought, stopping at the local chippy on her way to pick up a fish and chip supper. She was glad to shut the door on the day.

She indulged in a glass of white wine with her meal, and after washing up, finally summoned the courage to ring Jackman.

* * *

By the time Jackman spoke to Marie, he'd digested what Rory had told him. He'd expected nothing less of him, in fact he wondered if he'd overstepped the mark by requesting that Rory carry out the post-mortem personally, but he had felt he owed it to Sarah to provide the very best.

For a few moments they discussed the pathologist's findings, and then he became aware that Marie had more news for him. 'Okay, Evans, cough up.'

He heard her draw in a deep breath. Then she told him of Orac's sinister discovery from Sarah's laptop.

'I knew it! She was being targeted by some psycho!' His brain reeled.

'Jackman? How much do you know about Sarah's past?'

Marie's words brought him back to earth. He thought for a moment. 'Well, she . . . I . . .' He stopped. 'Not much, Marie. In fact, surprisingly little. To me, she had no past. Sarah was a wife and mother, the centre of her family. I know she and my brother met at some charity function, and that both her parents had either died or gone abroad, I'm not sure which, but they were not at the wedding.' He sounded embarrassed. 'And I suppose that is more or less it.'

'So you know more about me than you do about your own brother's wife?'

'Okay, Detective, what are you getting at exactly?'

'I hate to say this, but you, or we, really need to make some serious enquiries into Sarah's past.'

Jackman sat back in his chair. She was right, but it wouldn't be easy. 'My brother will be key to that, but he's at breaking point. I'm going to have to tread carefully. Although,' he thought about Ella Jarvis, 'Ella knew her better than anyone as far as I can tell. I'll start with her.'

'And your mother?'

'Maybe she knew more than me, but I get the feeling she saw Sarah much as I did, very much in the present.'

Marie sounded tense. 'Jackman, shall I bring these printouts to you tonight? I've looked through them and I really think you should see them. I sense that this man, if it is a man, had something over Sarah, something from way back in her past. The things he says refer to a particular incident. They are not random threats about trivial things.'

Jackman was still at his brother's house. He glanced at the clock and saw it was just after half past nine, and he hadn't even stopped to eat. 'That's asking too much of you, Marie. Look, I'll drive into town, grab something to eat and call in to you on my way back to Mother's house, if that's all right?'

'Fine. I'll be here,' Marie said.

* * *

He arrived an hour later, full of apologies but clearly excited about something. Marie led the way through to the lounge and offered him a coffee.

'Please. I could do with a caffeine hit right now.' He flopped down onto her sofa and let out a long, loud sigh. 'What a day!'

'But you've found something?' Marie called out from the kitchen.

'Her phone, Marie! I've found it, and she didn't try to trash it either.' He got up and walked into the kitchen. 'I think she wanted it found. It was in a drawer in the hall table right by the front door, almost the last drawer I looked in. I only noticed it on my way out. Talk about hiding something in plain sight.'

'Have you checked the call log?'

'Full of stuff from an unknown caller. In one day alone he rang her fourteen times. Whoever this wicked bastard is, he drove her to do what she did, just as certainly as if he'd shot her point blank.'

Marie handed him a steaming mug of coffee. 'And when you read the emails, you'll get an insight into his scary mind-set. It's unnerving, to say the least.'

'Poor Sarah, what she must have gone through.' He turned to go back into the lounge.

'Did you actually stop and get some food, Jackman?' Marie asked.

He looked at her blankly. 'I, er, no, I must have forgotten.'

'I can do you an omelette and oven chips. You have to eat, *you* know that.'

'No, honestly, I'm sure my mother will have left me something. Thanks anyway.'

Marie went and fetched the folder of printouts. 'I hope you didn't mind but I took copies for myself. There are some interesting quotes. I thought I'd look them up, they just might give us a clue as to what kind of person we're looking for.'

'A psychopath, I suggest.'

'Apart from the obvious.' Marie sat down opposite him. 'I've got a small mystery of my own too.' She told him about the dead man on the disused footpath.

For a while he said nothing. Then he looked at her anxiously. 'What are the odds of having two supposed suicides within two days, and both seemingly involving some kind of coercion?'

'Pretty rare, I'd say. The same thought had occurred to me. But where's the connection? Not that I even know who the dead man is.'

'You have to make that a priority, Marie. There is a chance he is connected to Sarah, and at least that would mean we're only looking for one psycho, not two.'

'Whoopee, I do like a glass-half-full attitude.'

'Seriously, Marie. You know we don't believe in coincidences. Unless we're unlucky enough to find ourselves looking for two vindictive killers at one time, we need to look at a possible link.'

'I quite agree, and don't worry. I'll be hitting this case like a runaway train in the morning. And you, DI Jackman, should get some food into you and have some sleep, then tomorrow you can work your socks off to discover everything you can about Sarah's past. Oh, what was her maiden name, by the way?'

Jackman looked perplexed. 'Do you know, I don't think I've ever heard it mentioned.'

Marie stared at him. 'You do know this is pretty unusual, don't you? You are a policeman. Policemen notice things. We listen to everything people say, and we remember. It sounds to me as if your sister-in-law didn't want anyone to know that she even had a past. No parents? No previous name? No chat about silly things that happened when she was young? It's like Sarah Jackman didn't exist before she married your brother.'

CHAPTER EIGHT

When Jackman arrived back at the family home, he was surprised to see his mother sitting at the kitchen table waiting for him.

'I kept you something, Rowan. I guessed that you'd miss dinner.' His mother went over to the stove and produced a large soup bowl from the warmer. She was wearing one of his father's dressing gowns over her silk pyjamas. It was something she had often done when he was a child, and for a fleeting moment it made him feel almost nostalgic for family life.

'You didn't have to wait up, Mum.' Jackman gratefully accepted a bowl of delicious smelling chicken casserole and a thick wedge of fresh bread.

'I can't rest, son. The whole situation is unbearable. I've been wondering why you asked about Sarah's recent state of mind, and now I'm imagining all sorts of things. Do you suspect foul play of some kind?'

Jackman laid down his fork and looked at her worried face. 'Yes, I do, and all the time I'm uncovering new facts that confirm it.'

'Oh dear. That's good news and bad, at the same time.'

'If I can prove it, it will be a huge relief to James and the boys. It will count for a lot just to know that their mother didn't leave them voluntarily.'

His mother looked shocked. 'Who would do such a terrible thing?'

'I don't know, but I intend to find out.' He took a mouthful of food. He hadn't realised how hungry he was. 'Mum, how much do you know about Sarah's past?'

His mother took a long time to reply. Finally she said, 'Not much, Rowan, and that's because when James first told us he was going to marry her, he asked your father and I never to pry into her private life, her life before she met him, that is.'

Jackman screwed his face into a frown. 'Why on earth ask that of her future in-laws?'

'He said that something traumatic had happened in her past, and talking about it dredged up old fears and worries.' She gave a little shrug. 'So we agreed of course. What else could we do? We liked her from the moment we met her. We decided that if James was happy, then that was all that mattered. It wasn't much to ask in the grand scheme of things.'

Except that whatever happened, it finally came back from the past, and it killed her, thought Jackman darkly. 'He never said anything like that to me.'

His mother gave him a rueful smile. 'He didn't have to, did he? You two were never as close as I'd have liked, and you were both so involved with your careers that frankly, you never spent much time together anyway.'

'That's harsh, Mum.' It hurt, but Jackman had to admit that she had a point. 'I do love James, of course I do, he's my big brother, but we have grown up to be very different men.'

'You were *always* very different! Different babies, different toddlers, different boys, teens, and young adults.' Harriet laughed softly. 'Chalk and cheese.'

He sighed. 'I want to help him now, but I'm going to have to ask him to share whatever he knows, and I'm not sure that will be easy.'

'I'm certain it won't, although his mood has improved somewhat this evening. He's not so fraught. He's calmer, at least.'

'And he's prepared to return home?'

'Now that he knows Ella will be supporting him, yes. Even in the state he's in, he wants what is best for Ryan and Miles, and they want to go back to school.' She gave him a tired smile. 'But don't worry, I'll keep a close eye on him. My friend Clara is covering for me at the stables this week, so I have more time.'

'You look as though you need someone to keep an eye on you. You're exhausted, Mum.'

'We'll get through it. We're a tough family, all things considered.'

'True. I'll be in and out of Rainham Lodge, and I'll make sure Ella has everything she needs.'

'Bless you, Rowan. Now, if you've finished that, go get some sleep. You can't function properly without food and rest.'

'You sound just like Marie! She's told me that once already tonight.'

'Sensible woman. Take heed! And now, off to bed.'

He did as he was told, but took the folder of emails with him.

At around one a.m., he was still staring at them, and fervently wishing he had left them downstairs. He didn't know what had happened, but he did know that they were dealing with a very sick son of a bitch.

* * *

Yvette called out softly, 'Susie? Are you awake?'

'Yes, I have been for hours.'

'Me too.'

Yvette turned over to face Susie's side of the bedroom. 'Worried about Mum coming home tomorrow?'

'Partly. I mean I'm terrified that she might be taken ill again, but I'm more worried about the boys.'

Yvette wondered why they still called them "the boys" when by now their ages ranged from thirty to forty-five. 'I wish Mother had never said all that about not resting until Brendan's name is cleared. It has fired up Dale and Liam all over again.'

'I know. I feel the same. I just wanted Mum's last days to be peaceful and full of love, not riddled with tension.'

'I bet you can't wait to get back to your kids and your Stevie?'

Susie sighed. 'We all said we'd be here for Mum to get her over this bad patch. After all, she was always there for us, through thick and thin.' She shifted and the bed creaked. 'Stevie understands, and he's so good with the youngsters. He knows it's not for ever.'

'It's still good of you, Susie. And it's good of Kenny's wife too. I'm really pleased you're with me right now. I don't think I would have coped without you.'

'Don't be daft! Of course you would.'

Yvette wasn't so sure. 'Dale and Liam scare me, Sue. They are so . . . so intense, so driven. And if I'm truly honest, I've lost heart. Brendan is never coming back, and we can do nothing to make it happen, so what is the point?'

'Don't let them hear you talk like that, Yvie. They want us all to be together for this last hurrah.'

'The bloody crusade! I wish it was all over,' Yvette said. 'You can't tell me that you aren't worried by the look in Dale's eyes?'

'Honestly? It terrifies me. And Liam is even worse. Hell, he was only eight when it all happened, but I think he's the most obsessed. I have no idea what they will do next. But I'm here for Mum, so I'll stay, and say all the right words, until this is finished.' She waited for a moment then added, 'And you'd be well-advised to do the same.'

Yvette drew her knees up to her chest and pulled the duvet tighter around her. It was sound advice. She knew how her family felt about loyalty. But even so, she felt a growing apprehension that something dreadful was going to happen.

CHAPTER NINE

Jackman had driven to Rainham Lodge to see the boys off. It was their first day back at school, and he felt sick with anxiety about what they might be facing there. But then kids could surprise you. Whatever, he felt that he should be there to add his support and let them know that their uncle was around for them.

A smiling Ella loaded them into the car, checked that they had everything they needed and waving through the open window, sailed off down the drive.

'One small step,' he murmured to his hollow-eyed brother.

There was no answer. James seemed almost locked-in, which wasn't what Jackman needed right now.

'Ella has left us croissants and coffee, so come on, brother, you need to eat.' Jackman took his arm and gently propelled him towards the door.

In the kitchen, James sat at the table and stared blankly across the room.

Jackman heated the croissants, poured the coffee and placed the two plates and mugs on the table. 'No arguments, James. Eat!'

James reached for the marmalade and placed a small helping beside the pastry, then picked up the glass jar and stared at it. 'Sarah made a load of this for the local church to sell at a Macmillan charity morning.'

His voice was toneless, and Jackman wondered what on earth the doctor had prescribed. 'I know. Ryan sold me two jars, and I probably only eat one a year!'

James didn't reply. He didn't touch his food. 'This can't be happening. What did I do that was so *wrong*?'

Jackman put his coffee cup down. 'You did nothing wrong, James, so don't go there. None of it is your fault.'

'Then why does it feel like it is? I feel like I'm paying for some terrible sin.'

Jackman took a breath. This could be the way in. 'James? There is something I need to tell you, and I'm going to need your help.' He didn't wait for a reply. 'I believe that what happened to Sarah stemmed from an incident in her past. You have to tell me all you know about it, the thing she didn't talk about.'

For the first time, Jackman saw a glimmer of interest in his brother's eyes. He sensed that he had thrown James a lifeline, one that meant he wasn't to blame after all.

'I would, but I don't know myself.'

Jackman stared at him. 'What? You never asked?'

James picked a corner off his croissant and nibbled at it. 'Quite early in our relationship, Sarah told me that something had happened to her. She was involved in something that affected her so badly that she couldn't talk about it. She said that maybe one day she'd explain, but it might be that she'd never be able to do so. It was my choice as to whether or not we went forward or called it a day.'

'And you chose to stick with her?'

'I loved her, Ro. I still do. It seemed a small thing to ask, and it wasn't the past that I was interested in, it was our future together.'

'Weren't you curious?'

James sipped his coffee. 'A little, I guess. But I'd promised not to ask, and that was that. We moved on, everything was perfect, or so I thought.'

'Sarah had a secret side to her, James. I believe someone decided to remind her of it, and it was all too much for her.' Jackman made another pot of coffee.

'But what on earth could she have been mixed up in? She was such a sweet girl and the best wife and mother ever.'

Jackman didn't want to guess. He'd seen cases that would shock the life out of his brother. He knew how devious and destructive people could be. 'Can you tell me anything at all about her? Or her family?'

James was reverently spreading Sarah's marmalade onto his croissant. 'Like what?'

'Her parents? Siblings? Where she came from? Anything, really.' Jackman was already feeling frustrated at having to wring every bit of information from his brother.

'It's all a bit of a grey area really. I don't think she had any siblings, and her parents — well, I've never actually met them. You know yourself that they never even came to the wedding.' James sounded apologetic and slightly embarrassed. 'I think they moved abroad somewhere, although I'm not certain. They could be dead for all I know.'

A feeling of despondency crept over Jackman. How could he never have noticed that his own sister-in-law had no past? He tried to remember conversations they had had, but all he could recall was talk of the children and holidays. Days out. And work, of course. She did talk about her job, but had he really listened? She had been some kind of area manager for a company that supplied art and craft materials for primary schools, hence her travels around the county. She cut her hours when she had the children and finished up job sharing with another woman who also wanted a shorter working week. He wondered if the woman was a friend as well as a work colleague.

'She did talk to Ella a lot.' James suddenly seemed to wake up. 'Especially when she was suffering from postnatal depression after Miles' birth. Ella was the only person she could tolerate around her, and I think she might have opened up to her more than she did me.'

'Then as soon as she's back from the school, I'll talk to her.' He poured his brother another coffee. 'Are there any personal papers or photographs belonging to her anywhere?'

James frowned. 'No. Strangely she never brought a single photo with her when we married and settled down here. That was odd, now I think about it, because she was always taking pictures of the kids, and me, and the dog and the garden and days out. She has boxes full of pictures and a massive file on the computer, but they all relate to our time here at Rainham Lodge.'

Jackman wondered what on earth had happened to make Sarah blank out her entire existence prior to meeting James. 'Whatever happened had to be pretty serious, didn't it?'

James nodded slowly and continued to tear small pieces from his croissant.

'Look, I know this is the worst time for you, but I want you to try to think of anything that could help me find out what happened.' He looked intently at his brother. 'If I'm right, someone coerced Sarah into killing herself. Do you understand that, James? And I have to find out who that person was.'

James stopped chewing and stared back. 'So it was nothing to do with us, with our life together?'

'Help me out here, bro! Forget the guilt. There's a very dangerous person out there, and I need your help badly.'

'Okay, I'll do my best, I promise.'

'This is for Ryan and Miles as well, you know. They need to grow up knowing the truth about their mum, not what the papers and the media are going to make of it.'

James nodded slowly. 'You're right.'

'Think, James. Was there any subject she shied away from? Any topic of conversation that she avoided? Something she couldn't bear to watch on TV?'

James's brow knotted in concentration. Then he said, 'Funnily enough, there was only one time when she really looked scared, like wide-eyed fearful. And that was when I told her that my little brother, Rowan, was a policeman.'

Jackman tilted his head to one side. 'Why?'

'Oh, she covered it up. She said she was simply sur-prised, considering that both Father and I are in finance, but I knew her shock was genuine. She was frightened at the thought, I know it.'

So, whatever happened all those years ago probably involved the police. 'Thank you, James. That's something that I can follow up.' Jackman's mind started to race. She might be on their files or on the PNC. But as a victim, or a perpetrator of a crime?

* * *

Gary Pritchard and PC Kevin Stoner peered around the crowded tables of the drop-in centre. They were looking for one face in particular.

'She comes here most weekdays, for a hot drink and a sandwich.' Kevin went up to the serving hatch and smiled at the volunteer standing behind it. 'Ron? Has Cassie been in today?'

Ron, big, beefy and wearing a Leicester Tigers rugby shirt, shook his head. 'Not yet, mate. She's been getting later and later. Reckon it's the arthritis catching up with her.'

Or the meths, thought Gary. He knew Cassie of old. She had been on the streets for as long as he could remember. She was a sad case, but weren't they all? Recently both he and Kevin had noticed a decline in the old lady. Once lippy, sarcastic and argumentative, she was now almost taciturn. Even so, if you wanted to know anything about street peo-ple, Cassie was the one to ask. Whether she told you or not was another matter, but she missed nothing, and she had taken a shine to the polite, good-looking PC Kev, as she called him.

'Speak of angels.' Gary pointed to the entrance. Cassie, dressed in more layers of ragged clothing than he would have thought possible to get on, was fighting to get her battered trolley through the doorway.

Kevin hurried over and helped her, only to receive a short tirade about her not being helpless yet and if she wanted help, she'd ask for it. Kevin grinned at Gary, took a tenner from his wallet and went back to the counter. He handed it to Ron. 'Give her whatever she wants, plus the change.'

'I'm assuming you two want something?' said Cassie, looking at Gary. 'And not being stupid, I'm guessing it's about the riverside death.'

Gary noted that she didn't say suicide or murder, just death. 'We'd appreciate your help, Cassie, if you wouldn't mind?'

'Do I have any choice?' she muttered.

'There's a free breakfast in it, and maybe a few quid for yourself.'

She sat down heavily. 'Okay, fire away!'

Kevin leaned forward. 'We need anything you can tell us about the man who died.'

'Food first.'

Kevin jumped up and went to the counter, 'Give her the works and plenty of tea.' He returned to the table. 'Ron's bringing it over for you.'

Cassie rearranged some of her layers of clothing and sat back, like some elderly dowager duchess giving court. 'We've seen him around all week, but he wasn't used to the streets, you know? He was scared, very scared.'

'Surely, if you were new to this sort of life, it *would* be very frightening?' asked Kevin.

'Not like *he* was, me duck. We tried to talk to him, but he was having none of it. And we saw him with a man a couple of times, and he were a stranger too, and none of us liked the look of him. Very odd, he was.'

'How do you mean, odd?' asked Gary, 'In what way?'

'Well dressed, but kind of dark, like a funeral. In his forties, I'd guess. Face like an undertaker. But it were his eyes that got you. Staring eyes, like he was on something, only you knew he wasn't. And I could be wrong, but I'm sure he was the reason for the dead man to be so frightened.'

'Have you seen the other man since?'

'Nor sight nor sound. He's gone.'

Gary glanced at Kevin and raised an eyebrow. 'Would you recognise him again, Cassie?'

'I'll see him in my dreams, duck.' She shivered. 'Oh yes. Once seen, never forgotten, that one. And if I sees him again, I'll be straight down that cop shop of yours and you can lock him up.'

'Why would we want to lock him up?' said Kevin.

'Because pound to a penny, he's responsible for that poor man dying.'

At that point Ron arrived with a plate of eggs, bacon, sausage, tomatoes and hash browns, and a big mug of tea. 'Courtesy of these gentlemen, Cass, and here's the change for you.'

'I should think so too,' she grumbled.

But Gary noticed a twinkle in her rheumy eyes, and she didn't hesitate to dig in. 'So the man who died, he didn't speak to any of you?'

'Not one of us.' She showered her dinner in salt and pepper and lavish quantities of tomato ketchup. 'Tell you something though, the fear that came with him, it's still out there, in the alleyways and the town lanes, especially after dark. None of us slept well last night.'

'Death does leave a shadow sometimes.'

Gary looked sharply at Kevin, surprised at the depth of feeling in the young man's words.

Cassie stopped chewing and looked at him shrewdly. 'Nicely said, PC Kev. You're a bit of a philosopher on the quiet, aren't you?'

Kevin shrugged. Privately, Gary agreed with Cassie. The young officer had been right. Death did leave a shadow over a place.

Gary took a five pound note from his pocket and passed it to her. 'If you see that man again, come and find us, and if you are worried about anything at all, we'll help if we can.'

Outside, Gary looked at Kevin, 'She saw a murderer, didn't she? And she knows it.'

Kevin Stoner nodded gravely. 'Let's just hope he doesn't know it too.'

* * *

Marie waited impatiently for the morning meeting to finish, so she could take a look at the CCTV footage of Sarah on the bank of the Thames.

She opened up the program on her computer and stared at the screen. She watched it through twice, and then, frame by frame, paused it. The second time she looked at one of these shots she froze it, then printed it off.

She was still staring at it when she noticed Robbie Melton looking over her shoulder. She looked up at him. 'Rob? Look at the CCTV clip, will you? And then slow it down, and tell me if you see anything strange on it.'

She stood up and let Robbie sit in front of the monitor.

A few moments later, he paused the footage on exactly the same frame as Marie. 'I'm not sure that she's alone, Sarge. I'm sure there is someone behind her. I'd place a bet on it. You can't see them, but,' he stabbed his finger on the print-out, 'well, she looks like she's glancing back at someone. You can tell by her anguished expression.' He bit on his lip and stared harder at the still. 'I suppose she could just be looking around, in case someone saw her. I should think the last thing you would want was someone calling it in and the River Patrol dragging you out before you'd finished the job. But my money's on the first option.'

'Exactly. It would never in a month of Sundays get past the CPS as evidence, but I'm damn sure we're right.'

Robbie grunted. 'This won't help anything, except to indicate that there was foul play.' He stood up so she could sit down again. 'Are you convinced that there's something sinister going on here, Sarge? Or are we reading too much into a fearful backward glance and the fact that the victim is our boss's sister-in-law?'

Marie shook her head. 'No, Robbie, the whole thing cries out that there's a crime going on here. Not a straightforward one, but I think when we find out more, we'll dig up something very nasty.'

'And if it was coercion or some dark kind of assisted suicide, then we're forced to consider a link with our vagrant.'

Marie nodded. 'Any luck with identifying him yet?'

'Charlie and Max are chasing up missing persons, and Rosie is working on a digitally enhanced image of the man showing him clean-shaven and tidy. Someone should recognise him.'

'Gary and Kevin are talking to one or two faces they know on the streets, and I'm going to ask them to trawl around the local charity shops, the Salvation Army and anywhere he might have picked up his "street" clothes. Forensics say they are all second-hand garments, but not overly worn.'

'Why would a man who obviously has money and takes care of his appearance, suddenly morph into a tramp? It doesn't make sense.'

'Gary's just rung me with the news that he was seen with another man, well-dressed and with piercing eyes. Our wannabe vagrant was apparently terrified of him.'

Robbie groaned. 'More puzzles! Give me a straightforward bloody murder any day.'

Marie laughed. 'Can you wait until Jackman gets back before you wish one of those on us? We're busy enough as it is.'

* * *

After telling Jackman how the boys got on, Ella made some tea and they sat and talked for a while. She listened to Jackman's questions, but said she couldn't be any help.

'We talked so much, but in retrospect none of it was about her past. She did tell me that there had been an incident when she was younger that was difficult for her to talk about. She said that she'd even had to ask James never to ask her about it. So I let it go. You don't want to hurt people, do you?'

'But you would've liked to know, wouldn't you?' asked Jackman.

'Too right. I was eaten up with curiosity. Maybe it's my nature, born nosey, but I even Googled her name to see if I could discover what it was.'

'I take it you had no luck?'

'None at all, and I'm no slouch when it comes to a bit of sleuthing on the Internet.'

Jackman smiled. 'Then you were in the right job, working for the police in forensics.' Jackman regretted his words as soon as he said them.

'I think I'm probably better suited to this kind of thing,' she said.

'Sorry, that was thoughtless of me. It's just that you were very good at what you did. Lots of people, including Professor Rory Wilkinson, really miss you.'

'Thanks, but I obviously don't have the stomach for it.' She steered the conversation back to Sarah. 'She did mention a school friend once, although it was just a passing comment. I don't think she realised what she had said, but I never forgot it, as it was probably the only mention she ever made of her early life.'

'Do you recall the name?'

'Pauline? Yes, that's it, Pauline Grover.'

Jackman raised an eyebrow. 'You have a good memory.'

'You need one, working with children.' She laughed.

Jackman thought she looked very attractive when she laughed. Hastily he dragged his attention back to the matter in hand. 'So did you Google her too?'

'How did you guess? Yes, I did, and again, nothing at all.'

'I guess not everyone likes social media.'

Ella nodded. Then she looked at him and said, 'Jackman, is there anything practical I can do to help you? I'm going to have a fair bit of spare time while the boys are at school.

James has a woman who comes in to clean, so once I've made sure their suppers are ready and their clothes are all clean and pressed, I'm pretty free.'

'There might be. I'd certainly appreciate it. I just need to fathom out where to start.'

'Just say. Meanwhile, I'll speak to the children, as I said. Luckily they are talking about Sarah quite openly, which is good.'

'And James is slowly becoming more aware that he has to pull his weight. Though I have no idea how he would cope if you weren't here.'

'Well, it was good for me. I was fed up mooching around, but I couldn't muster the energy to look for a new job. I think I was bordering on depression to be honest. Your mother's call was just what I needed to get me back into gear again.'

Jackman pushed his chair back. 'Well, as things are on a more even keel here today, I think I'll go into work for a few hours. I'll come back this evening to check on you all. Is that alright with you?'

'Fine. I need to get a schedule together for Ryan and Miles's after school activities and check what shopping we will need — oh, and settle in and unpack. It was all a bit of a rush.'

'Thanks again, Ella. It's good to have you here. You're a real lifesaver.' Suddenly his phone rang. 'Sorry, I need to take this. It's Marie.'

He listened while the tension swept through him.

'Can you get over here, sir? We've had a development.' Marie spoke fast. 'Robbie picked up an attention-drawn from DCI Cameron Walker in Beech Lacey. He's driving over now. I think you need to hear what he has to say.'

Jackman was already on his feet. 'On my way, Marie.'

CHAPTER TEN

DCI Cameron Walker and Jackman arrived at the same time. Jackman knew Cameron's reputation. He was a likeable detective and a fount of local knowledge. He was tall and solidly built, but a terrier when he got his teeth into a case. Not a man to be underestimated.

'Jackman! Nice to see you.' Cameron held out his hand. 'Sorry to hear about what happened.'

Jackman gripped the outstretched hand. 'Not exactly the best time of my life.'

They pushed through the front doors and Jackman led the way upstairs to the CID office. Marie already had three steaming beakers of coffee ready on her desk.

'We'll use my office.' Jackman picked up a beaker and turned to go.

'Can I bring Robbie in on this, sir?' asked Marie. 'Only he made the connection first.'

'Of course. Just tell him to bring another chair.'

Cameron Walker looked around the book-lined office in envy. 'This is nice!' He took in the leather-topped desk, the captain's chair and the bookshelves. 'Very nice indeed. How come I only get a glass-windowed cupboard with chipboard furniture?'

'Because you didn't trail around auctions, car boots and house clearance sales, then smuggle it all in here in the dead of night,' said Marie. 'Our boss is really a squirrel.'

Jackman grinned. 'So what have you got for us, Cameron?'

'Bottom line, a case almost identical to yours, only our lovely contented partner and mother jumped off the roof of a London department store.'

Jackman exhaled loudly. 'Phew! A local woman?'

'From Beech Holby, a few miles from Beech Lacey, where I live. And from what Marie told me over the phone, the scenario is pretty well a carbon copy.'

Jackman sipped his coffee and stared into it in silence. He wondered why two local women would kill themselves in London.

'The good news is that we're a bit further ahead with the investigation than you. Our death happened two weeks ago, and the woman did leave us some clues to work on.'

'What was her name?' Jackman asked.

'Forester. Suri Forester.'

'What a coincidence. My brother told me earlier that Sarah's maiden name was Woodman. A forester is a woods-man, isn't he?'

'Even odder,' Robbie interjected, 'Suri comes from the Hebrew for princess and is the Yiddish version of Sarah. A friend of mine copied the name from a couple of celebrities who called their baby Suri.'

Jackman supressed a shiver.

'The story gets darker,' Cameron said in a low voice. 'That is not her real name, and I suspect Sarah Woodman wasn't your sister-in-law's real name either. Both changed their names because of something that happened to them years ago, something that neither of them *ever* talked about.'

'Witness Protection Programme,' whispered Marie.

Cameron Walker nodded. 'We thought that too, but it's not easy to prove. Everything is so hidden. It's like groping around in the dark.'

Jackman recalled his brother saying how scared Sarah had been when he told her Jackman was a copper. She must have wondered what would happen if he started to dig into her past! It was the answer to so many questions.

'My team are tracking her history and I'm reliably told they could have some answers by later today,' Cameron said.

'Are you happy to work in tandem with us on this, Cameron? Share whatever we get?'

'Absolutely.'

'I'm happy for you to lead,' Jackman offered.

'Let's be a double act, shall we?' suggested Cameron. 'There's a good fifteen miles between here and Beech Lacey, it's not just two minutes round the corner. You run this end, I'll keep on with our investigation and we'll keep in constant contact.'

'Yes, that's good. What if we each arrange a liaison officer to collate everything that comes in and share it straight across?'

Cameron nodded. 'Fine. I've got a lad who is happier on a computer than anywhere. He can do that standing on his head.'

'And how about Rosie McElderry for this end, sir?' Marie added. 'It would be right up her street.'

'Perfect.' Jackman smiled. A very satisfactory arrangement, and it still left Robbie, Max and Charlie on the ground.

'Sir?' Marie looked at him. 'I haven't told DCI Walker about our other death yet. The murder or suicide on the river path.'

'Ah, yes. We have no idea how, but this might just be connected. Marie, would you do the honours?'

Marie recounted the story of their John Doe, adding, 'But as yet, no one has come forward to identify him, or even report a man of his description as missing.'

'Could be a connection, I suppose,' mused Cameron. 'It's a bit too much of a coincidence otherwise, isn't it? Two killers with the same rather weird modus operandi? It's unlikely.'

'I agree,' said Jackman. 'We'll keep working on that one and let you know whatever we find out.'

Cameron stood up. 'I'd better get back. Thanks for the coffee — though I have to say it's no better than ours.' He pulled a face. 'Since we exist on the stuff, you'd think they'd provide something drinkable.'

Jackman smiled and held out his hand. 'We really appreciate your help, DCI Walker.'

'Ditto, and it's just Cam. Less of a mouthful. Bye, Marie and Robbie, nice to meet you both.'

The door closed behind him, and Robbie said, 'What a nice guy! Not like some DCIs I could mention.'

'He's really laidback, but he's a damned good policeman. No one on his team ever asks for a transfer, that's for sure,' said Jackman.

'Bit like you, sir.' Marie grinned at him.

After Robbie had left, Marie said, 'Do you think Sarah was a witness to something, sir?'

'It ticks the boxes, doesn't it? You tell no one, not family, not friends, you start again — new name, new life. It's the biggest secret you ever have to keep, for it could cost you or those closest to you their lives.'

'It's not talked about much, is it? Not even in our own circles.'

'I can understand that. Although there are lots of false theories about it — like the huge sums of money that are paid out to the witnesses on the programme, which is not true at all.'

'A friend of mine looked into joining the witness protection unit, but it meant giving up all work on criminal investigations. She would've been working solely on protecting and hiding vulnerable witnesses. She started the training but decided it wasn't for her. She reckoned they expected the witnesses to go through a really heart-wrenching process, ruining their lives all for the sake of justice and putting some scumbag behind bars.' Marie paused. 'So do we think that's what this is all about? Someone discovered her new identity, and that of another local woman, and threatened them?'

Jackman frowned. 'We have to go back to the beginning now. Find out who the girls were and what crime they witnessed. Then we might be able to get a handle on who was terrorising them.'

'And keep trying to identify our dead pseudo-vagrant.'

'Him too. That's a pretty full workload, Marie. But now Ella is staying at my brother's house and the boys are back at school, I will be on duty again as from tomorrow, okay?'

'Music to my ears, sir.'

* * *

Dale and Liam pulled on their jackets. Kenny watched them hurry out.

'What are they up to now?' Yvette's voice came from behind him, startling him.

He gave her a rueful smile. 'God alone knows. Best not to ask.'

Yvette sank down on the stairs and rubbed at her aching shoulders. 'I've just been handing out leaflets again, over to the north of Saltern High Street this time, but I know they'll just end up in the gutter or the litter bins.'

'Mum appreciates what you are doing. Just hang on to that thought. You're doing it for her.'

'You're a sweet man, Kenny.'

'Rubbish! But I do understand how you feel, Yvie. We've been fighting for so long, and no one gives a damn about an old case, do they? It's history now, and we're just another sad family who can't let go, can't face the truth that one of their own was a murderer.'

'You don't believe that, do you?'

Kenny yawned. 'That Brendan killed that girl? Of course not! If there was a sweet man in our family, it was Brendan, not me. Naughty, it's true, and a bit of a lad, but kill a teenager? No way. Not in a million years. But I do believe that the rest of the world just wants us to fade away.'

Yvette stood up. 'Want some tea?'

'Susie's just making Mum a cup. Let's join them, shall we? But not a word of this in front of Mum, okay?'

'As if. Susie and I have agreed we'll make all the right noises, don't worry about that.'

'It's not me you have to worry about, Yvie, it's Dale and Liam.'

'Oh I know that, Kenny. I know that all too well.'

Kenny painted a smile onto his tired face and followed her into the kitchen. It was strange, but as the two women succumbed to exhaustion and dejection, the more fervently Dale and Liam pursued the crusade. If he had to hear the word "retribution" one more time, Kenny thought he would scream.

* * *

Around four in the afternoon, Marie took a call from Rory Wilkinson.

'I'm ringing to talk to you about men's underwear.'

Marie heard a stifled giggle and smiled. 'Wonderful! My favourite topic of conversation.'

'Good. Well, your vagrant-that-clearly-is-nothing-of-the-kind was, in my opinion, quite a well-off man, and here's where the underwear comes in. He had on charity shop clothes, but obviously drew the line at crappy under-garments. His boxers alone would have cost him over thirty pounds, and his T-shirt was Dolce & Gabbana and no copy I assure you. It retails at over £200.'

'For a bloody T-shirt!' Marie exclaimed. 'You're kidding me!'

'My dear Sergeant, there are young men roaming the streets of our capital city, who frankly look like dossers, in ripped jeans that cost nearly a thousand pounds a pair. You want designer fashion wear, you pay for it.'

'I think I'll stick to the High Street, thanks, Rory.'

'Good decision. Now, back to your mystery man. Max was right about the classy haircut. Generally he was in very good shape, well nourished, with expensive dental work.' He took a breath. 'And that could be how we identify him. He had some specialist implants — and guess what! We now have implant recognition software, radiographic recognition of dental implants, *and* assessment of batch numbers. Whoopee!'

'You are a genius.'

'Don't state the obvious, please. Of course I'm a genius. But when I said *we*, I was talking about forensics in general. I don't actually have the software here, but I know a woman who does. I shall grovel and creep — much as you do when you need something from me — and hopefully I'll have some answers by tomorrow.'

'I can live with that, Rory, and meanwhile our image of the man will be going out on the local news tonight. I can't believe that no one is missing him.'

'And why dress as a tramp and get yourself killed? I'm not joking when I say look for this man in the higher income bracket. He was no hand-to-mouth labourer or benefits cheat. He had money, no question. Intriguing, isn't it?'

'Baffling.'

'Well, I must bid you farewell, dear lady. I need to go and polish up my sycophantic skills in order to obtain information on those implants for you. Ta-ta for now.'

Shaking her head, Marie replaced the receiver. Conversations with Rory were rarely dull. She wondered if she should relay what she knew to Jackman, who had left to visit his nephews, but she decided it could wait until she had something more definite.

'Sarge? While you were on the phone, Orac tried to get hold of you. She wondered if you could go down to her underworld kingdom before you leave.' Charlie grinned at her. 'I'd be happy to come with you . . .'

'What is it with you guys? You are all obsessed with that woman!'

Charlie laughed. 'Maybe.'

'Well, sorry, but I can cope alone, thanks.' Marie looked at the clock. She'd better go now. Time was getting on.

Down in the basement, she really did feel as if she had wandered into a dark and creepy parallel universe. The area was quiet. That, and the dim lighting in the corridors made her want to walk on tiptoe and speak in a whisper.

Orac beckoned from her lair. 'First, I should tell you that I haven't yet tracked down whoever sent Sarah's emails, though I'm edging closer. Have you made any inroads into her secret life?'

Marie took a seat in front of a bank of flickering screens. 'Some. We suspect that her name is an alias.'

'Oh, it is.' Orac flashed those disconcerting eyes at her. 'Until she was sixteen, the lady's name was Heather Miller.'

Marie's mouth dropped open. 'How on earth . . . ?'

'I might not have tracked her stalker yet, but I have made considerable progress with the woman herself. I carried out some checks on the name Sarah Jackman, and discovered from her marriage lines that she was apparently born Sarah Woodman. I then found an anomaly in the electoral roll and a couple of other databases, and a question came up regarding her National Insurance number. I went through a few of the more official channels, and came up with a change of name.'

'Wow! Impressive!'

'It's what they pay me for.' Orac gave her a half smile. 'Although they don't pay me nearly enough!' She turned to face Marie. 'I'm not sure how your DI Jackman will take this, but his sister-in-law is not the person he believed her to be.'

Marie nodded. 'He knows that already. He just wants answers, no matter what. He thought she might possibly be in the witness protection programme.'

Orac drew in a deep breath. 'I don't think that's actually the case.'

Marie frowned. 'What else could it be?'

'She disappeared voluntarily, off her own bat, as it were.'

'At sixteen?'

'Yep. Sixteen, almost seventeen.'

'I don't get it.' Marie felt totally confused.

'I need to do some more work. I'm going to stay on tonight until I get to the bottom of it, but it is my belief that she and another girl witnessed something dreadful, or at the very least saw someone leaving the scene of a crime.'

'Another girl! Of course! Another girl died in similar circumstances a couple of weeks ago. Her name was Suri Forester and she lived in Beech Holby.'

'Ah! That makes my life easier, and it confirms my suspicions. I just need concrete proof. I think, by the morning I will be able to tell you precisely what occurred over twenty years ago to change the girl's life.'

As Marie hurried back to the CID room, she rang Jackman on her mobile and swiftly told him about Sarah's change of name. He sounded as intrigued as she was, and she knew neither of them would sleep that night. She felt like a kid on Christmas Eve, unable to wait for the morning to come. Except, what she'd unwrap would probably not be very nice.

CHAPTER ELEVEN

Jackman decided that unless there was some reason to with-hold information he would keep his family — James in particular, but also Ella Jarvis — up to date with how the investigation was proceeding. Naturally he wouldn't pass on anything sensitive, but he felt they deserved to know why Sarah had acted as she did, if only to dispel any guilt they might be feeling concerning her death.

And so, as night fell, he found himself back at Rainham Lodge. When she was a SOCO, Ella had signed the Official Secrets Act, so he felt he could talk to her openly. After the children had gone to bed, they sat together with two large glasses of wine, and discussed the possibility of someone hav-ing driven Sarah to kill herself.

Ella thought about it and nodded slowly. 'She was always cagey about her past. I thought it must have been a case of sexual abuse, which would explain the never-men-tioned parents.' She sipped her wine and settled herself into the sofa cushions. 'I had it in my head that her father had been the cause of the trouble, which is why I never tried to pry. Now I wonder if she almost encouraged my suspicions, so as to cover up the real reason for her secretiveness. It's

74

quite hurtful to have been lied to for years, but I guess that confirms just how serious she considered the threat to her safety to be. She dared not open up to anyone.'

'Undoubtedly.' Jackman told her they believed her real name was Heather Miller. 'I swear it wasn't in her nature to hurt or lie. And her love for the children and James was undeniable.'

'Oh, I agree. She adored them, idolised them. She would have done anything for them.'

'Done anything for them?' Jackman mused. 'I wonder . . .'

Ella sat up, wide-eyed. 'You think she killed herself to protect her family?'

'It's a possibility, isn't it?'

'So the threat of violence or vengeance was directed at them, not her?' She frowned. 'But wouldn't that mean they might still be in danger? If you are dealing with a mental case, what if he isn't satisfied with just Sarah's death?'

'Let's not get ahead of ourselves.' In his mind, Jackman was already arranging safe houses and round-the-clock protection for his beloved family. He hastily dragged himself back to reality. 'I'm pretty sure that it was a personal attack on Sarah. I don't see that it would do much good to intimidate her family when she's no longer around.'

'Sins of the fathers?' volunteered Ella grimly. 'It has happened.'

'I know, but—'

'You say there was another death locally, very similar to hers?'

He nodded. 'Beech Lacey are investigating an almost identical case. We will be liaising closely with them.'

'Was her name Pauline Grover by any chance?'

'No, it was Suri Forester.'

'Oh, so not Sarah's old friend, the one she mentioned accidentally?'

Jackman's mind clicked into gear. Could that have been Suri's real name? The one that Cameron Walker was looking for? He glanced at his watch, pulled his phone from his pocket and found Cam's number.

After he ended the call, he stared at Ella. 'You are right! The DCI at Beech Lacey has just heard from his sergeant — they have traced Suri Forester back to a change of name by deed poll, from Pauline Grover.'

Ella blinked, and then exhaled. 'Two teenagers, so terrified they abandon everything and become different people. Phew! That is scary.'

As if willing the hours away, Jackman looked at his watch. 'First thing I'll do tomorrow is take a thorough look at the young lives of Heather and Pauline.'

Ella set down her wine glass and leaned towards him. 'Jackman? Do you think we're in danger here?'

He hoped he looked reassuring. 'If I think that for one moment there is the slightest danger to you or any of my family, you will be protected. I promise you that.'

She smiled wryly. 'Okay, just being a trifle paranoid. It'll pass. I just couldn't bear to think of those children having to deal with any more upset while they are still trying to come to terms with their terrible loss.'

To Jackman, such a thing was unthinkable. 'Tomorrow morning I'll get the whole team working on this. I was going to anyway, but there is considerably more urgency now. We need to know what happened so long ago, then we can really get to grips with who might be behind this nightmare.'

Ella drained the rest of her wine. 'I trust you, Jackman. And don't worry. I'll keep the children close. And I'll ask the school to be extra vigilant.'

'Without scaring the shit out of them.'

'Naturally. I'll just explain that until there's a verdict from the coroner about their mother's death, it would be prudent to be observant. I'll talk up our concerns for their general wellbeing.' She gave a short laugh. 'I shan't be telling them we suspect an axe murderer lurking in the climbing frames!'

Jackman laughed, but it faded quickly. They sat in silence. He looked at Ella's worried face and wondered if her thoughts were as dark as his.

* * *

While Jackman was preparing for bed, Marie was still sitting at her kitchen table, looking at a hot whisky toddy and the copies of the emails sent to Sarah by the man — or woman — who hated her so much.

She had already skimmed through them, but now she went over them slowly, trying to find some clue hidden in the words.

She sipped the warm drink, her mother's recipe, and wished it could dissipate the chill that the messages brought.

Insidious, threatening and full of menace, they were shocking to read. They mentioned nothing concrete, but all alluded to something the sender knew had happened, for which he blamed Sarah. There were numerous references that sounded biblical: *His mischief will descend upon his own head . . . If what you do is evil, be afraid.* Another, *Time's glory is to unmask falsehood and bring truth to light* seemed more like a literary quote, possibly Shakespeare. She turned the pages, wondering how Sarah must have felt. Did she believe that she was to blame for this thing that had happened? Marie sighed. In the end, the author of this dreadful barrage had got his way. Sarah had paid for what he accused her of.

She read the last message aloud:

O daughter of Babylon, you devastated one, how blessed will be the one who repays you with the recompense with which you have repaid us. How blessed will be the one who seizes and dashes your little ones against the rock.

The paper shook in her hand. Dash your little ones against the rock? She took a long swallow of the fiery whisky. Now she knew why Sarah had so readily thrown herself into the deep waters of the river Thames. The evil bastard had threatened her children.

Marie thought of the other woman. Had it been the same with her? Cam Walker did say she was a mother, didn't he? Marie swore. She drained the rest of the drink, pulled the papers together, and stood up. She needed to try and sleep. Jackman was back tomorrow, and they had a hell of a lot to talk about.

* * *

The church wasn't the only place he felt calm. He also liked woods, being sheltered inside a natural cathedral of tall trees with only the sounds of nature around him, but they were hard to find on the fens. Tonight the church was locked, so he chose a point far out on the marsh, a place that few people knew about. It was a miserable spot, bleak and almost impossible to find. With one rough lane in, it was inhospitable and the track to the raised sea bank was overgrown with nettles and brambles. Just below the bank, there was a Second World War pillbox, its pitted walls covered with lichen and its roof with self-seeded couch grass and weeds. If he climbed on top, he could see across to the flat expanse of marsh, and sometimes, if the tide was in, the silvery grey waters of the Wash. Other than the occasional poacher, no one would attempt to come here in the dark. It was why he loved the place, to sit on top of the pill box and see a vast expanse of nothing extending out before him. Out here it was possible to believe in nothing, to forget all loyalties and purpose, other than the impulse to destroy. But he had purpose, he reminded himself. He had loyalty, and he *believed*. He believed in himself.

The power he felt when those two women jumped was indescribable, immense. Such power he had over them!

He took a deep breath of the air, heavy with salt, held it, and let it out slowly.

He had watched them do it. He had seen the looks on their faces. He had seen them relinquish the strongest impulse of all living beings. Self-preservation.

When you know where love lies, true, selfless love, you can also destroy. *That* was the source of his power. Love as a lethal weapon. He began to laugh, louder and louder. There was no one to hear.

* * *

It was late when Ella finally got to bed. The boys had been restless, Miles had cried for almost half an hour. She sat with them, listened to their questions, and tried very hard to say the right things, things that would help. She had used the word "dead," rather than "asleep." She knew it was important that they appreciated that their mother was never coming back. She thought Ryan understood, but Miles lived in a fantasy world, where the wizard would always wave a wand and restore the hero to life at the very last moment. He had to be made to realise that that didn't happen in real life.

Ryan had asked, 'Was Mummy cross with me?'

'No, sweetheart!' she said. 'Your Mummy loved you very much. Why did you think she was angry with you?'

'Because she was acting funny all week.' He stared hard at his duvet and refused to look her in the eye.

'How do you mean, funny?'

Finally he looked up at her, pain and bewilderment in his eyes. 'One minute she was mad at me, then she would hug me so hard I couldn't breathe. It was really weird.'

'Adults do act weird sometimes, Ryan. We have a lot to worry about and sometimes we take our worries out on the wrong people. That was most likely it. She told you off, then she was sorry she had so she hugged you.'

He pursed his lips. 'I suppose.' Then he brightened. 'Yes, that would be it, wouldn't it? I mean, she did say she loved us more than anything in the world.' Almost immediately he lay down and snuggled into his pillow.

She got ready for bed, thinking how different the two boys were. Ryan was serious and practical. He enjoyed games, he played, but he was calculating and measured in everything he did. In short, he was his father's son. Miles, on the other hand, was easy-going and fun-loving, gregarious, artistic and full of imagination, just like Sarah.

She had believed that Miles would give the greatest concern, but now she wasn't so sure. To her knowledge, Ryan hadn't shed a single tear. He hadn't had a tantrum, nor did he seem especially sad. Apart from that single question earlier, he just seemed to swallow the whole thing and store it away in his mind. Did that mean he couldn't deal with it?

She lay in bed and listened in case Miles was still crying. The house was silent. It was good to know that Jackman was just a few doors away. He had tried to ease her worries, but she was good at reading people, and knew Jackman was as concerned as she was. She must remember to tell him what Ryan had said. It added to the supposition that Sarah had done what she did to protect her children. It was a terrifying thought.

Ella turned on her side and lay awake, her eyes open in the dark.

CHAPTER TWELVE

That morning's meeting went on for almost three-quarters of an hour until Jackman finally wrapped it up and delegated the tasks for the day.

'So, Rosie, you are our contact with Beech Lacey. I want you to work closely with their liaison officer, DC Darren Smith. Make sure nothing gets overlooked. Every new piece of info that comes our way is passed directly to them, and vice versa. Okay?'

DC Rosie McElderry nodded enthusiastically. She had a quick brain, and this job would be a refreshing change for her. 'Great, sir. I'll ring Darren and we'll set up a system.'

'Good. Now,' he looked around, 'Charlie, I want you and Gary to concentrate on identifying our John Doe. We're certain there is a connection to Sarah, but until we have an ID we are dancing in the dark.' He handed him Rory's pathology report. 'Professor Wilkinson now thinks he has a way to identify him through dental implants, so chase him up on that. Find out who this man is — and fast.'

Jackman turned to Robbie and Max. 'You two are going to concentrate on the time when the two women took the names Sarah Woodman and Suri Forester. It won't be easy but, Max, you should tie up with Orac on this.'

Max's eyes widened and he grinned. 'Gotcha, boss! I'm on it.'

'I bet you are!' Rosie flashed him a warning glance. She had been Max's girlfriend for the past year.

'Marie, you and I will continue this conversation in my office. There are some loose ends to tie up, and then we'll start to dissect my sister-in-law's early life and find out all we can about her friend, Suri Forester. Okay, guys. To work! And I expect something for the four o'clock meeting.'

* * *

Marie closed the office door behind her. She had already told Jackman about her suspicion that someone had been with Sarah when she died. Jackman had looked at the CCTV footage again and his face had spoken volumes. It wasn't absolutely certain, but there was a good chance Sarah was looking at someone standing behind her.

Jackman was reading through his emails. He gave a sigh of relief. 'The inquest has been opened and adjourned.'

Marie smiled. 'As we hoped, but it's good to hear it from the horse's mouth.'

'I think we have Rory to thank for that. The coroner established identity and the fact that the cause of death was drowning, but following the pathologist's report, he adjourned to await the forensic and full toxicology reports. He also commented that the police had advised further investigation, so the verdict will wait, pending the results of their inquiries.'

'Great. We have a bit of leeway.' Marie looked at him. 'Okay, sir, what's the problem?'

He sighed. 'Ruth Crooke. The super's not certain that I'll be able to maintain a professional attitude. She's worried about a possible conflict of interest because Sarah is, sorry, *was*, my sister-in-law. I've assured her that we were never close, and pointed out that the reason for that was my commitment to my career, but she's considering asking me to stand down and let someone else take over.'

Marie groaned. 'Oh hell! How do you feel about that little bombshell?'

'Sodding-well pissed off!' Marie almost smiled. Jackman very rarely swore.

'Can I help at all? I can speak to Ruth, if you like. She and I get on pretty well after that case involving her niece. I've even learned to let the heavy sarcasm go over my head.'

'I have to keep hold of this case. I have to.' Jackman sat back and folded his arms.

Marie didn't say it, but she could see Ruth's point. It was too close to home. What if the man behind it all decided to target other members of Jackman's family? There was no way he could remain in charge if that happened. 'How long has she given you?'

'Today. That's all. Just today.' Jackman looked desperate. 'I've got to see her first thing tomorrow with a full report on where we are. She'll decide then.'

'So we need to buckle down and get some answers. You know Ruth, sir, she'll not do it lightly. If we can show her something within twenty-four hours, I'm sure she'll let you run with it. So come on, give me some work to do instead of fretting over something that might never happen.'

Jackman straightened up. 'You're right, Marie. Sorry about that.' He gave her a tired smile. 'Not enough sleep last night. In fact, practically no sleep at all.'

Marie smiled back. 'Same here. Orac said she would stay late at work until she found the connection between Sarah and her friend Suri. I've been wondering all night what those two teenagers might have been involved in.'

'Right. Well, I thought you should trawl through police reports of serious crimes from the time just preceding Sarah's change of name.'

'And look for cases that involved fifteen- to sixteen-year-old girls?'

'Yes, and not just as possible witnesses. It hurts me to say this, but check anything that has them as victims or even perpetrators. If someone wants retribution, it could be because of something they did, rather than what they saw or suffered. I can't believe that of Sarah, but we have to consider the possibility.'

'Absolutely, sir. And an open mind will be exactly what Ruth will be watching out for.'

'I had thought about that myself,' Jackman said smugly. 'I'm conducting a fair investigation but also covering my back.'

'Good. And so you should. Sir, was Sarah a local?'

'Hard to say, although she did have the accent. Not too pronounced, but I'd say it was natural and not acquired.'

'Narrows my search somewhat. So what will you be doing?'

'Trying to trace anything I can about Sarah when she was Heather Miller — birth certificate, christening, school records, health and hospital notes, anything to give us an idea of who she was before she became Sarah. Cam Walker is doing exactly the same with regard to Pauline Grover. The moment either of us sources something, our carrier pigeons, Rosie and Darren, will pass it over.'

'Neat. So, let's get to work. I hate to say it, but the clock is ticking.'

* * *

Just after eleven, Charlie almost fell into Jackman's office. 'We've got him, sir! Our John Doe's got a name.'

'Good lad!' Jackman hadn't expected a result so soon.

'You'd better thank Prof Wilkinson, sir. He found us the dentist who fitted the implants, and all we did was contact them and get his details. The dead man's name is Bernard Seaton, and he lived out Harlan Marsh way. Gary and Kevin Stoner are on their way there right now.'

'Excellent. Tell them to come directly to me when they return.'

'Will do, sir.'

Charlie hurried back to his desk to begin checking Bernard Seaton's background.

Jackman returned to his work with a little more enthusiasm. At least the swift identification of the dead man would earn him a few brownie points with the superintendent. If they could add another step forward, she might rethink her plan to remove him.

He stared at the screen. Just how many million Heather Millers were there in the world? He cancelled the search and went on to check school records. If he knew where she came from it would help, but right now it was pretty random. He hoped that Marie and Robbie were having more luck than he was.

* * *

'I hate coming back to this area.' Gary Pritchard's voice was uncharacteristically sombre.

'But you lived here for years, didn't you, Gary?' asked Kevin.

'I did, but apart from my sister and my lovely dogs, it wasn't a happy place.'

'Oh, yes, I forgot. Harlan Marsh was where they found all those bod—'

'Let's not go there, Kev. It's too painful.'

'Sorry, mate. That was a very bad case, wasn't it? I wasn't thinking.' Kevin changed the subject. 'Do you know the address we're looking for?'

Gary gazed across the miles of flat fields, mostly full of kale, sprouts and various kinds of cabbage. 'I know the entrance to the lane, but in all honesty, I've only ever been down there once. It goes nowhere. It's one of those strange roads that curves around the fen for miles, and then ends in an overgrown turning place with nothing but farmland as far as the eye can see.'

Kevin stared at the silent satnav. 'So, we are looking for a house called Marlins. And it looks like we are on our own with finding it.'

85

Gary took a left turn into Hurn Bank Lane. 'As far as I recall from when I worked this patch, there are only three or four houses down here.'

Kevin stared down the lonely road. 'Blimey, this is pretty bleak, isn't it? I wouldn't like to live here.'

'You want to see it when the rain is being driven by a sixty-mile-an-hour wind! The day I came here it was blowing a gale, and it gave a whole new meaning to the word "miserable," believe me.'

They drove for almost a mile and a half, passing only one dwelling, a farmworker's ramshackle cottage called Utopia, which made Kevin laugh for several minutes.

The next one looked slightly better. The nameplate "The Willows" hung, appropriately, from a huge willow tree.

'Two down,' muttered Kevin. 'And another one in sight around the next bend.'

Gary slowed down and negotiated a sharp bend with deep dykes either side. 'This has to be it. The address I visited was the last house before the dead end, and I don't think it was called Marlins.'

They turned in to a semi-circular gravel driveway and Gary pulled up outside the front door.

'Oh my!' exclaimed Kevin. 'It's a diamond stuck in a turd!'

The house was big and well-cared for, with a triple garage and a carport with a dovecote on the roof. 'Our tramp's house?' asked Gary.

'It's called Marlins, and our dentist informed Charlie Button that the man's implants were some of the most expensive you can buy, so, yes, I'd say this is the Seaton residence.'

They rang the doorbell and heard it ring inside the house, but no one answered.

'Long way to come just to turn round and go home again,' said Kevin thoughtfully.

'There might be someone out the back. You go right, I'll go left.' Gary started off towards a gate at the side.

'You won't find anyone in!'

Gary jumped. 'Where did you come from?' He stared at the elderly man who had materialised behind him. He was wearing a waxed jacket and had a Jack Russell on the end of a faded and frayed leash.

'We looks out for strangers around here. I saw the police car as it went past my place.'

'So you know Mr Seaton?'

'Bernie? Sort of. Not well. He's a bit of a recluse. That's why he bought this pile stuck out here in no man's land.'

'He lives alone, in this big house?' asked Gary in surprise.

'Yes. Quite alone. No cats, no dogs, no budgie. Nothing.' The man looked fondly down at his own dog. 'He must get lonely, although a few weeks back he had a visitor come regular like. Must have been a relative, I suppose, but he never said.'

'Did he say where he was going, sir?'

'Just away, no more than that. Asked me to keep a watch on the place; keep me eyes open.'

The man was around seventy, guessed Gary, fairly well dressed but his clothes were far from new. 'Can I have your name, sir?'

'Derek Keats, Officer. I live next door in the Willows.'

Gary decided that the man was no threat and that he wanted him on side. 'Well, listen, Derek, I probably shouldn't be telling you this, but as Mr Seaton obviously trusted you . . .' Gary paused, then added, 'And remember, this didn't come from me, and it still has to be confirmed, but a gentleman who we believe to be Bernard Seaton has been found dead.'

'Oh dear, oh dear.' The old man rubbed at his wrinkled cheek. 'That's very bad news.'

Kevin joined them and produced a copy of the digitally enhanced photograph. 'Is this Mr Seaton, sir?'

The man screwed up his eyes and squinted at the picture. 'It's not the best likeness, but yes, that's Bernie alright.' He looked at Gary. 'What happened to him?'

'I'm afraid we can't say as it's an ongoing investigation, sir. But we are going to have to take a look around his home.'

Gary looked at Kevin. 'Ring this in, Kevin. Now we know this is his house, we need a forensic sweep done.'

'I have a key.' Derek Keats fished deep inside a breast pocket of the old jacket and produced a shiny Yale key. 'In case of emergencies, he said. And I guess this constitutes an emergency.'

Gary smiled. 'It will also save any damage, sir. Thank you.'

As soon as he stepped inside, Gary knew that something was wrong. On first glance it would have looked quite normal, until you noticed small indications of damage. A photo torn into shreds. A piece of what must have been valuable china crushed almost to powder. A leather-bound book burnt in the fireplace. Someone had selected particular items and systematically destroyed them.

Gary and Kevin pulled on latex gloves and looked around. The hall opened onto a big open plan lounge-dining room that led into a massive conservatory. It was light and airy, and stank of money. Nothing was cheap. The carpets were rich and thick, the curtains beautifully hung on ornate poles and the furniture must have cost a fortune.

'A tramp?' Kevin whispered.

'No way was our Bernie destitute.' Gary's eyes narrowed. 'I don't like the look of that, do you?'

A single hardback chair had been placed in the centre of the dining area. Two lengths of rope were still attached to it — one piece hung from the back, and the other from one leg.

They moved closer, careful not to disturb anything.

'Someone was tied up here, and I'm assuming it was Bernard,' mused Gary. 'While someone else walked around his home smashing and annihilating his precious possessions. What do you think?'

Kevin nodded. 'That's what it looks like. But why?'

'I suggest our "visitor" wanted something badly.' Gary looked at the torn photograph. 'It's a child. A little girl, and it's pretty old, certainly not taken on a modern day camera. I'd say it was a treasured memory.'

'And matey-boy shredded it.' Kevin grimaced. 'Ouch. That would have hurt.'

'So would this.' Gary bent down and peered into the fireplace. Beside the old burnt book there was a bundle of letters, still with a singed strand of ribbon around them. 'Love letters, unless I'm just being a romantic old fool.'

Kevin looked over his shoulder. 'Love letters, for sure.'

Gary heaved in a deep breath. 'This man, whoever he was, hated Seaton so much that he tortured him, not physically, but by destroying the things he held dear.'

'I wonder who this Bernard Seaton really is?' Kevin said. 'Shall we take a look around? See if he has an office? He's sure to have some paperwork that might give us a clue.'

Gary shook his head. 'I'd love to, Kev, but this is a crime scene. We'd better wait for the SOCOs to get here or we'll be accused of trashing the evidence, if there is any. Hopefully the others back at the office have already traced his history now they have his name.'

On their way back to the hall, Gary noticed some letters placed on the hall table. He looked through them and passed the pile to Kevin. 'Forget my last comment. Look at these!'

'Ah, I see what you mean. They're not addressed to Bernard Seaton at all, but to Philip B. Seaton, and this one,' Kevin pointed, 'says, "to P. B. Seaton, QC." Hell, he was a Queen's Counsel!'

'So he was a barrister, was he? That shines a very different light on why someone might have hated him, doesn't it?' Gary reached for his radio. 'The team need to hear this, unless they've made the connection already.'

'And here come the CSIs.' Kevin was looking down the lane. 'I'll just go and check that our friendly neighbour and his dog are out of the way, and tell him not to broadcast the news just yet. We don't want the press on the doorstep before we've had time to process the scene.'

'Good thinking, lad.' Gary called in their discovery, and waited for the scene-of-crime officers, wondering what other secrets this beautiful lonely house would offer up.

CHAPTER THIRTEEN

Information was beginning to stream into the CID room, and Jackman retreated to his office to collate what they knew in time for the four o'clock meeting.

He was in full flow when a soft tap on his door interrupted his efforts. He swore under his breath, and barked 'Come in!' But when he saw who it was, his face softened and he broke into a smile. 'Laura! Come in and sit down.'

Laura Archer, the force psychologist, returned his smile. 'I know you are busy — well, run off your feet — but that's actually why I'm here.'

He tilted his head and looked at her. 'I don't . . .'

'Your nephews and your brother are not the only ones who need support, Jackman. I'm here for you too. So, how are you coping?'

Jackman exhaled. Where to begin? 'I would say fine, and that I'm on top of things, except for the fact that I am under extreme pressure to get results fast or I'm off the case. That is where the stress comes from.'

'Conflict of interest?'

He nodded glumly. 'Even though I saw less of Sarah than I do of our dog handler! And I see him perhaps once a fortnight. I just want the truth to be found, most of all for my family's sake.'

'And if that truth is uncomfortable?'

'It will still be the truth, Laura. That's what really matters.' He sat back and stretched out his legs in front of him. 'I can find a way to explain the truth to Ryan and Miles, but I can't explain guesswork and lies, and I won't lie to them.'

Laura gave him a long look. 'You seem to be approaching this in a practical and healthy way. I'd say your added incentive will actually assist the investigation rather than hinder it. If it will help, I'm on my way to speak to your superintendent about another matter, and I will tell her that you have my full support to continue as OIC on this case.'

'If you can swing this, Laura Archer, I will take you to the Watermill Restaurant and treat you to the best meal of your life!'

'The Watermill? That will set you back six months' pay! I'll settle for that little French restaurant in Bridge Street, thanks. Their Sole Meunière, with a bottle of Sancerre, is like rising to heaven.' She paused. 'And we needn't wait. We could go there anytime — if you like?'

Jackman blinked. He contemplated her soft light brown hair and cornflower blue eyes and decided that there was nothing he'd like more. 'That's a date — after the case.'

'And if the case goes on forever?'

'Then we renegotiate.' He grinned at her. 'Now I have another incentive to get a fast result.'

Laura stood up. 'I have to go, but remember, if you feel at all shaky, you have my number. Don't hesitate to call me, anytime. Okay?'

Jackman thanked her. He opened his mouth to remind her about the dinner date, when there was a loud rap on his door.

Marie stuck her head in. 'Sir! You'll want to hear this! Oh, apologies, I didn't realise . . . Hi, Laura, sorry to interrupt, but sir, we've worked out the connection between the two girls, *and* our pseudo-vagrant!'

Jackman felt a rush of excitement. He glanced at his watch. 'It's almost four. Is everyone here?'

'Apart from Gary, who is still at Seaton's house.'

'Then get them together, and I'll be right there.'

* * *

While Jackman addressed the team, Marie could see Laura Archer and Ruth Crooke in earnest conversation in the corridor outside the CID room. A few moments later, they both slipped quietly inside and leaned against the wall at the back.

'So, Marie? Would you please bring everyone up to date on the latest findings.'

Marie walked up to the front and stood next to the whiteboard. 'Earlier today we confirmed that the man found dead on the towpath was called Bernard Seaton of Harlan Marsh. Since then, a search of his home has revealed that he is actually a retired QC by the name of Phillip Seaton. Gary Pritchard and Kevin Stoner have since told us that Seaton was apparently held hostage in his own home and made to watch as his precious personal items were destroyed. A neighbour noticed that a strange man was visiting Seaton regularly. Seaton was known to be a recluse, so we believe that the visitor was the man who assaulted him.' She took a breath. 'The neighbour's description of this visitor corresponds to eyewitness reports of the man who was seen with Seaton while he was living rough here in Saltern, so we suspect that this is the man who "assisted" Seaton's supposed suicide.' She looked across to Robbie Melton. 'Robbie?'

'Yes, Sarge.' He stood up. 'I've checked back on a series of high profile cases that Seaton dealt with when Sarah Jackman was a teenager, and have come up with one definite possibility.'

Everyone looked at him expectantly.

'Seaton was the prosecuting counsel at the trial of a man called Brendan Symons. Symons was convicted of the rape and murder of one Lyndsay Ashcroft and given a life sentence.'

Marie took up the story. 'And we believe that this is the connection because there were two key eyewitnesses to the attack — two teenage girls.'

She waited for the murmurs of surprise to die down.

'And the time scale fits?' asked Jackman.

'Perfectly, sir. The girls were never named. Due to their age, and the fact they had witnessed the rape of one of their school friends, they were allowed to give their evidence *in camera*. They were only ever referred to as Girl A, and Girl B.'

'When was this?' asked Jackman.

'Mid-nineties. But that wasn't the end of it. I remember that the media had something new to say about this case almost every week. And then Brendan Symons, who protested his innocence to the last, hanged himself in his prison cell'

Jackman whistled softly. 'And the family took up a crusade that is still rumbling around in the press. I saw something about it only the other day. But listen everyone, don't make assumptions at this point. It would be very easy to assume that the family are behind it all, and maybe they are, but you mustn't get sidetracked. This is a complex case, and there will be a lot going on that we know nothing about. This is a massive step forward, but possibly just the start of the investigation proper. Okay?'

There were nods.

'So the girls were put into the witness protection programme for their safety?' asked Charlie.

Marie pulled a face. 'Too soon to know. It seems probable, but as you know, they don't just hand out information. You have to go through the correct channels and obtain the proper authorisation, and I haven't had time to pursue it yet. My initial enquiry yielded nothing, but naturally I will be following it up. Plus there is always the chance that they, or their families, might just have taken it upon themselves to up sticks and find a new life. We need to do a lot more investigating in that area.'

'Thanks, Marie.' Jackman walked back to the front. 'Seaton's house is being carefully searched and forensics are carrying out a sweep. We're hoping to find some reason for Seaton's sudden strange transition from a prominent barrister to a recluse, hidden away in the bleakest part of the fens.'

'And then to street dweller,' added Max.

'That was never of his choosing, I'm sure. He was made to do that. We just need to know why, and who made him do it.'

'Are we assuming that the same man caused all three deaths, sir?' Rosie asked.

'We assume nothing yet, but I think that's the conclusion we'll come to. It's all about retribution. We have a maverick wandering around Saltern-le-Fen, a vigilante with a twisted desire for revenge.' He looked at each of them in turn. 'What we don't know is how far he is prepared to go to assuage his hunger for revenge. He's dealt with the witnesses, and the prosecutor. Is the judge next? Or the jury? Or the officer in charge of the investigation?' Jackman swallowed. 'This is very serious and we need to put all our efforts into identifying this killer as speedily as possible.' He looked up. 'I need to speak with the superintendent, but if you would all remain here for the time being, I will be back shortly to issue your duties. Marie will fill you in on the rest of the details. Thank you all in advance for what I know will be your whole-hearted dedication to getting this man off our streets. Marie, take over, please.'

Marie wondered if they'd done enough to keep Jackman on the case. Surely they couldn't have done any more? She guessed that Laura might have put in a good word too. Why else would she have been talking to Ruth just prior to their meeting?

She smiled. When she had walked into Jackman's office earlier, had she been mistaken or was there a ripple of electricity in the air? For some time now, Marie had been on the lookout for a suitable partner for Jackman, and Laura was the perfect candidate for the Evans Eligibility Test! Why hadn't she thought of her before? She was intelligent, professional and caring, plus she was pretty and dressed well! Laura made Marie feel like a hod-carrier by comparison. Also, Marie really liked her. Well, if they needed a little push . . .

* * *

Ruth Crooke began the moment the door closed behind them. 'I suppose I'd better put you out of your misery, Rowan. You have a stay of execution, okay? I'd be a fool to lose the momentum that you've built up.' She narrowed her eyes. 'But if at any time you feel that your position as Officer in Charge is at all compromised, you stand down immediately. Is that understood?'

A weight lifted from his shoulders. Jackman nodded furiously. 'I'll treat this case professionally, ma'am, I promise.'

Ruth paced her office. 'The very thought of the Brendan Symons case rearing its head once again fills me with horror. They are a tricky family to deal with, and if the rumours in the media are correct, the mother is far from well. You will need to tread with the utmost care, Rowan.'

'You sound as if you've had dealings with them before, ma'am.'

She looked glum. 'Several times, and I'd rather not repeat the experience.'

'I haven't had time to go over the case, ma'am. Is there anything particular about it that I should know?'

Ruth sat down and nodded to a chair. 'I think I'd rather you read the reports yourself and drew your own conclusions. The case divided the officers who were working it. Young Brendan was a bit of a tearaway but he had never been in trouble before. Some believed his claim that he was innocent, and others thought him as guilty as sin, and that he was using his cheeky good looks to literally get away with murder.'

'And when he killed himself, how was that perceived? As an admission of guilt? Or the fact that he couldn't face a life sentence knowing he was an innocent man?'

'Again, divided. Most thought he was guilty and he couldn't live with himself after what he'd done.'

'I'll read the transcript after the meeting, and see for myself.' Jackman stood up. 'I'd better get the guys sorted out. Thank you, Ruth. I won't let you down.'

* * *

Jackman finished delegating the tasks and saw Marie beckoning to him.

'While you were with the super, I heard from witness protection.'

'That was pretty damned quick!' exclaimed Jackman.

'Only because they were adamant that no one connected to the Lyndsay Ashcroft murder trial was put on the programme.'

'Blast!' Jackman growled. 'Does that mean we've got the whole thing wrong?'

'No, sir, just that the two anonymous girls were not considered to be under threat. Brendan Symons was safe behind bars serving a life sentence, and their identities had been kept under wraps. It wasn't considered necessary.'

'Right. Then I think it's time we acquainted ourselves with exactly what happened to Lyndsay Ashcroft, don't you?' asked Jackman.

'And then get the super to access the names of those two young witnesses. Until we know for sure that they really are Sarah and Suri, we could be chasing our tails.' Her eyes sparkled. 'Not that I believe that's the case for one minute. We are on the right track, sir, I know we are.'

CHAPTER FOURTEEN

Marie was right. They collated all the information — from Orac, DCI Cameron Walker at Beech Lacey, Ruth Crooke, and whatever they had found themselves — and by seven that evening they had the strange story of Sarah and Suri.

Engrossed in the work, not one of the team asked to go home, but they did accept the offer of pizza, courtesy of Jackman. He summed up what they knew as they ate. 'The start of it all is the murder of Lyndsay Ashcroft back in 1995. Ruth Crooke has been told that the names of the two teenagers who gave testimony at the trial were Pauline Grover and Heather Miller, or Suri and Sarah as we know them. The murder took place in a small town called Nettleby in the north of the county. The teenager who was killed went to the same school as the girls, and Brendan Symons, the young man who was convicted of her rape and murder, lived in a neighbouring village. He was known to all three girls.' He sipped at his coffee. 'Phillip Seaton was the prosecutor, and apparently he did a very good job of not only securing a conviction, but making sure that Symons got life.' He glanced across to Gary Pritchard. 'You found some very interesting evidence at Seaton's house, didn't you?'

'I did.' Gary put down his half eaten slice of pizza. 'The man kept records of everything and filed dozens of letters, many of them poison pen letters. He had evidently been hounded for many years, accused of bringing about the death of an innocent man. I think it was just irritating to begin with, as it rather comes with the territory, but Seaton's wife died suddenly, and not long after, his only son went off to Australia to work. At this point the threats intensified, and under pressure, Seaton cracked. He gave up work and moved away. He began using his middle name, and refused to speak to anyone from his past. He emerged as Bernie, the recluse of Harlan Marsh.'

'But his nemesis found him,' Robbie added sombrely.

'He did.' Gary snatched a bite of pizza. 'Even though he was ex-directory, he started getting phone calls. I know this because he kept a diary for a while. Sadly he gave up just before his persecutor's first visit, or I'm sure we would have a description to match the one his neighbour gave us, and our snout Cassie's.'

'Any suggestions as to why Seaton finished up on the streets?' asked Max. 'That's the weird part. After all, even though he was a recluse and a bit on the odd side, he still dressed really well and was careful with his appearance.'

Rosie laughed. 'Still thinking about that awesome haircut?'

'Yeah! He had values. He was no spring chicken but he took care of himself.'

'*And* his house,' added Gary. 'Apart from the articles that were destroyed, the place was immaculate. And he had some smashing gear too. Lovely paintings, beautiful ornaments and really classy furniture.'

'Would you say his surroundings were important to him, Gary?' Jackman asked.

'Very much so, sir.'

Jackman nodded. 'Then maybe that's how the killer manipulated him.'

Robbie looked up from his food. 'Like threaten to torch the place? Something like that?'

'Possibly,' Jackman said. 'His wife and son were gone, and his possessions were all he had left.'

'But surely that wouldn't cause you to kill yourself?' Charlie asked. 'I mean, I completely understand if your kids are threatened, but belongings can be replaced.'

'Don't forget that this was a sustained psychological attack, over a very long time. Who knows what state his mind was in by the time he died?'

'True. I hadn't thought of that.' Charlie picked up his pizza, then put it down again. 'Do you think he had OCD?'

Jackman shrugged. 'Gary? You've seen his house? What do you think?'

Gary frowned. 'I didn't think of it at the time, but yes, quite possibly. I said immaculate, but it was really almost too perfect. A place for everything, and everything in its place, as they say.'

Charlie grinned. 'Then you are right, sir. A threat to his perfect home might really get to him. Just mess up his sock drawer and he'd probably feel like topping himself.'

Jackman tried not to smile. 'A tad on the callous side, Charlie, but I catch your drift.'

'It would take a master manipulator and a lot of patience to carry off something as insidious as that,' Robbie interjected. 'Sir, do you know the history of the Ashcroft murder? Was the convicted man's guilt ever in doubt?'

'No. His DNA was everywhere at the scene, and with two eyewitnesses identifying him under oath it was pretty well cut and dried.'

'But the family never doubted his innocence, even with all that damning evidence?' Robbie looked perplexed.

'Tomorrow we will go over the whole transcript together.' Jackman drained his coffee. 'I'm as puzzled as you as to why the family are still so adamant after all these years. And if it's not the family behind the deaths, someone else also believes that Brendan Symons was wrongly convicted.'

'Someone who loved him, maybe?' murmured Marie.

'A woman?' Gary asked. 'Surely not.'

Marie shrugged. 'Why not? But it can't be. We know for a fact that it was a man hounding Seaton. The neighbour saw him visiting just before Seaton disappeared.'

Rosie added, 'Men are capable of loving other men, in any number of ways. I'm thinking hero worship, comradeship, brotherly love, apart from the straightforward good old-fashioned sexual sort.'

'I agree,' Max added. 'You would have to have very strong feelings indeed to keep up a hate campaign like this one for so long.'

'Why wait all this time?' asked Charlie. 'Why not start to even the score immediately after Brendan killed himself? It's been twenty years since his suicide.'

'He's got a point, sir,' said Gary. 'I know all about revenge being a dish best served cold, but why let the people you hold responsible have twenty good years of life and freedom?'

'There could be a valid reason. Maybe he's been in prison. He might have sat in jail plotting retribution until he was let out,' Jackman said.

Marie looked pensive. 'I keep thinking about that terrible quote of his, about "seizing and dashing your little ones against the rocks." Couldn't this really be a calculated long-term plan, something truly terrible? What if the killer waited until his targets had something really precious in their lives so he could use that against them?'

'Could anyone be that wicked?' asked Rosie, then added quickly, 'Don't answer that, I know the answer.'

'The big question is, does it end here?' Jackman exhaled. 'The two witnesses and the prosecutor are dead. Is that enough for him?'

'I suspect not.' Robbie looked grim.

'Me neither.' Marie folded up the empty pizza boxes. 'This whole thing just screams insanity, and no one can second guess what a psychopath will do next.'

'Laura could give us her opinion,' volunteered Jackman. 'Remember her old mentor, Professor Sam Page? He's a retired psychologist specialising in memory. Maybe he could give us some input too.' The thought of seeing Laura again gave Jackman goosebumps.

Robbie nodded. 'Good idea, sir. It would be good to get some insight into the kind of person we're dealing with.'

'Surely it *has* to be one of Brendan's family?' Max balled up a paper serviette and lobbed it at a wastepaper bin, smiling when it went in. 'I like the idea of a stricken, lovelorn, lost soul, but it's much more likely to be a blood relative wanting revenge, isn't it?'

'It certainly could be, which is why we will be interviewing them. And when we do, mind, it's eggshells all the way. The super says they're tricky, and I didn't like the look in her eye when she said it.'

Charlie leaned back in his chair. 'Sir, regarding the murder trial, what were the grey areas you mentioned?'

Jackman glanced at the clock. 'Don't you guys have homes to go to? Annie and her cleaning staff are waiting to come in.'

Max shrugged. 'Ten more minutes won't make too much difference.'

'Briefly then, the teenager was found in a wooded copse on the edge of the town. She had been beaten and then strangled. Brendan never denied seeing Lyndsay that night and admitted that they had made love. He was adamant that it was consensual, and that they had been planning it for weeks. It was her first time.'

'And her last,' whispered Rosie. 'Poor kid.'

'Exactly. Brendan flatly denied killing her. He said they had planned to leave the area separately in case they were seen together, which they didn't want. He swore that she was alive when he left her. Alive and happy.'

Gary frowned. 'So, if they were so careful to keep this a secret, how come Sarah and Suri saw them? You said they were eyewitnesses.'

'There had been a party that evening, a very clandestine affair arranged by a couple of young men from Brendan's village. They'd broken into a disused stable at the back of one of the lads' homes, and because his parents were away for the weekend, they organised drink and some music and invited a select few girls from Nettleby. Lyndsay was invited, along with Sarah and Suri, but Lyndsay only stayed for a very short time. Her two friends went out to look for her and thought they saw Brendan's motorcycle hidden in a small stand of trees. They sneaked into the copse and saw Lyndsay and Brendan together. The girls admitted giggling together when they realised that they were actually going to "do it," as they put it.'

'And curiosity got the better of them,' said Rosie.

'They were both still virgins. They said they knew they ought to leave, but they were so fascinated, they stayed to watch.' Jackman could picture the stifled giggles and the wide, disbelieving eyes. 'When it was over, they slipped away before they were noticed. But when Lyndsay didn't come back to the party, they started to get worried. After a while they went back, and that was when they saw Brendan's bike heading off. Then they found Lyndsay, dead, in the same spot she had been in with Brendan earlier.'

Max pulled a face. 'That didn't exactly sound like rape to me. Surely, the girl had consented? Wouldn't the girls have seen if it was rape?'

'That's what Brendan said. But, the post-mortem found considerable bruising and damage. It was decided that what the witnesses saw was only part of what happened. It seems that he wanted more, Lyndsay objected, and he raped her. She would have called out for help, and he silenced her by hitting and then strangling her. Then he ran away.'

'Phew!' Charlie grimaced. 'Nasty.'

'The forensic evidence was undeniable. Brendan's was the only DNA found.'

'And the two girls saw them together,' Marie concluded. 'And also saw Brendan leaving the scene later. Case closed.'

'Except that they never actually saw him hurt her. What they described was an inexperienced attempt at lovemaking.'

'I hate to get too personal, but initially did he actually . . . ?' Gary asked tentatively.

Jackman nodded. 'Yes, he scored.'

'If they were, as he said, planning this "event,"' Max asked, 'Wouldn't he have used protection?'

'He did, but he made a serious beginner's error and put it on wrong.'

'Disaster!' Rosie winced and shook her head.

Jackman nodded. 'And that was what put the nail in his coffin.' He looked up at the wall clock. 'Now I really think we should call it a day. Tomorrow we'll get an action plan together and tackle this head on. We cannot afford to let this killer melt into the shadows. We have to identify him and apprehend him, and to do that we have to take this murder case to pieces.' He pointed to the pile of thick files on the desk in front of him. 'He's hidden in here somewhere. We need to dig him out, before he does any more damage.'

* * *

He sat on top of the pillbox and gazed across the dark marshland. There was a hint of dampness in the air, a thin misty sea-fret was coming in, but he didn't mind. As long as it was silent, devoid of any trace of humanity, he was happy.

He hadn't meant to come here tonight, but a strange, uncomfortable sensation had invaded him, a feeling of being trapped in his own home, in his own skin. The next thing he knew, he was riding across the fen on his powerful motorbike, heading towards the seclusion of this wild and miserable spot that he had come to rely on when the church was closed.

Earlier, he had felt almost manic with delight. If he closed his eyes, he could still see the sublime terror on the faces of the two women the moment before they jumped. The feeling of power had never left him, and he knew he would never forget it.

With the lawyer too, it hadn't been the death that excited him, it had been his control over that man. He had him take to the streets, made him sleep on cold, hard pavements, despite his fastidiousness. He sighed contentedly. As soon as you understood what really mattered to a person, then you had control over them. The actual death had been something of a let-down, although it had been amusing to watch those shaky little trial cuts, before making the final killing slice. He hadn't wanted to step in, but by then it was getting tedious, and he didn't want any of those nosey street people coming across them. No, best by far was the prosecutor's reaction when he destroyed his beautiful possessions and his fragile memories. The pain. The pleading and begging. And then the dandy's degradation at having to ask the Salvation Army for clothes. *So* satisfying. Over time, he had managed to compel the smug prosecutor to desert all his affluent friends, sell his three-storey town house, and go scurrying to that desolate spot deep in the fens, to a place where he knew no one, and more importantly, no one knew him. The women had paid the ultimate price for what they did so many years ago, but the prosecutor had truly suffered.

He hoped that Brendan and Lyndsay were somewhere above, looking down. He hoped they understood that he was gathering in the sinners and making them pay. He sometimes pictured the two of them as avenging angels, fire flying from their pointing fingers and fearsome golden lights flashing from their scornful eyes.

After all these years, hot tears still formed behind his eyelids when he thought of Lyndsay. After she was gone he had believed his life was over too. But like a miracle, her passing had made him rise, a phoenix emerging from the ashes of her death. He had found the strength and courage to mould a new identity from the wreck of a child that he had once been. And what a man he had become! A man capable of sowing the seeds of destruction in the minds of others. A man of power. A man of infinite patience.

He kicked his heels against the lichen-covered sides of the old concrete pillbox and stared unseeing, into the shadows that drifted over the marsh. Suddenly he realised that this wasn't the finale he had planned for, but just the beginning.

He was far from finished. How far would his powers take him?

Murder, and the motives behind it, had always fascinated him. He had read extensively on the subject and had come to the conclusion that he was quite different from others who killed. All the studies described killers as lacking in human feelings and emotions. In order to function in society, they had to emulate what they saw in others, and some became good at it. But he did have emotions, and they were deep. He could communicate. He attracted people to him, and they admired his drive and conviction, shared his beliefs. He was no loner. He was curious and outgoing. His house was open to all and he had any number of friends.

He was nothing like the men and women he had read about, he was simply different, and that alone gave him enormous power.

Thoughts of power led him to consider his last "experiment." This particular plan of vengeance had taken a very unusual turn. The police knew nothing about it yet, although they would probably bump into it fairly soon. The longer it took them to find, the nastier it would be for them.

Now to his next target. He had one other planned demise, but after that? Which one would give him the most pleasure to bring down and destroy? He was here tonight to settle the matter, or at least narrow his selection to two or three. He wiped the chilly droplets of rain from his face and supposed that, like so much in life, in the end it all came down to love.

CHAPTER FIFTEEN

Each night, as darkness shrouded Rainham Lodge, Ella grew nervous. It made no difference whether James was there or not. It was up to her to keep Miles and Ryan safe. She felt alright when Jackman was there. But tonight he wasn't around, and she didn't know if he was coming.

Ella finished ironing the boys' school clothes and put the board away. No matter what she did to distract herself, her thoughts flew back to Sarah. Had she really taken her own life to protect her sons? Ella was convinced that the answer to this was yes. Sarah worshipped her children. If someone had threatened their lives, she wouldn't have hesitated for a moment. She would have put them first. Deep in thought, Ella set down the iron to cool. Sarah's suicide was a selfless act, but it was also very risky. The man who had been hounding her was undoubtedly a psychopath, and most probably a liar. She could have died for nothing, having left her children in an even more vulnerable position.

Ella shivered. This was a bad way to think when you were alone. Maybe she should ring Jackman. He had asked her to, if she felt concerned about anything, but she was reluctant to interrupt his work just because she felt a bit spooked. He needed to throw every ounce of energy into finding the man who drove Sarah to her death.

She went back into the lounge and looked around for something to do. She was far too restless to concentrate on TV or listen to music. Perhaps she should use this time to tidy some drawers and cupboards. She had James's full permission to do whatever she wanted, and she might find something interesting. So why not?

An hour later Ella was sitting at the kitchen table, staring at an old-fashioned Olympus Pearlcorder. She had found a microcassette inside, and despite desperately wanting to listen to it, hadn't yet pressed play. It had to be Sarah's. Ella had found it in a shoebox with some other personal stuff of hers. For some reason Ella couldn't bring herself to listen to her friend's voice. Instead, she made a cup of tea, and while it cooled she rang Jackman. Maybe he should be the first one to hear it. It could be nothing at all, a collection of favourite recipes or something. It could also be Sarah's deepest thoughts, recorded at the lowest, darkest point of her life.

It was almost ten thirty when Jackman arrived. Even though Ella knew he was dying to listen to the recording, first he asked about his nephews. She told him briefly about Ryan, but added that she would speak to James if she became really worried. Now to the Pearlcorder.

'I haven't touched it. I used disposable gloves to replace the batteries.'

Jackman smiled. 'Once a SOCO, always a SOCO.'

This time the reference to her earlier job didn't hurt. Jackman pressed play.

It was bad enough hearing Sarah's voice, but far worse was what she said. Ella sank onto her chair and stared at the little machine.

'I know what I saw! We weren't lying, neither of us! So why is he saying that we were?' The voice was strained, she was obviously close to tears.

'And why is he punishing us? Why is he saying such terrible things? Making such horrible threats? What does he want from us? We can't say anything different today to what we said all those years ago. We can't say something other than the truth, can we?'

There was a long pause, and the sound of Sarah blowing her nose.

When she spoke again, she sounded calmer. 'I'm going to leave this recording with my things, just in case the worst happens. If you find it, give it to my brother-in-law, Rowan Jackman. He will know what to do with this information. Perhaps it might help him to understand. He will want to understand, I know that. When I was almost sixteen, my friend Pauline and I watched another friend called Lyndsay, and a boy called Brendan, making love in the woods. Half an hour later we found her dead body and we saw Brendan running away. We told the police and, sorry Jackman, it was the worst thing we ever did. We should have kept what we saw to ourselves. Apart from the trial, which was pure hell, Brendan's family threatened us, and now someone, we don't know who, is persecuting us, saying we're liars and whores and deceivers. He says we must pay the price for perjuring ourselves. And . . .'

They heard her gulp as she fought back a sob. ". . . and this was after we'd been living new lives for twenty years! How he found us I have no idea, but if anyone is interested, my real name is Heather Miller and I was a witness for the prosecution in the trial of Brendan Symons—"

Jackman switched off the tape. 'Are you alright? You look very pale.'

'It's such a shock, that's all. To hear it from her own lips. It's like she's talking directly to you.' Ella stood up and went to fill the kettle. 'I could do with a hot drink. Tea or coffee?'

'Tea, please, and yes, it's horrible, but thanks to you, we are now in no doubt about what happened.' He looked at the recorder. 'I think you've heard enough. I'll listen to the rest later.'

She turned to face him. 'No, Jackman, I need to hear it. I need to know what kind of man is out there, possibly watching Sarah's children. I have to know what we're dealing with.'

To her relief, he nodded. 'I understand that.' He looked at her intently. 'But I really don't think he's watching this house, and as I said before, if we think that for one moment any of you are in danger, you'll be straight out of here, I promise.'

They spent the next half hour drinking tea and listening to Sarah's account of how, after Brendan killed himself, both she and Pauline were mercilessly bullied and picked on until life became unbearable. Their names had been withheld at the trial, but it was a small town, and Brendan's village was even smaller. People knew exactly what had happened and who was involved. In the end, they ran away. They were well into their teens by that time, and they moved down to the south of the county and rented a flat together. Still scared, they changed their names, managed to get jobs, and became Sarah and Suri, two young women who had a future again. In Sarah's words, "you always live in a kind of parallel world when something like this happens." But in the end she found a loving husband, wonderful friends and after she had Ryan and Miles, the only place she wanted to be. Then, when she had almost reached the point of no longer looking over her shoulder, *he* came along, and the nightmare began all over again, only this time it was a hundred times worse.

Jackman paused the tape and took a deep breath. 'It's hard to imagine how she managed to transform herself so successfully. I would never have known that she had such terrible secrets, and I'm a detective!'

'Me neither, and I worked for her and we were friends.' Ella swallowed. 'Sometimes I felt like I was her only really close friend. She seemed so warm, so grateful for the time I spent with her.'

'It looks as though she and her friend Pauline didn't see too much of each other after they settled down to family life.'

'Maybe it was too painful, being reminded of their past. I think I'd want to make a clean break too, wouldn't you?'

'Possibly, although you never forget a thing like that. There are so many little triggers that would bring it all rushing back. For the sake of my sanity, I think I'd want to keep the person who suffered alongside me really close.' He leaned forward and rested his elbows on the table, 'As far as I can gather, Sarah only ever made one mistake, and that was mentioning the name Pauline Grover to you.'

'And she never realised it. It was just thrown into a casual conversation and forgotten. She certainly never mentioned knowing anyone called Suri.'

Jackman sat back. 'Are you up to hearing the rest of it?'

Ella nodded. 'Let's do it. We've come this far.'

The last part of the tape was nothing less than harrowing. It was very disjointed and clearly recorded over a period of time. Sarah described the horror of being threatened, and worse than that, of her children being threatened too. She regretted smashing her laptop, and hoped that someone other than her husband or children would find this recording. She was clearly close to breaking point, and Ella felt quite sick by the end of it. Her last words were just, "Please forgive me." And then the tape came to an end.

They sat in silence for a while. Then Ella said, 'He's the most wicked man, isn't he?'

Jackman sighed. 'I can sometimes understand murder, when it's done in anger, in the heat of the moment, if, say, someone you love has betrayed you. It's never excusable, but at least I can see how it happens. Anyone can break if the pressure is too great to cope with. But such shocking callousness and premeditation is beyond my comprehension. I'm almost afraid to meet him. He's the very epitome of evil.'

Ella had the odd feeling that the killer saw his actions as being just and righteous. As if it was his sworn duty to right a terrible wrong, like a crusader. She explained this to Jackman.

He agreed rather doubtfully. 'The problem is we don't know what this terrible wrong is, other than that it revolves around Lyndsay and Brendan. Was it one, or both of them that lit his fuse? Who or what is he trying to provide posthumous atonement for?' He shook his head. 'There is so much more to all this. Things we know nothing about. We have a long way to go before we can look this man in the eye.'

That was something Ella hoped she would never have to do.

Jackman stood up. 'I'm sorry, Ella, I have to go home tonight. There are things to deal with back at Mill Corner, and I've an early start tomorrow. Will you be okay?'

'James will be back from a meeting with your father quite soon, and yes, I'll be fine. Don't worry.'

'I do worry.' He looked at her.

Ella wondered why such a good and eligible man was single. She watched him go, feeling rather sad for him. He should be going home to a loving hug and a warm bed, not to "deal with things," probably stuff like leaving money for his daily help and putting the bins out. *What a waste!* Ella closed the door and heard his car drive away. She had said she was fine, but she wasn't. She would've been much happier if Jackman had stayed.

CHAPTER SIXTEEN

For once, Ruth Crooke made no mention of Jackman leaving the investigation. He had cornered her in her office just before the morning meeting.

'Hearing what happened to Sarah in her own words confirms that we have a vendetta on our hands, and it's being orchestrated by a devious fanatic with considerable cunning. How you are able to brainwash another human being into taking their own life is almost beyond comprehension.' She shook her head.

'He's a master manipulator, Ruth. I'm terrified to think what he will do next.'

Her face was drawn and grim. 'We have to assume he will continue to wreak vengeance on those closely connected to the Lyndsay Ashcroft murder case. I'm going to have to take this to the chief super, you know. I think that everyone who was involved in incriminating Brendan Symons has a right to be told what's happened here.'

'It could cause panic, but, yes, I'd want to know if some murdering zealot had me in his sights.' Nevertheless, the last thing Jackman wanted was the press having a field day with such a fantastic story. He said as much to Ruth.

She stared into space for a few moments, frowning. 'That's very true, Rowan. If all the people connected to the case started being over-suspicious of anyone who tried to get near them, our man might well turn his attentions on us. After all, he will blame us for interfering with his crusade.'

'So it's a double-edged sword, isn't it? We could draw his attention away from innocent victims and become victims ourselves, putting those closest to us in danger. A real rock and hard place situation. Still, I guess that's what we are here for, isn't it? To protect life?' He looked at her.

'It is, but I still need to take advice. Meanwhile, you crack on. I'm thinking that interviews with Brendan Symons's family are going to be a priority?'

Jackman nodded and stood up. 'Without a doubt. Not something I'm looking forward to, but it should be sooner rather than later. After daily orders, I'll take Marie and we'll pay them a visit.'

'Yes, Marie will be perfect if the interview gets tricky. Good luck, Rowan, and remember what I said about them. Tread warily. They still bear a grudge.'

'I'm wondering how much to tell them. What do you think?'

'I'll leave that to you. You'll need to gauge their reactions, but I know you'll be diplomatic.'

Jackman returned to the CID room. It was almost time for the meeting, but he wanted to tell Marie about Sarah's recording before he spoke to everyone.

Marie was sitting at her desk, staring at her computer screen. She looked up as he approached. 'Still with us?' she asked hopefully. 'Ruth isn't still twitchy about you as OIC, is she?'

'Fingers crossed, the super seems pretty okay with it at present.' He moved closer and lowered his voice. 'And that's mainly because I've found a witness who confirms categorically that Sarah was literally being hounded to death.'

Marie's eyes widened. 'Really? Who?'

'Sarah.'

'What?'

He took a breath. 'She left a tape recording. Ella found it and rang me last night. It's pretty harrowing, but there's no doubt about what happened, and it's most certainly to do with Lyndsay Ashcroft's murder. I'm going to play it to the team, but I wanted you to know first.'

'Appreciated.' Marie stared at him. 'So are we looking at the Aggrieved Family Symons as suspects?'

'They are first in line to be interviewed. And you, my friend, have the honour of accompanying me, immediately after the meeting.'

'I'm overwhelmed at your kind offer, though I'd be very happy to let someone else have the pleasure.'

'Me too, but sadly the buck stops with us. Ruth's orders.'

'Bugger.'

'And here I was thinking my sparkling personality would more than compensate.'

'Sorry, boss, but no, it doesn't.' She glanced up at the clock. 'Time to go address the troops.'

* * *

Jackman gave Robbie, Max and Rosie the job of finding everything they could about the Lyndsay Ashcroft trial. Charlie and Gary were to look into why Brendan Symons hanged himself.

Jackman and Marie drove up to the north of the county to speak to the Symons family.

'I've never been to this part.' Marie overtook a slow-moving vehicle and put her foot down. 'Nettleby Oaks sounds like quite a small village.'

Jackman nodded. 'I've not been there either, but from reading some of the transcripts, it sounds more like a hamlet. I looked it up before we left Saltern and the area's very rural, not like the fens, but still sparsely populated. Nettleby is a bigger village. It has a school, a few shops and a couple of places to eat.'

'And that's where Lyndsay came from?' asked Marie.

'That's right.'

'What do we know about the Symons family, Jackman? I had a brief look at a couple of old reports, but apart from all the press coverage of their fight to clear Brendan's name, there wasn't much on the people themselves.'

'They are a tight-knit bunch. From day one, they were adamant that Brendan was wrongly convicted.' Jackman exhaled. 'According to Ruth, there were quite a few coppers who agreed with them.'

'Even in the face of all that forensic evidence? That's a bit odd, isn't it?'

'Brendan was a likeable young man. He never denied having sex with Lyndsay, he just swore he never hurt her. Some of the interviewing officers made notes on their records that he seemed genuinely devastated about the girl's death. One or two were never completely convinced that he was guilty.'

'And the family? What are they like?' Marie turned onto the B road that would take them to Nettleby.

Jackman opened his notebook. 'The father has passed away since the trial. That leaves the mother, Sheila Symons, and three brothers, Dale, Kenny and Liam — and two daughters, Yvette and Susie.' He stared at his notes. 'And there is also a small band of loyal friends who supported them throughout the trial and still do, as far as I can make out.'

'Are we walking into the lion's den?'

'I think that sums it up, Marie. We need to be extremely wary.'

'Lovely! Maybe they'll be out.' She paused. 'Surely they don't all live at home, do they? They must be well into their thirties and forties by now.'

'Two, Kenny and Susie, are married, but I have no idea about the others. According to our records, Dale and Liam are still registered at the mother's address, but I've no idea whether they actually live there.'

'But they still keep up the campaign?'

Jackman nodded. 'They have never given up, not for a single day.'

'This doesn't bode well, does it? I can see why we need to be uber-diplomatic.'

When they finally found Nettleby Oaks, the description "hamlet" seemed an exaggeration. Five House Lane, where the Symons family lived, was just that, a leafy lane with five farm cottages clustered together, overlooking a tapestry of tree-lined fields.

'Bit different to our part of the county,' murmured Marie, bringing the car to a halt. 'Prettier, but I definitely prefer our wide open spaces.'

They walked up to number two and Jackman rang the bell.

They heard people moving around inside, but it was a while before anyone answered.

The woman who opened the door looked at them suspiciously. She was short and plump, with short dark brown hair and hazel eyes. She was wearing faded jeans, a man's shirt and a V-necked sweater. 'Yes?' She stood waiting, hands on hips.

'It's the bloody police, Sue, you can tell a mile off.' A tall man came up behind the woman. His expression, too, was far from welcoming. 'What do you lot want?'

Jackman forced a smile and he and Marie showed them their warrant cards. 'You are right, sir, we *are* the police. We need to speak to Mrs Sheila Symons on a matter of some urgency. Is she at home?'

'Unless you've come to tell us that our brother's name has been cleared, no, she isn't.'

'And you are? Dale or Kenny?' asked Jackman. Liam, he knew, was younger than this man.

'Dale Symons. But none of us wants to talk to you, so I suggest you just sod off.' He made to close the door, but the woman put her hand on his arm.

'Shut up, Dale. They said it was urgent. The least you can do is listen to what they have to say.'

'They've never said anything important before,' Dale grumbled. He turned his back on them. 'You talk to them if you want, but leave me out.'

'I'm Susie. You'd better come in.'

She led the way to a small sitting room, crammed with furniture. Sofas, armchairs, dining chairs and beanbags took up every square inch. Sue gestured to a seat. 'Sorry about my brother. He still feels very strongly, as we all do, that the police let us down badly.'

'The case was before my time, Susie, but I have to say that we do respect your family for continuing to campaign for your brother Brendan.'

Susie's expression softened very slightly. 'He never killed that girl, Detective. He was a sweet, sweet boy. He couldn't even put an injured bird out of its misery, and he cried for days when our dog died. You never knew him, but I did. I loved my brother and I *know*, deep in my heart, that he never hurt Lyndsay Ashcroft. He just wasn't capable of it.'

She was clearly sincere. But her love for her brother didn't make him an innocent man.

'Susie, we really need to speak to your mother. Is that possible?' Marie asked. 'It's very important.'

Susie looked uncertain. 'Our mum . . . she's ill, very ill. I don't want her bothered. Can't you tell me? And maybe . . . no, I'll get Yvette and Kenny. They are with Mum now. Whatever you have to say, you can tell us together.'

She left the room. Jackman frowned at Marie. 'They are all here, even the married ones. What does that tell you?'

'That the mother is dying,' Marie said flatly. 'Ever felt like a sitting duck?'

'Never so much as right now,' he whispered. 'This, as the super said, is going to be tricky!'

Susie came back into the room, alone.

'Mum wants you both to go up and see her, but—'

'We'll try not to tire her out, I promise.' Jackman looked at her, his expression compassionate. 'She's very poorly, isn't she?'

Susie's eyes filled with tears. 'She's not got long.' She swallowed loudly. 'But she's a very strong woman, and she says she wants to hear what you have to say.'

They followed Susie up a steep staircase and into the front bedroom. It was uncomfortably warm. Jackman saw a small open fire on the far side of the room, burning brightly in a cast-iron grate.

Sheila Symons was propped up in bed against a mound of pillows. Her face was sallow and gaunt, but her eyes were shrewd and bright.

Susie pointed to a tall and skinny, dark-haired woman. Like her sister, she wore faded jeans and a sweater. 'This is Yvette, and my brother Kenny.' She gestured to a rather mousey man who sat close to his mother, holding her hand.

'Mum? This is DI Jackman and DS Marie Evans. They are from Saltern-le-Fen, and they want to talk to you.'

'Get them something to sit on.' The old woman's voice was cracked but strong, her tone said she was used to having her orders obeyed.

Susie scurried off and returned with two straight-backed chairs.

Jackman noted that Dale was not in the room, but he suspected that the older son was still somewhere within earshot. The other brother, Liam, was absent. He coughed. 'Mrs Symons, we won't take too much of your time. There has been a rather disturbing development in Saltern, and it appears to be connected to the murder of Lyndsay Ashcroft. Hence we felt the need to come in person and explain what's happened.'

'Is this "development" something that could lead to my son's name being cleared?'

'At this stage, Mrs Symons, we're very much in the dark about what it means. I can't give you false hope.'

'I thought not.' The woman sighed. 'Okay, get it over with. What's it all about?'

Jackman glanced at Marie. She nodded very slightly. He explained that someone had taken the law into his own hands and was causing the deaths of people involved in the prosecution of Brendan.

No one in the stuffy, hot room spoke.

Dale burst into the room, shouting. 'So now you are accusing us of murder too! You pigs! You're not satisfied with wrongly accusing my brother and sending him to his death!

118

You now come here, accusing us of taking the law into our own hands and executing the people who put my brother behind bars!' His eyes were wide and his nostrils flared in anger. Then he stood with his hands at his sides, apparently at a loss for words, swearing under his breath.

'*If* you've finished!' His mother looked at him, hard. 'I think that's quite enough of that.'

'You'd be just as angry if they didn't tell you, Dale, so let's listen, shall we?' Yvette said. Jackman thought she seemed the most reasonable of the lot.

Dale slumped back against the far wall.

'It was necessary to warn you about this, Mrs Symons, as we'll naturally have to make enquiries. Please be assured, we're not targeting you or your family. We will be speaking to dozens of people involved in the old case.'

The old woman nodded, and asked Kenny for a drink of water. 'How are these people being killed, Detective Inspector? And who has died?'

Jackman hesitated. They would see it in the news before long anyway, so he might as well tell them. 'The two unnamed witnesses, who were only teenagers at the time, and the prosecuting barrister are dead. Someone hounded and terrorised them until they took their own lives.'

There was a collective intake of breath. Yvette whispered, 'Oh, dear God! Heather and Pauline? Both dead?'

Marie spoke softly. 'One drowned and the other fell to her death. You knew them?'

Kenny looked up at them. 'Of course we did. It's a small community, isn't it? We always knew, but after the trial it all came out anyway. It's true, we did make life hard for them, but . . .'

Sheila Symons shifted uncomfortably in her bed. 'This is terrible news, Officers. For their families of course, but it's also devastating for us. We will be the obvious suspects. People will think that we've finally decided to take our revenge. The whole thing will flare up again, and we'll lose the goodwill of all the people that believed in our cause.' She coughed, and the sound was rasping and painful, and she sipped more water.

'We should leave.' Jackman stood up. 'But, please, if there is anything you can do to help us, anyone you know of who's ever shown signs of being fanatical about what happened, and I don't mean committed, as your family is, I mean seriously overzealous, please do contact us. We'll leave you our details, and as I said, we will need to talk to all of you very soon. We'll phone and make arrangements.' He gave the old lady the warmest smile he could muster. 'I'm sorry we've tired you. Please accept our sincerest apologies.'

He thought he heard a snort of derision from Dale, but Sheila Symons nodded. 'I appreciate you coming, even though your news is far from good. We'll think about what you've asked.'

In the hall, Jackman gave Susie his card. 'This person is ruthless. We have to catch him. I'm just sorry that we'll have to come back for detailed statements regarding all your whereabouts. Please do understand, they will be as much as to prove your innocence and to rule you out of our enquiries, as to assign blame. Okay?'

Susie nodded. 'Why? After all this time, why now?'

'We don't know, but we fear he hasn't finished.' Jackman's voice was like granite. As she closed the door, he noticed that Susie looked sickly white.

Back in the car, Jackman let out a long breath. 'Did I do the right thing? Telling them so much?'

'There was no other way, Jackman. You did what you had to do, and I think the old lady really did appreciate it. She might still believe that Brendan was innocent, but she's no psycho killer, not that I can be quite so sure of the wild-eyed son, Dale.' Marie pulled a face. 'He's a bit of a fire-cracker, isn't he?'

Jackman gave a short laugh. 'You can say that again. I'll be very interested to get each of them on their own.'

Marie started the engine. 'You and me both, guv. I can hardly wait.'

CHAPTER SEVENTEEN

'Something bothering you, sunshine?' Max gave Rosie's shoulder a gentle squeeze.

'Just worried.' Rosie didn't react to Max's touch.

'About?'

'This man. This deviant.' She turned and looked at Max. 'The criminals we usually get don't bother me. I can see what makes someone rob, deceive, beat people up and generally behave badly in certain situations. Sometimes I can even get their reasons for killing. But this guy . . .' She gave a shudder. 'This guy is off the scale. It scares me.'

Max pressed her shoulder again. 'Hey! Come on! Where's my fearless girl? He's just another crazy. Hell, we've had our fair share of them over the years, haven't we?'

'I know we have, but he's different, you must be able to see that!' Rosie sounded almost accusing.

Mildly concerned, Max sat down beside her. This wasn't the Rosie he knew. 'Of course I can see it, flower, but I'm not giving him the satisfaction of getting under my skin. He's an evil bastard and I hope we nail him before he turns someone else's mind into mush.'

'I hate the thought of someone taking advantage of another person's weaknesses. It's so cruel.'

Max nodded. 'Mind-benders. They've no moral values at all.'

Rosie frowned. 'I'm not sure he sees himself like that. I've been looking at the messages he left Sarah, and I swear he believes that he has some kind of divine right to punish the wrongdoers. Sure, we realise it's all to do with the Ashcroft murder, but is he on a crusade to avenge the murder of Lyndsay, or to avenge the conviction and subsequent death of Brendan Symons?'

Max scratched his head. 'We need to know a lot more about that trial, don't we?'

'Exactly.' Rosie grimaced. 'Until we know what he's killing for, we won't know where to look for him.'

'What if he's just picked on that case simply because he felt that there was a serious miscarriage of justice? He may have no connections with anyone.' Max shrugged.

'Wait! He might *know* it was a wrong verdict, because he knew the real killer! He could even *be* the killer, and has been cheated out of his notoriety!' Rosie stared at Max. 'Is that a possibility, or am I just sleep deprived?'

'It's a possibility, but we need to keep digging.'

'DC Cohen. DC McElderry.' Ruth Crooke stood in the doorway. Her face was set. 'I need you to follow something up for me.'

Max and Rosie jumped up and hurried over to the superintendent.

'Ma'am?'

'In the absence of DI Jackman and Marie, I need to pass something on to your team. It has been decided to tell all those who were involved in the Ashcroft trial that they could be in danger and to take precautions.'

Max nodded. 'Fair point, ma'am. They have a right to know if they are under threat.'

'The jurors have been contacted and several people from the original prosecuting team, plus the judge who presided and passed sentence, but one man is missing from the list. We cannot locate the foreman of the jury, and to be frank, as the man who delivered the guilty verdict, he could well be the next victim.'

'You want us to find him, ma'am?' asked Rosie.

'As fast as possible, DC McElderry — unless you think our man has finished playing judge, jury and executioner?'

'No, Super, I don't think he's finished at all,' Rosie said. 'Don't worry, we'll find him.'

The superintendent gave them a memo with a name and an address on it, turned and strode towards the lifts. The words, 'What part of "as fast as possible" don't you understand?' floated back to them in her wake.

Max and Rosie hurried back to their desks.

'I always said she had eyes in the back of her bleedin' head,' grumbled Max.

'I see why she's worried, though. She might have a point about this man,' she looked at the memo, 'Isaac Whitman, being next in line.'

'Then we better get to him, hadn't we? Before our Mighty Avenger does a mind-fuck on him.'

Rosie winced, but made no comment. She grabbed her bag. 'We have an address in Horncastle. Let's start there, shall we? I'll drive.'

'Wilco.' Patting his pockets for his phone, Max hurried after her.

* * *

Gary stared at the results of the inquest on Brendan Symons, and shook his head. 'Poor little devil,' he murmured.

'You are talking about a convicted killer, Gary. Should I be worried about you?' Charlie Button looked up from his screen.

'Maybe, maybe not.'

'You doubt the verdict?' Charlie spun his chair around to face Gary.

'I see grey areas, and I hate grey areas.' Gary swiped the printout with the back of his hand. 'Guilty or not, this kid had never been in trouble before, then he's thrown into the deep end of a Cat A prison. Not just any Cat A, but one that houses some of the most dangerous male prisoners in the country. No wonder he cracked.'

'The inquest states that his death was given as asphyxia due to compression of the neck following hanging from a ligature. How on earth did he manage that?' Charlie frowned.

'Torn-up shirt fashioned into a rope secured round his neck, then the other end tied to the top bunk. Not difficult if you are desperate. And the blood can be cut off in as little as seven seconds so you pass out, and then die.'

Charlie grimaced. 'That's horrendous.'

'The governor's report states that Brendan hadn't reported any abuse or given them cause to monitor his safety.' Gary snorted. 'Not surprised. He'd have been too bloody scared to report anything. I can't even imagine the emotional stress he went through.'

'Gary? What you said about grey areas. Do you really think that lad might have been innocent?' Charlie asked.

Gary sat back in his chair. 'Son, I hope that he *was* guilty, because then his fate would in some way be justified. But if, just if, he had told the truth, then I can totally understand why his family have carried a torch for him all these years.'

'They say that unless you are a chronic recidivist, being incarcerated is pure hell, on a lot of levels. So if you were jailed for something you really hadn't done, well . . .' Charlie shrugged, 'it would blow your mind.'

'And prisons are high crime areas. The amount of drug-dealing, theft, robbery, assaults, threats of violence and sexual abuse is much greater than on the outside.'

'And if you were squeaky clean when you went in, it would be the shock to end all shocks,' said Charlie thoughtfully.

Gary shuffled some papers on his desk, and pulled out a note with a name and address on it. 'I checked this out earlier. It's the contact details of an old lag I helped put away years back. Mackie finally saw the error of his ways and after

124

spending half his life in various prisons, he went straight. I've calculated that he was inside in the same prison at the time when Brendan Symons took his own life. It's a big prison, but news travels like wildfire in those places. I'm going to see if he remembers anything in particular about Brendan.' He stood up and reached for his jacket. 'Hold the fort, Charlie. He only lives on the other side of town, I won't be long.'

* * *

Mackie Cairns clearly wasn't over the moon to find Gary on his doorstep, but reluctantly invited him in.

They went into a small sitting room that housed a television, a battered coffee table, a faded beanbag and a shabby sofa. Gary wasn't offered tea, but from a quick glance into the kitchenette on the way in, he decided that was lucky.

'I'm not after information, Mackie — well, not the sort of thing I'm usually after. I just wondered if you could recall if there was any funny business going on up in Durham when Brendan Symons hanged himself.' Gary laid a ten pound note on the coffee table.

'There's always "funny business" going on in the big house, PC Pritchard. You should know that.' Mackie was a tall, heavy man with unruly hair and a craggy face. After his last stint inside, he had abruptly turned his back on crime and got himself a job as a mechanic in a local garage. Considering that one of his past vocations had been as a getaway driver, he knew plenty about cars. Plus, he had kept his hand in while in prison, studying engineering.

Gary steeled himself for the usual banter before he got an answer, but this time Mackie seemed almost reflective when he spoke about Brendan Symons.

'There was a strange atmosphere in the place around the time that lad was brought in.' Mackie eased himself down onto the beanbag, allowing Gary to have the sofa. 'As you well know, no one's guilty in prison, they all swear they never did it, but Brendan divided the inmates. Some of them decided he was a baby-faced assassin, a rapist and a killer, end of story. Others . . . well, others thought he was either a bloody good actor, or he really was innocent.'

Gary nodded. 'It was much like that on the outside, Mackie. Two camps.'

'Yeah, but everything is so much more intense in the slammer. Things get out of proportion, then they turn nasty.'

'And did things get bad for the kid?'

'He was a pretty boy, PC Pritchard. I don't need to spell out what that means, do I?'

Gary shook his head. 'No, you don't.'

'Thing is, someone took a fancy to him, but Brendan wasn't having any, and he made an enemy of a very nasty man indeed. Then someone else took him under his wing, but I never believed it was out of kindness. I thought it was to get one over on Brendan's first admirer. Whatever, it screwed Brendan's head up even more.'

'I notice you forgot to mention the names, Mackie.'

'No, PC Pritchard, I didn't *forget*.'

'Point taken.' Gary knew not to pursue it. He grinned. 'As a matter of interest, which camp were you in?'

Mackie shifted his bulk on the unstable beanbag. 'After all the years I've clocked up in the can, I think I've learned to read between the lines.' He looked up at Gary. 'If he killed that girl, I'm a monkey's uncle. And I'm no monkey.'

Gary drew in a deep breath. 'Somehow, I knew you were going to say that, but I really hoped you wouldn't.'

'Why? Because it means that the man who did kill her is still free?' Mackie picked up the tenner and pocketed it.

'That's another thing. No, it's more that Brendan, a young man with his whole life ahead of him, died for nothing, and his family have to live with the stigma of having spawned a murderer.'

'You are a right old softie, aren't you, PC Pritchard?'

'I hate injustice, Mackie, that's all. I can still cut it with the heavy mob when I need to.'

Mackie looked unconvinced. 'Why the interest, after all this time?'

Gary raised his eyebrows. 'Can't say, Mackie. Ongoing investigation.'

Mackie hesitated, then added, 'This didn't come from me, but there was one other rumour going round the block at the time, and that was that Brendan's suicide was, er, how can I put it? *Assisted*?'

Gary froze. There had been absolutely nothing in any of the records to suggest that Brendan's death had been anything other than a desperate measure to end his suffering. 'What d'you know, Mackie?'

'No more than what I've told you. But if I were a betting man, I'd wager that Brendan Symons wasn't alone in his cell when he died.'

'Is that even possible, after lockdown?'

Mackie gave a hearty laugh. 'It didn't happen after lockdown, and even if it had, *anything* is possible in prison if you know who to bribe.'

Gary left, feeling that a heavy weight had just descended on his shoulders. They moved heaven and earth to get the bad guys put away, now he wondered exactly what kind of place they were sending them to.

* * *

Jackman and Marie were busy working out a rota for the Symons family interviews when Gary arrived back at the station.

Marie frowned at him. 'Oh dear! That is not a happy face.'

'No.' Gary flopped down into his chair. 'I've just heard something very disturbing.'

Jackman looked up from his computer screen. 'That sounds ominous.'

Gary exhaled. 'Someone who was on the same block as Brendan Symons has told me that it was suspected that the lad's suicide wasn't exactly textbook. The word he used was "assisted."'

'Shit!' Marie exclaimed. 'But what about all the official reports? Even the family are sure he took his own life. Are you certain this source is reliable, Gary?'

'I'd stake my next month's pay on it being kosher, Sarge. This guy is a born-again ex con holding down a job and keeping his nose clean. He's helped me before, and he's solid.'

Jackman let out a long whistle. 'How many more "assisted" suicides are we going to find?'

'But they can't be connected, can they?' Marie asked incredulously.

'I don't think that's the case,' Gary said. 'I think this was a prison thing. The kid got caught between two rivals, and from what I gather, he was collateral damage. Someone wanted him badly, and someone else "helped" him find a way out. That or it was a case of, if I can't have him, no one will."

'It's still another travesty of justice, isn't it?' Jackman's face was grim. '*If* it's true. And we'll never prove it.'

'A load of cons admitting something like that! I don't think so!' Marie snorted.

'I know it's just hearsay,' Gary added, 'but it gives us more of an insight into what the mood was like at that time.'

'Did your guy tell you anything else?' asked Jackman.

'He said he thought the kid was innocent. And I trust his judgement.' He looked hard at Jackman. 'So maybe the Symons family were right all along. Did you get any vibes when you met them, sir?'

'Angry family, Gary. Hard to read. Marie and I both have mixed feelings about them.' Jackman described their visit. 'Where are Rosie and Max, by the way?'

Robbie looked up from the pile of paperwork that he was working on, 'The super sent them on an errand, sir. The foreman of the jury at the Ashcroft trial is unaccounted for. He's the only one who hasn't been notified of possible danger. She's asked them to try and locate him.'

Marie threw a worried glance at Jackman. 'Why does all the news today sound so menacing?'

'The deeper we dig, the darker it gets,' Jackman proclaimed.

'Very profound, sir,' Gary said. 'Anyone fancy a doughnut?'

* * *

Max straightened his tie and pressed the bell. The address they had been given was a neat semi-detached in a quiet road that ran behind the busy high street. He pointed to the garden. 'Holiday, maybe?' he said to Rosie. 'I mean, all the flower beds are weeded with the edges done, but the grass hasn't been cut for a week or two.'

He rang and they waited, but there was still no answer. Rosie went next door.

The woman who opened the door was in her thirties and wearing startling pink gym kit. 'Just caught me, I'm off to Zumba. She stared at Rosie's warrant card. 'Oh. Is something wrong?'

'It's Mr Whitman. Do you know if he's on holiday? We need to contact him rather urgently.'

'I'm afraid I can't help you there.' The woman looked worried. 'I said to my Pete, it's not like Isaac to go off and not tell us. He does go away quite a bit. He has a caravan in one of those seaside parks on the East Yorkshire coast, but generally we feed his fish and put his bins out for him. This time he never mentioned a holiday, but we haven't seen him for weeks.'

'Do you know if he has any close relatives that we could contact?'

'He has a sister who runs one of the little antique shops in the town. It's called "Bygone Treasures," I think. Her name is Victoria Whitman.' She glanced at her watch. 'I can't really tell you any more.'

Rosie smiled. 'Thank you for your help. We'll go and see his sister. Enjoy your class.'

The door closed, and Max asked, 'What's Zumba?'

'Dance fitness. Bit too vigorous for me.'

Max grinned lasciviously. 'Oh I don't know. I've always found you pretty vigorous.'

'Shut up, Max, or I'll be arrested for assaulting a police officer. Now, where is this antique shop?'

'This is Horncastle, you know, it's full of antique shops. Why don't we go into the first one we see and ask?'

They left the car and took a footpath through to the busy, narrow high street.

'Okay, this will do.' Rosie pointed to a bookshop that boasted antiquarian, second-hand, and collectible books. Inside, it looked like a fire hazard just waiting for a match. Volumes were stacked from floor to ceiling, in wobbly towers, on shelves and bursting from cupboard doors.

'People buy this crap?' muttered Max, wrinkling his nose. The dusty tomes gave off a musty smell.

Rosie brushed cobwebs off a dog-eared Rupert the Bear Annual, and shook her head. 'Pass.'

It took a few moments to locate the proprietor, hidden behind a stack of National Geographic magazines. Rosie had to fight back the urge to tell him they were from the Health and Safety Executive.

'Sorry to disturb you, sir, but can you tell us where we can find a shop called "Bygone Treasures?"'

Relief flooded the man's face and he replied eagerly, 'Oh yes, it's about five hundred yards up the high street, opposite a little teashop called "Going to Pot."'

She heard a snort, thanked the man hastily and hustled Max out.

Bygone Treasures was locked, with a big "closed" sign on the door.

Frowning, Rosie stared at the shabby exterior. 'I'm not getting a good feeling about this, what about you?'

Max tried the door, but it was firmly locked and bolted. 'Let's go next door, see if they know anything.'

The shop assistant in the small boutique gift shop shook her head. 'Victoria did mention going on a buying trip. She goes to the big flea market in Lille to bring back pieces for the shop, but she always pops in and tells us when she's off. We have a key, just in case of emergencies. These are old buildings and things do go wrong.'

Rosie thought of the bookshop and smiled. 'We have concerns about her brother, Isaac. Do you know him by any chance?'

Tracey nodded. 'Nice man, very supportive of his sister. They are twins, you know. Not identical, but so much alike.' She stared at them. 'He's not in any trouble, is he?'

'Oh no, not at all. We just need to contact him rather urgently.'

'You've tried his home? He lives just off the high street in Lime Walk.'

Rosie nodded. 'Same story there — goes away a lot but this time he hasn't told the neighbours.'

Tracey took a deep breath, opened a drawer under the counter and produced a shiny key. 'It's for the back door. Vic always bolts the front one from the inside and leaves the back way. You get to it down the alleyway two doors up the street. Please do let me have it back, won't you?'

Rosie assured her they would, though she was doubtful. With every minute that passed, she was feeling more and more concerned. She knew that the killer liked to target his victims' weak points, and what could be more of an Achilles heel than a twin sister?

* * *

While Rosie and Max hurried down the alley, Yvette and Susie were making tea. Susie's hand shook slightly as she added milk to the mugs.

'I'm still shell-shocked after that visit from the police.'

Yvette nodded. 'Me too. I can't stop thinking about it. And it's made me even more worried about Dale and Liam.'

Susie straightened up. 'Surely you can't think they would do anything that terrible? Not our brothers!'

'Sorry, Susie, but I told you they scare me. To be honest, I don't know what to think anymore. Someone is taking things into their own hands, and if it's not one of us, who else could it possibly be? Who would care so passionately?'

Susie sank onto a kitchen chair and stared at the milk carton as if willing it to speak. 'There *were* others, Yvie, you know that. There still are. We have loyal supporters who, like us, have never given up.' She paused. 'I thought some of them were more driven than we were. I can name three or four that I always thought were too involved, almost unhealthily so.'

Yvette sighed. 'I know who you mean. Let's pray it's one of them and not our family. But you have to agree that the boys aren't making things any easier for us. They need to back off.'

'We should have a family gathering and tell them.'

'And do we give the names of our supporters to the police?' Yvette asked.

'Absolutely! We need to take the heat off the family. We must do all we can to help the police, even if it does go against the grain after all we've suffered.'

'To protect the family, and to try to give Mum some answers before . . .'

'Exactly, Yvie. Before it's too late.'

CHAPTER EIGHTEEN

Considering the state of the rest of the building, Max was surprised to find a modern UPVC replacement door at the back. He glanced at the lock. 'Diamond Standard, snap-proof lock. Victoria doesn't want any thieves getting their sticky hands on her bygone treasures, that's for sure.'

He took the key from Rosie, unlocked the door and stepped inside. Again, he wrinkled his nose. He hated the smell of old places. Max liked smart. He liked new. He found the stench of mildew, must and decay disgusting, and this place smelled of them all. Yet, he loved old architecture, and appreciated ornate structures and beautiful design. Just not up close.

They were standing in a small kitchen area. Its old butler sink and retro cabinets in cream and green were pure nineteen fifties. On a small pine table, covered in a plastic cloth, were unwashed plates, cups and cutlery.

'Not good,' he whispered. 'Not good at all.'

'Should we ring this in?' Rosie was staring at a mouldy loaf and a packet of rancid butter, still open on the table.

'Better see what we've got first, I guess.' Max grasped the doorknob and opened it.

The smell hit them immediately, and it wasn't musty old antiques.

Max was afraid. Not for himself and what he might find, but for the effect it would have on the already shaky Rosie. This case had upset her from the word go, and he was terrified that the coming revelation would send her into freefall. 'You were right, flower. We need to ring this in. You go contact the guv'nor. I'll check this out.'

'On your bike! We do this together.'

'Rosie! I—'

'I know what you are trying to do, Max, and I love you for it. But when we're on duty, I'm a policewoman first and your girlfriend second. We do this by the book. We investigate, observe, touch nothing and report in. Okay?'

Max said nothing, but he wanted to tell her that it was the policewoman he was worried about. She had already told him she couldn't cope with the type of punishment this killer dished out. With a sigh, he pushed the door open and they entered a dingy hallway that led into the shop itself. The smell intensified and he gagged. Not daring to look at Rosie, he went into the shop and quickly checked around. He could see nothing untoward, which just left upstairs.

He hesitated at the foot of the stairs, and Rosie pushed past him. 'For heaven's sake, Max, let's get this over with. We know it's going to be shitty, let's just do it.'

Upstairs they found two doors, one half open and the other closed. They glanced at each other. Rosie pushed the closed one and it swung open.

They stood in the doorway and stared.

It was as if they were looking at a dimly lit tableau in some waxwork museum. Every item in what had apparently been a stockroom had been pushed against the walls and stacked haphazardly in piles.

Apart from two chairs and a table.

The chairs were Victorian with intricately carved high backs. They were set opposite each other, one each side of a narrow heavy oak table, and both were occupied.

Rosie grasped his hand and he heard her take a deep shaky breath. 'Oh dear Lord! What has he done this time?' she murmured.

Together they stepped closer, but kept a good distance from the scene, ostensibly to protect the integrity of the crime scene, but Max didn't want either of them getting too close. After joining the force, Max had quickly discovered that he was unable to look death in the face. He could cope with the most terrible accidents, and even gruesome murders, but he couldn't face the eyes of the dead.

'What's actually happened here? And why is it so hot?' The quiver in Rosie's voice told him she was struggling to stay calm.

On the table were two big plastic beakers that Max presumed to have held water, and a mass of packets of tablets. Most were opened, their foil strips empty.

A man and a woman, who he assumed to be Isaac and Victoria, were tied to the chairs with wide bands around their waists, and ropes around their legs. Their upper arms were strapped tight to their bodies but their lower arms and hands were free.

'The heat is coming from those two portable electric heaters,' Max swallowed hard, 'and knowing what's happened with our other victims, I'm thinking he somehow coerced them into taking lethal doses of drugs.'

'That's what I thought. The bastard!' Rosie was close to tears.

'We've seen enough. Time to call it in.' Max turned away.

She nodded. 'We've seen too much.'

Max pulled her back through the door. He looked at her face and made a vain attempt at gallows humour. 'Any guesses at what old Rory Wilkinson will say when he sees this? How about, "I'll not be attending any of *their* dinner parties!" or maybe—'

'Shut up, Max! Just shut up.' Rosie ran down the stairs and out of the back door. Max closed the door on the grisly scene and went after her. He found her sitting in the yard with her back to the fence and her head in her hands.

Max sank down beside her and put his arms around her. She was shaking with sobs. For once, Max managed to keep his mouth shut and just held her close.

* * *

'Just heard from Max.' Jackman stood up and called across the CID room. 'The killer has struck again, this time two victims at one location.'

'The jury foreman?' asked Marie.

Jackman nodded. 'And his sister. SOCOs are on their way there now, and the local bobbies have secured the area for us. Marie? I need a private word.'

She followed him into his office, not liking the pallor of his face.

He closed the door and without waiting to sit down said, 'Max rang, and he's worried sick about Rosie. She's taken this one really badly.'

'What? Our Rosie?' This just didn't ring true. Had the killer done something truly horrific this time? 'Does Max know what the problem is?'

'He said that she's been edgy about this case ever since we started investigating. The killer's callousness and ruthlessness has really got to her. Then, seeing these two bodies . . .' Jackman began to pace the room.

'Are you thinking about pulling her off the case, sir?'

'It's worse, Marie. Max said she's talking about chucking it all in. Giving up her career.'

Marie gasped. 'Rosie's a first-class detective! She can't mean it.'

'We all have one case that hits us harder than most, and maybe this is hers. We'll get her through it, if that's what she wants.' Jackman shrugged. 'But for now, we have a double killing to attend to. Are you ready?'

'As I'll ever be. Lead on, boss.'

On their way to the car park, Jackman told her what Max had said. 'Rosie sounds in a bad way, Marie. Max said she couldn't stop crying, and that's not like her. I've just checked and the FMO is coming in later, maybe he can talk to her.'

'Good idea. He's a nice man, I'm sure he'll help her.'

Before she could continue, Jackman's phone rang and he stood still, frowning.

'Yes, Ms Symons, of course I remember you.'

Marie waited, wondering why one of the Symons family was ringing Jackman on his mobile.

'Later this afternoon? Well, four thirty would be good. I have something to sort out now, but I'll be back by then. Okay, see you later.' He ended the call, looked at Marie and shrugged. 'Yvette Symons says that the family will talk to us, but she wondered if she could be first, and she'd prefer to come to the station.'

'So the rest of the family don't hear what she has to say,' Marie added.

'That would be my guess. She sounded as if it was urgent.'

Marie got into the car. 'Does she know something, do you think?'

Jackman started the engine. 'Let's hope so.'

* * *

Rory Wilkinson was already at the crime scene when they arrived.

'You do like to shower me with different versions of death, don't you? And the weirder the better, it would seem.' He peered at them over the top of his glasses.

Jackman and Marie were still trying to take in what they were seeing.

'Bizarre,' muttered Jackman.

'Grotesque,' added Marie, fighting back the urge to retch. The stench in the hot, airless room was overpowering.

'Indeed. And our fiendish killer decided to confuse the poor pathologist even more by sealing the doors and windows tightly and leaving two electric heaters on full. Silly things like that play havoc with determining time of death.'

Jackman stared at the two bodies. Their bonds held them in an upright sitting position, although their heads had fallen forward. He saw that they were holding hands across the table. Touching. 'Who died first, Rory? Any idea yet?'

'I'd say most probably the man, although I need to do extensive tests.' He drew in an exasperated breath. 'Putrefaction. The whole time of death thing is going to come down to the rate of decay, and because of the hot, stuffy atmosphere, even that will be difficult.'

Jackman noticed that Rory wasn't his usual jovial self. The foetid air must be getting to him too. 'Have they been here long, Rory? I'm not asking for the impossible, I just want to get some idea of what happened.'

The pathologist stood back and looked steadily at the dead woman. 'They've probably been here for around ten days, but I don't think they've been dead for more than two.' He shrugged. 'I know that sounds odd, but I think they were imprisoned here for quite a while, maybe even two weeks. The fatal doses of tablets were not taken until two or three days ago.'

Marie looked at the empty packets. 'What are the tablets?'

'Paracetamol, Amitriptyline, an anti-depressant, and Oxazepam, an insomnia medication by the looks of it. We'll do a toxicology report, just in case the packets are a red herring and they've been given something completely different. Nothing would surprise me.'

'Me neither.' Jackman glanced at Marie. 'I think it's time we got out of here before one or both of us throws up and contaminates the scene.'

Marie moved smartly to the doorway.

Rory chuckled behind his mask. 'Lightweights!'

'Sorry, but the smell is absolutely disgusting.'

'I daresay you'd be a bit pongy too if you'd been made to sit in a chair for a fortnight.'

Marie groaned. 'This killer is too sick for words. I've never encountered anyone so . . .' She spread her hands, at a loss for words.

'So inhuman?' finished Jackman. 'I think that's what's got to Rosie.'

Rory looked up. 'Ah, young Rosie McElderry? You need to watch that lass very carefully, Detective Inspector. The bad old years of stiff upper lip and soldier on regardless are long gone. I saw her when I arrived, and unless I'm very much mistaken, she needs help.'

Jackman nodded. 'The FMO is coming in later. I'll make sure they have some time to talk.'

'Good. Now, since you weedy children are deserting me, I'd better get on. I'm sure these two souls will be much happier in my morgue than they are in this stuffy room.'

* * *

Marie felt as if she would never escape that terrible smell. It seemed to envelop her, and it clung to her clothes and her hair. All she wanted was to go home and take a long, hot shower, but Yvette Symons was due right now.

Yvette was punctual to the minute, and soon Marie was sitting alongside Jackman in interview room two.

Yvette seemed to have prepared exactly what she wanted to say, and began immediately.

'There is no doubt that my brothers Dale and Liam are still totally committed to our cause, and because of that I'm sure you will be very thorough when you check out what they were doing at the time of these deaths. However,' she paused and looked at each of them, 'there are certain people who have spent years helping to find a way to clear Brendan's name. Susie and I both agree that . . .' she looked down, 'that they . . .' She let out a sigh of exasperation. 'Oh, how can I say it? Frankly, Inspector, we don't know why they have been so motivated for so long. They seem to be even more passionate about it than us!'

'Some people love a good cause to grab hold of,' volunteered Marie.

'Susie said exactly the same thing. They need some kind of crusade in their lives to give them meaning.'

Jackman nodded. 'That's very possible. So, do any of these supporters give you cause for concern?'

Yvette seemed to relax now that her point had been made. 'I could be maligning them, but they all seem a bit full-on at times.'

'Names?' asked Jackman.

Yvette placed a sheet of paper on the table and pushed it across. 'I'd rather this stayed between us, if that's okay? If your investigation includes checking the people who have helped us, then these names would come up anyway, but they are the ones Susie and I agree are perhaps a little worrying.'

Marie leaned over to look, but the names written on the paper meant nothing to her.

'I recognise one name,' said Jackman. 'He's a doctor, isn't he?'

'Retired doctor, yes. Mark Courtney. He's a very intelligent man, Inspector. But actually we found him rather overpowering. We are working folk and sometimes he seemed more concerned with theories and big words. Still, he really knew how to put together a speech for the newspapers or for anything legal. He was Dad's right-hand man until our father died, then he supported Mum when she took over the campaign.'

'And he still does?' asked Marie.

'Oh yes. In fact, now Mum is ill he's taken on a lot of the organisation.'

Marie frowned. 'Wouldn't it be better if a member of the family did that?'

Yvette looked at her rather sadly. 'Probably, but it's been so long now. I have to admit that I've had enough. So have Susie and Kenny, though don't tell them I said so.'

Jackman's voice was gentle. 'You still believe that your brother was innocent though, don't you?'

Yvette looked worn out. 'He never did it, end of story. But we have no evidence, and Brendan is never coming back, so what are we really doing it for?'

'For justice,' said Jackman quietly.

Marie knew that Jackman was thinking of Gary's informant, the man who swore that Brendan was telling the truth.

Yvette frowned and stared at Jackman. 'Am I imagining this? Is a policeman telling me we could be right?'

'I'm just saying that I understand why you are doing it. You are convinced he was wrongly convicted, and that his incarceration caused his death. I think you have every right to protest.'

Yvette let out a little laugh. 'Why weren't you around when we started this? We might just have won a retrial.'

Jackman raised his hand. 'I wouldn't go that far.'

'No one listened to us. No one!'

Marie thought Yvette was about to cry. She said, 'We're listening now.'

Yvette took a handkerchief from her pocket and wiped her eyes. 'Could you help us?'

'Who knows what we may turn up as we investigate these deaths? But frankly, Yvette, I doubt we will ever get irrefutable proof after all these years,' Jackman said evenly. 'But don't give up hope.'

He picked up the sheet of paper with the names on it: Mark Courtney, Christian Ventnor, Art Pullen and Jeremy Shaw. According to the Symons sisters, each man was either extreme or militant.

'Thank you for bringing them to our attention. We will definitely interview them.' Jackman smiled. 'Regarding the rest of the family, is there anything we should know? Like how to approach Dale without getting an earful.'

'Liam's the one you need to watch. He's wild, always was, and I think he'd be lost without the cause.'

'What about Kenny? He didn't have much to say when we visited you.'

'Don't let him fool you, Detective.' Yvette raised an eyebrow. 'He's a sweet man, and he has a lovely wife, but he's eaten up with worry about our mum. It's all he can think about. He's very smart, the best educated of all of us. He even went to university, but something made him drop out. He's a teacher now, but he's taken a leave of absence to care for Mum.'

'Interesting. So you are all at home, for your mother's sake?' Jackman asked.

She nodded. 'We are, but it won't be for long.'

Marie could believe that. Sheila Symons had looked about as ill as it was possible to look without receiving a visit from Rory Wilkinson. She yearned to find out the truth about Brendan Symons, and to do it while his mother was still around to hear the news.

After Yvette left, Marie was alone in the CID room. The others had finished for the day and Jackman had gone to report to Ruth Crooke. She thought about the case. It was damaging them. Though Jackman seemed to be firing on all cylinders, he was obviously deeply affected by the death of his sister-in-law and consumed by worry about the safety of the rest of his family, especially the children. And Rosie, who had taken on thugs single-handed, and had once bravely gone undercover to find a perverted killer, was all at once as weak as a kitten. Who would be next? Max? Head over heels in love with Rosie, he would be worried sick about her and wouldn't be able to fully engage with the investigation. That left Robbie, Gary, Charlie and herself. Could the four of them take on this sadistic freak? She doubted it.

'How come you're looking so thoughtful?'

She hadn't heard Robbie Melton come in. 'I thought you'd gone home, Rob. I was just thinking that this case is really taking its toll on the team.'

'Rosie? Mmm. I heard Max telling Gary that she was in with the FMO earlier. Then he told us what had happened. It doesn't sound too good, does it?'

'Jackman is right though, isn't he? There is always one case that seems to hit harder for some reason.'

Robbie nodded slowly and sat down beside her. 'As far as that's concerned, I've written the book, and I very nearly didn't come through.'

Marie closed her eyes. How thoughtless could she be? Poor Robbie had been terribly affected when his partner Stella North was shot. He had all but thrown in the towel, but Marie and Stella had been good friends, and Marie had persuaded Jackman to bring Robbie into their team. It turned out to be fortuitous for everyone. Robbie Melton was a damned good detective, and getting him into a different division, away from all the ghosts and memories, had been the saving of him. 'Sorry, Robbie, that was thoughtless of me.'

'No, it's a fact, isn't it? Most coppers will tell you they have something that still gives them nightmares. I'm no special case.'

Marie patted his arm. 'Actually, you *are* special, Rob. You're a fighter, and you did get back on the horse.'

'I'm glad I did. And I hope Rosie does the same. She's a tough kid. Let's hope she bounces back from this.'

Marie nodded. 'I'll get Charlie to take over liaising with Beech Lacey. Would you work with Max for a few days, Rob? Keep an eye on him. I reckon he'll be pretty cut up at seeing her like this. I'm sure he could use a friend.'

'Of course I will.' Robbie smiled at her. 'They are pretty close, aren't they?'

'Yup. I reckon that if they weren't so career-minded, they'd be engaged by now.'

'Would it matter? They aren't high rank, so there's no problem with having a relationship, is there?' Robbie asked.

'Oh, there's nothing to stop them, but I know from personal experience that it isn't easy. It's the hours and the shifts, the unpredictable nature of the job. It worked for Bill and me, but we were in different jobs within the force. Even so, there were times when we hardly ever saw each other.'

'Think they'll get married?'

Marie shrugged. 'Who knows? They certainly suit each other.' She grinned at Robbie and punched him playfully, 'You're a right little match-maker, aren't you, Rob? I bet you like slushy films too!'

'So what if *When Harry met Sally* is my favourite film? I love a happy ending, that's all.'

'Nothing wrong with that. Now, how about giving a happy ending to a very sad woman with just a few weeks left to live? Gonna help me?'

Robbie looked at her suspiciously, 'Um, I think so . . .'

'I guarantee that if this works, you'll really feel like you're in a slushy film.'

'*If* it works.'

Marie tutted. 'It will work. Sheila Symons *will* have a happy ending.'

'We're talking about the woman who has been the bane of every policeman's life for the past twenty years? *That* Sheila Symons?'

'The very same. But it's what I want, okay?'

'And what DS Marie Evans wants, DS Marie Evans gets.' Robbie threw up his hands. 'Okay, tell me what to do.'

CHAPTER NINETEEN

Ella Jarvis hadn't had the best of days. First the washing machine broke down, then just after lunch the school phoned her saying that both boys had been particularly unsettled. Ryan had got into a fight. Nothing serious, just a scuffle, but he was so angry afterwards that he had to be taken out of class. Miles had been tearful all day, and nothing seemed to placate him, so at two, Ella had picked them up and brought them home.

She let them watch their favourite film, *Zootropolis*, and promised to make them banana waffles with honey. People would say she was encouraging bad behaviour by rewarding them, but the kids were suffering, and she wanted to do whatever she could do to make things better for them.

'Can we wait and eat dinner with Daddy tonight, Auntie Ella?' Miles asked.

'I'm not sure what time he'll be home, sweetheart. Shall I ring him and ask?'

Miles shrugged and walked away. 'If you like.'

Ella sighed. James wasn't spending enough time with the boys. Yes, he was struggling, but he had to find a way to hide his grief and have some thought for his sons or they would see it as yet more rejection.

She phoned James from her room so the boys wouldn't hear. He said he was in the middle of a complex business deal and he could well be late.

Ella hung up and immediately rang Jackman. 'I hate to ask this when I know how busy you are.' She explained about James.

'Of course, I'll be there. Six thirty okay? I'll stay until the boys have gone to bed.'

Ella ended the call. She wondered why James couldn't be more like Jackman, who made time while hunting a dangerous killer.

'Auntie Ella?' Ryan stood in the doorway.

She looked at his serious little face and her heart went out to him. 'Come in.' She patted the bed beside her.

Ryan sat down. 'I'm sorry I got into a fight.'

She put her arm around him. 'It's not like you, Ryan, so you must have had a good reason.'

'A kid in my class said my mum was a sinner and she wouldn't go to heaven. She said she'd burn in hell.'

Ella swallowed. 'Well, all I can say is, whoever said that was talking out of their bottom.'

Ryan gave a little giggle.

Ella held him tighter. 'Your mummy wasn't a sinner. She was a good woman and a loving mother. Don't you dare listen to anyone who says different. She's looking down on you from heaven, and she'll always love you.'

He looked up. 'So she won't burn in hell?'

'No, Ryan. Your mummy has died, and that's very sad, but she's at peace now.'

Ryan nodded. 'Did my brother ask if Daddy will be home for dinner?' Before she could speak, he said in a flat voice, 'He'll be working. Miles is stupid sometimes.'

'He is working, that's true, but Uncle Rowan is coming instead.'

'Yay! Do you think he'll play *Cars 3* with us?'

'Is he good?'

'No, he's rubbish, that's why we like to play him.'

146

'Ryan?' Ella asked, 'Do you know why Miles was so upset today?'

Ryan pulled a face. 'He's having bad dreams.'

'Oh no. He should call me when that happens. What are they about? Do you know?'

Ryan hesitated. 'He dreams he sees Mummy's bad man.'

Ella drew in a breath. 'Mummy's bad man?'

'Uh-huh. Mummy warned us never to talk to strangers cos there are bad men out there.'

'Well, that's quite right, but she only meant you to be careful. We've all told you not to speak to strangers or get into cars, or to take anything from anyone you don't know, haven't we?'

He wrinkled up his face. 'Yes, but it wasn't like that, Auntie Ella. Mum meant someone *really* bad. We saw him once. Now Miles sees him all the time, in bad dreams.'

Had they really seen someone? Ella swallowed and said calmly, 'Will you tell Uncle Rowan about it when he gets here?'

The little boy nodded seriously. 'Yes, but we'd better do it man to man. Miles will get upset, so I can't say in front of him. I'll tell Uncle on my own. You can look after Miles.'

She nodded gravely. 'That's very sensible, Ryan.'

'*After* we've played *Cars 3*.'

Ryan jumped up and ran off. Ella sat on, feeling sick.

She listened out for the boys playing downstairs, and then rang Jackman again, relating what Ryan had said. Jackman told her not to worry, he'd come as planned and they'd take it from there. Ella hung up, very relieved that she had Jackman to rely on. If it was up to James to sort these things out . . . well, it didn't bear thinking about.

* * *

Jackman sat in his office and stared at the table, wondering what to do. Then he thought of Laura Archer.

She answered his call immediately, sounding very upbeat. Her old mentor, Sam Page, was with her, having dropped in for a chat. 'Do you think Sam and I might be able to meet the children?'

'I think that would be a great idea, Laura. What if I suggest that we all go this evening? I'll pick up a takeaway, so we don't put Ella to too much trouble. We could eat and then you could evaluate the problem.'

Jackman heard Laura speak to Sam, who agreed, and they arranged to meet at Laura's place.

'Choose something that the boys love to eat,' she said, 'and then we can all relax and get to know each other a bit. And try not to worry, Jackman. This could just be a bogeyman dream. It would be perfectly understandable under the circumstances.'

Jackman knew that to be true but still he worried. He glanced at the clock, rang Ella and hurried down to his car.

* * *

Robbie opened the door to his apartment. He hung up his jacket, kicked off his shoes and looked around. Stella had once said that his expensive and classy pad had all the warmth of a Premier Inn. He had never mastered the art of making the places he lived in homely. He certainly didn't want chintzy wallpapers or floral curtains, but he would have liked to live somewhere that was welcoming and warm to come back to.

He went to the kitchen, opened the freezer door and stared at the stacks of ready meals. He pulled out a lamb moussaka and checked the fridge to see if there was any salvageable green salad. He washed the few leaves, nuked the moussaka and sat at the breakfast bar to eat. The kitchen looked very "male." Its black marble surfaces and black, silver and white tiled walls were cold and clinical. He needed to do something to make this place a home. *A plant?* He snorted. It would take more than a plant to give some life to the place.

He finished his dinner, put the plate and cutlery in the dishwasher and wondered why on earth he was feeling this way. Usually he was quite happy with his domain. Perhaps it was the talk about Max and Rosie, and Marie describing her life with

Bill. His relationship with Stella North had been the closest he had ever had. They were nothing more than colleagues, but he had loved her. After two years he still missed her, but he had moved on, and now he was content. His unease had to stem from the case they were working. Marie was becoming more and more certain that there had been a miscarriage of justice, and Brendan Symons had died an innocent man.

Robbie had never been a drinker. His parents' embarrassing drunken capers had turned him into a teetotaller right from his teens. Then he met a man named Harvey Cash, a witness in a murder case and an alcoholic. Something in Harvey's situation had moved him and he couldn't forget the man. Later, he and Marie had gone to Spain for a holiday, and they helped Harvey give up the booze and get his life back on track. While they were there, Marie had introduced him to a drink called a Tom Collins. While Harvey sobered up, Robbie learned that an alcoholic drink could be pleasurable.

Five minutes later, he was sitting on his leather sofa, sipping his cocktail and thinking about Marie. When they went away to Spain together, the mess room jokes about toy boys had been endless. But Marie didn't care. They were friends, and they needed a break, that was all.

But recently Robbie found that he was looking at her differently, his gaze lingering. He had started to worry about her when she rode her powerful new motorbike, nicknamed Harvey after their friend. Robbie took a mouthful and the ice made his teeth sing. Suddenly it was clear to him why he wanted his home to seem more welcoming. He didn't want Marie to see it like Stella had, cold and inhospitable as a hotel room. He drained the rest of his drink. Alright, so he needed help with the place. Well, he knew exactly who to ask.

* * *

On the way to Rainham Lodge, Jackman, Laura and Sam discussed the possibility that Miles really had seen the man who'd terrorised Sarah.

Jackman glanced at Sam in the rearview mirror. 'We can't discount the fact that the child could have seen him. After all, it seems he must have been stalking Sarah for quite some time. So how do we go about this?'

Sam leaned forward. 'We start by making friends with the boys, and putting them at their ease. The more comfortable and relaxed the child is, the more likely he is to open up.'

Laura held up a large bag of drawing materials. 'I've brought these. I suggest that after dinner, you and Sam talk to Ryan, Jackman, while Ella and I do a spot of art therapy with Miles.'

'Ah, like we do when gathering evidence from child witnesses.'

'Exactly. It often produces some quite revealing disclosures,' Laura said.

'I've used it with children with autism as well,' Sam added, 'with remarkable effect, I have to say.'

'How are the boys doing generally, Jackman?' asked Laura.

'I gather it's a bit of a rollercoaster. Up one minute, down the next. Ella had to fetch them out of school today, which is the first time that's happened.'

'It won't be the last, I'm afraid,' said Sam. 'Things will upset them — an unkind word or a sudden memory — but it's all part of the grieving process. Children can be incredibly resilient. Given time, they might just surprise you.'

'My brother doesn't help. God knows, I can't blame him. I mean, he's just lost the love of his life, his lodestar.' Jackman didn't want to criticise his brother, but he resented the way James was behaving. 'He promised to try to do all he could to help me discover who did this to Sarah, but instead he's immersed himself in work. Almost always now the kids are in bed and asleep by the time he comes home, then he's off and out early. I'm scared they'll start to blame themselves.'

'Ella would appear to be the positive energy in their lives at the moment,' Sam said.

Jackman nodded. 'Thank God, my mother brought her in. She's holding the whole thing together.'

'How do the boys regard Ella?' asked Sam.

'They call her Auntie. She was once their nanny, and I think she's a mother substitute now. Is that a bad thing?' Jackman glanced at Sam.

'Not at this stage. They need someone to nurture them, and they trust Ella. In time, they will adapt to their loss. Terrible things happen to families the world over, and yet people go on.' Sam sounded sad, and Jackman wondered if there was something more personal behind his words.

Laura turned to look at Sam. 'I sometimes wonder if a mother figure is quite as important as we like to think. If a child has someone in their life that they can look up to, a support figure, that's what counts.'

Sam nodded. 'That's a valid point. Same sex couples and widowed husbands often do a fantastic job of bringing up their children, simply through their love and care. Do I sense another research paper coming on, Laura?'

'Not exactly. I'm busy working on a paper on narcissistic parenting at the moment.'

Sam chuckled. 'Ooh, interesting stuff! I'd be fascinated to read that when it's finished.'

Jackman stared at the road ahead, terribly aware of Laura Archer's body so close to his.

* * *

Ella had told the boys that their uncle was bringing two friends with him, and a big bucket of popcorn chicken. She suspected it was the chicken, but the two of them seemed perfectly happy at the prospect.

She, on the other hand, would have been happier to see Jackman alone. She couldn't help resenting the fact that Jackman had brought in professional help. Or was that it? Wasn't it just that she liked being with Jackman, just the two of them? Maybe she was imagining things, but she felt they had developed an easy, comfortable comradeship together.

Headlights scoured the drive, and Ella stood up. All at once she felt ashamed of her thoughts. She was scared too, afraid of what these "professionals" might bring to light.

CHAPTER TWENTY

Very soon the interviews would begin. By now the police would have made all the right connections. They would know that the suicides were not what they seemed, and that the common denominator was the death of Lyndsay Ashcroft. Now they would be looking for someone who believed that the murder trial had failed them.

He stood up and went to pour himself a drink. It was strange to be so at ease, not to feel the need to cross the fens to his quiet place, or slip unnoticed into the church. For once, he was happy to remain at home and contemplate his next move. He sipped the bourbon, his favourite. Wild Turkey Rare Breed cost over fifty pounds a bottle, and was worth every penny. He liked the name too. Rare breed. Just like him.

He rested his feet on the coffee table, which was strewn with books and documents. He liked to study murder, especially the psychology of killers. Of course, he was looking for someone like him, but he was gradually coming to the conclusion that he was one of a kind, that his method was unprecedented. This was deeply satisfying. It took true genius to make your victims kill themselves.

He lifted his glass and drank a toast to himself. 'Here's to the creator of the complicated death!'

He hoped that the police would interview him. And if they did, should he extend the game and watch them chasing their tails? Or should he give Jackman all the information he needed? He slowly swirled the amber liquid, causing flickers of golden light to tremble in the crystal glass. Ultimately, he *wanted* Jackman to know. It was just a matter of when.

He placed the glass on a coaster, picked up a folder from the table and paged through his long-term strategy. By now it was quite a thick volume and all but complete. It was unfortunate that the judge who'd presided over the trial had recently succumbed to cirrhosis of the liver, but it was consoling to know that he had been the cause of the judge's heavy liquor consumption. Years of constant irritation, the veiled threats to one's family and friends do take their toll.

He grunted. He had almost forgotten his final dilemma. He had always wondered what would happen when his slow revenge had reached its climax. Now he knew.

He was too good.

This wasn't his epilogue at all, it was his new beginning. It was impossible to give up now. He had found his reason for living. There was one small loose end to tie up, and then he would be his own man, free to start planning new enterprises.

He thought again of all the people he had come to know over the course of the years. People with complex lives and deep emotional bonds. He looked at the folder on his lap. There was a whole section on the Jackman family alone, and what he didn't know about the detective's work colleagues wasn't worth knowing.

He stretched. Hmm. Decisions, decisions . . .

* * *

Much to Jackman's surprise, the evening got off to a flying start. The boys immediately took to Sam Page, and were clearly enchanted by Laura.

Only Ella seemed a little on edge.

After the meal, the adults joined the children in a game of Lego Jurassic World. After the games, Laura produced her sketchbook and coloured pens, and Miles happily started to draw.

'Not your thing, Ryan?' Jackman gently cuffed the boy's shoulder.

'Not really. I'm pants at art.'

'Me too. Couldn't even draw water.'

It took a while, then a small smile spread across Ryan's face. 'Don't give up the day job, Uncle.'

Sam joined them. 'Do you think this is a good moment to have a quiet word, young man?'

Ryan seemed to be trying to decide.

Sam lowered his voice. 'We don't want to upset Miles, do we? So perhaps you could tell your uncle and me about his nightmares. What do you think?'

Ryan nodded slowly. 'You're right, Sam. Would you like to see my bedroom?'

With a quick look at Laura and Ella, Jackman followed Sam and Ryan from the room. Miles didn't even look up.

Upstairs, Ryan explained what Miles had seen. Their mother had taken them to the park and sat on a bench with another mother while they played football. Then all at once she grabbed them and hustled them back to the car. They had protested because she hadn't even let them fetch their new football. 'We thought we'd done something wrong, but Mummy said it was nothing to do with us.' Ryan bit his lip. 'Then Miles suddenly said, "Was it that man by the gates?" and Mummy took hold of him and shook him and asked him what he had seen. She was so angry, and Miles just cried and cried.'

'Did you see him too?' asked Jackman gently.

'Sort of. I knew someone was there, but I was busy playing and I didn't take any notice. It was Miles who saw him, and because Mummy was so frightened, he thinks it was one of the bad men we were warned about.' He swallowed. 'Now Miles thinks the bad man killed Mummy, and he has nightmares.'

Sam put an arm around Ryan and said he'd been very brave to talk to them. 'Laura is getting Miles to draw different things. It's a way of getting someone to tell you something through pictures.'

'Is it important?'

'Very', said Jackman. 'Ryan? Have either of you seen him since?'

The boy looked down. 'A couple of times. Is this why you all came tonight?'

Jackman nodded. 'We came because we love you and we want to find out exactly what happened to your mummy.'

'That's good.' Then Ryan grinned. 'Is Laura your girlfriend, Uncle?'

Sam laughed and Jackman spluttered, 'No! What made you think that?'

'Nothing. I'm glad, though. She's very nice, but I think Auntie Ella would be a bit upset.'

Then he jumped up and left the room.

'Out of the mouths of babes . . .' Sam was trying not to laugh again.

Jackman sat on the edge of the boy's bed and stared at Sam, open-mouthed. 'What on earth . . . ?'

Sam chuckled. 'That boy is very perceptive, isn't he? Funnily enough, I was thinking the same thing myself earlier. Two fair damsels, eh? What a man!'

'Oh no, Sam, really, I mean, I never . . .'

'Just enjoy it. It's a predicament most men would give their eye teeth to be in.'

But Jackman's heart was sinking. Not now. He *had* to stay focussed on the investigation. He stood up and looked at Sam. 'Not a word, my friend, please? And now we must go and see what Laura's art therapy produced.'

'Of course. My lips are sealed.'

But as he left the room, Jackman could hear Sam's stifled laughter behind him.

Back in the lounge, Jackman looked surreptitiously from Ella to Laura, feeling very uncomfortable. Oh well, just as long as Ryan didn't come out with any further insights, he should be okay. Then he noticed the two women's solemn expressions, and knew that Laura's drawing session had paid off.

'Time for bed, lads.' Ella shooed her two charges towards the door. 'Say goodnight, and thank you for the meal.'

The boys thanked them and reluctantly made their way upstairs.

As soon as Ella came back into the room, Laura held up a drawing. 'He's a good little artist, which helps.'

'But we don't like his subject matter,' added Ella.

Neither did Jackman. He took the picture and peered at it. 'What did you ask him to draw?'

'Initially we kept it light, and had him drawing superheroes and animals.' She pointed to some brightly coloured pictures on the table. 'But then we asked him to draw something very good, and something very bad. This was the result.'

The paper was divided with a thick black vertical line. To the left, Miles had drawn an angel with a bright yellow halo and large white wings standing on a fluffy cloud with her feet surrounded by pink and red flowers. The word "Mummy" was carefully inscribed along the bottom.

On the right hand side the boy had drawn a much more complex image. Jackman could make out trees, swings and something that appeared to be a flying saucer and that he soon realised was a roundabout. Then there was a path with a lone football sitting on it. All that would have been fine, but Miles had added a tall figure standing at the end of the path. Jackman looked closer, shocked at the sinister atmosphere such a young child had managed to convey. The man was drawn entirely in black pen. He was standing straight as a pole and wore a long coat and a hat with a brim. But it was his face that made Jackman shiver. Miles had made him look like an alien, with a broad forehead, pointed chin, small mouth and nostrils and very large black almond-shaped eyes. Those black eyes seemed to stare back at Jackman from the paper. The title was, "The Bad Man."

'They *were* watched,' Jackman whispered to himself, 'Sarah and the children.'

'That's what we think too.' Laura glanced at Ella, who nodded.

Jackman pulled out his phone. 'Sorry, I need to talk to my superintendent,' he muttered, and walked into the kitchen.

Ruth Crooke answered almost immediately.

'Ruth, I think Ella Jarvis, my brother James, and particularly the two boys are in danger.' He told her about the drawing and waited for her answer.

'Normally, I'd say it's far from enough to warrant action, but with this dangerous individual still loose, and as I trust your judgement, it's either a safe house, or I can probably arrange to put a couple of officers on round-the-clock surveillance. It's up to you, Rowan.'

'I'll talk to Ella. She's here more than my brother. I'll see what she thinks and get back to you. And thanks, Ruth, I appreciate it.'

Jackman didn't return to the others immediately. He was haunted by Miles's picture, and something else too. The drawing was the work of a seven-year-old, and clearly just a stylised impression, but there was something about the figure that struck a chord in Jackman's memory. The moment he saw it, Jackman had the unsettling feeling that he knew this man.

* * *

DCI Cameron Walker smiled at his wife across the dinner table. 'I'm so glad to be home tonight.'

Kaye Walker gave him a reproving stare. 'And are you not glad to be home with me *every* night?' Then she grinned.

'Of course I am, but . . .'

'Joking.' Her smile vanished. 'I've not seen you so worried since your Darren got injured on duty. This investigation is really getting to you, isn't it?'

'That's an understatement. It's a bastard. The way this man destroys lives is beyond all comprehension. I don't think

I, or any of the other officers for that matter, have ever come across such a heartless, evil individual. I heard from Saltern just before I left. He's already taken another two lives.'

Kaye groaned. 'Oh no. More innocents?'

Cameron nodded. He knew he should not talk about his ongoing cases, but he and Kaye were practically joined at the hip and told each other everything. 'Not only that, but one of Jackman's brightest young detectives is traumatised after walking in on the killer's latest murder-fest. She was our liaison with Saltern, but the FMO has signed her off.' He chewed his steak thoughtfully. 'We've come off lightly here in Beech Lacey, with just one death. Poor old Jackman is on the firing line and well and truly taking the flak.'

Kaye sighed. 'I shouldn't say thank heavens, I know, but I will.'

'I know what you mean. Still, I have to help him all I can.'

'Oh, I know that. It wouldn't be like you to shy away from anything, or leave a fellow officer wallowing in the shit.' Kaye grinned. 'Excuse the vernacular.'

'I'm thinking we can help him out by taking over some of the background research stuff, while he gets down to the nitty-gritty. We have just about exhausted our lines of enquiry regarding our woman, but his team are way ahead on looking into the Ashcroft murder trial. I think he'd appreciate it.'

Kaye helped herself to more mustard. 'I'm sure he'll appreciate any help you can give him. What's he like, this DI Jackman? Is he like your friend, DI Nikki Galena?'

Cam laughed loudly. 'He's nothing like Nikki! Except for the fact that they are both damned good detectives. Jackman is a "gentleman" in all senses of the word. I like him. He even offered to share responsibility for this case, when he needn't have done. Nice guy.'

'Like you, my darling. Far too nice to be a DCI.'

'Well, I'm going no higher up that ladder, more money or not. I want to be a policeman. Things are already getting dodgy. I'm constantly being reminded to delegate, so I can spend more time on risk assessment and health and safety procedures.' He grimaced. '*Not* what I had in mind when I joined the force.'

Kaye smiled warmly at him. 'You love it! You know you do.'

Cameron frowned. In truth, the job wasn't what it was a few years back. There were so many areas where he believed they were letting the public down, mainly through lack of funds and manpower. He loved the job, but for how much longer?

CHAPTER TWENTY-ONE

Jackman, Laura and Sam waited until James arrived home from work, so as to back up what Ella had decided. Though privately Jackman thought his brother would agree with anything Ella said, simply because he was incapable of deciding for himself. He seemed to have lost all ability to concentrate on anything except business. Knowing how their father had behaved for most of their lives, Jackman knew he couldn't change him, but it still hurt to see what James was doing to his sons.

Ella had opted to stay in Rainham Lodge, as long as there was a police presence there, and Jackman had rung Ruth Crooke to arrange it.

It was gone midnight by the time he got back to Mill Corner, and now he was in early to prepare the daily orders. He wanted to get on with the interviews as swiftly as possible. They would start with the Symons family, and then tackle the "followers" that had continued to support them over the years.

Unfortunately, he was one officer down. Rosie had been signed off for a week, and when she would be fully fit for work again was anyone's guess. Jackman hoped that it was a temporary problem, but he kept thinking about Ella and how she'd walked off the job and never returned.

Deep in thought, he jumped when his desk phone rang. 'DI Jackman. How can I help?'

'It's more a question of what I can do to help you.'

Jackman recognised the deep voice of Cameron Walker, and breathed a sigh of relief.

'I've got two officers that I can put at your disposal, if that helps — oh, and one of them is me. Plus, I'll do the liaising directly, so that will free up another of your detectives.'

'Music to my ears, Cam. We have a string of people to interview and I get the feeling that time is not on our side. I can almost hear the killer's mind ticking over as he decides what horror to present us with next.'

'There aren't too many people left who were involved in that trial. Did you hear about Judge Henry?'

Jackman said he had. 'At least he was spared the wrath of our Grim Reaper.'

'Was he? I wonder?' Cam drew in a breath. 'Word on the grapevine says he changed a few years back, became "unsettled" and started drinking heavily. Maybe our man was quietly getting at him.'

'That could well be the truth,' Jackman said. 'Thing is, I can't see him stopping, can you?'

'With no righteous cause to fight for? Maybe he's run his course,' Cam said.

'I don't believe that for one moment.'

'Nor do I, but maybe there's a tiny chance he was only out to fulfil an oath of retribution. Once that's done, he'll close the book.' Cam grunted. 'Anyway, we can continue this debate when I get to you. We'll be there in half an hour, okay?'

Jackman thanked him and hung up. Cameron's help would make things easier. He was a very astute detective and had a reputation for dealing well with difficult interviews. 'Something is actually going my way,' Jackman whispered to himself.

'You know what they say about talking to yourself?' Marie grinned at him. 'Morning, boss.' She placed two coffees on his desk.

He looked up at her and smiled. 'You're early, and I'm very pleased you are.'

He gestured to a chair and proceeded to tell her about the events of the previous evening. He showed her Miles's picture.

'My God! That speaks volumes, doesn't it? And he's only seven? He draws better than me!' She took the picture from him and stared at it.

Jackman watched her eyes linger on the "Bad Man." Had she seen something there too?

'Why . . . ?' Marie frowned. 'Why do I think that I should recognise that figure? Is it a cartoon character? Or someone from a film?' She looked up at Jackman with a puzzled expression on her face.

'I felt the same, but a whole night of lying awake going over all the possibilities has produced nothing but mental exhaustion.'

Marie put the drawing back on his desk. 'It will come to me, I'm sure. And we can ask the others when they get in. Maybe one of them will know.' She sipped the hot coffee. 'I've been awake too, trying to look at our killer from a different perspective. I'm wondering if I might try a slightly different approach?'

Jackman smiled. 'All suggestions gratefully received! And we have Cameron Walker and one of his team joining us today, so we are back up to full power. Tell me more about your thoughts.'

'While the interviews with the Symons family and their cohorts are going on, I wondered if I might be allowed to dig deeper into the family histories of Lyndsay Ashcroft and her contemporaries? I know the others have been looking at the trial and all the media comments about it, but there is precious little in the old files about Lyndsay herself. Perhaps I can turn up something that leads to the source of the killer's reign of terror.' She scratched her head. 'And I'm going to approach it as if Brendan Symons really was telling the truth, if that's okay? It could just throw up someone else lurking in the shadows.'

Jackman considered her suggestion. 'Absolutely. I agree entirely. Someone has made it his life's work to bring down everyone who was connected with the case. His motive has to be about as strong and hate-driven as it's possible to get.'

'Hate-driven. Mmm. Interesting use of words.' Marie stared at him. 'I was thinking more about being driven by love.'

'A double-edged sword, I believe. If he loved either Lyndsay or Brendan, then that could transmute into hate for those who brought about their deaths.'

'And his voyage into vengeance begins.'

They sat in silence for a moment or two.

'Use Gary, he's good at reading people,' said Jackman at last. 'I'll take the rest of the team and our colleagues from Beech Lacey, and we'll talk to everyone involved with Sheila Symons's campaign. You never know, we might just find someone who overlaps with your historical enquiries. That suit you?'

'Great, thank you.' Marie finished her coffee and stood up. 'I'm sorry you feel your family could be under threat, Jackman, but that event in the park took place well before Sarah died.'

Jackman sighed. 'Oh, didn't I tell you? The boys have seen him twice since then, and the second time was two days ago, outside the school.'

* * *

Jackman thought he should talk to Sheila Symons first, and under the circumstances, decided he would do it alone. He felt that she might open up more, one to one. Knowing how ill she was, he had rung ahead but she insisted he come immediately.

On the drive to Nettleby Oaks, he tried to formulate his questions. He was aware that Sheila did not have long to live, and this might be the only interview.

He was invited in by Yvette, and he was careful not to mention her visit to the station. He climbed the stairs, and Kenny met him outside his mother's room.

'Mum's having a good day today, but please don't overdo it. The good days are few and far between.'

Jackman assured him he would keep it brief and Kenny opened the door for him.

Sheila was propped up on a mountain of pillows, looking considerably brighter than when Jackman had last seen her.

'I've spoken to the whole family, Detective Inspector, and I've requested that they share anything with you that might help your investigation.'

'I appreciate that, Mrs Symons.'

'Not that Liam or Dale will be anything other than hostile, I'm sure.' Her tone was almost apologetic. 'They have the campaign in their blood, they'll never give up.' She pulled herself up. 'And even though I know I won't be around to see an outcome, I'm glad they'll keep trying.'

Jackman sat in a chair close to her bed. 'Tell me about Brendan.'

Her face softened. 'You've heard the term "angels with dirty faces," I'm sure. Well, that was my boy. A little terror, but he had a heart of gold. He was a cheeky devil, but he charmed people. Brendan never killed Lyndsay, although I know they went together, if you understand my meaning?'

Jackman nodded. 'So did you ever have any suspicions about who did kill her?'

Sheila sighed. 'We've been over this a million times. If we could have provided another name, then maybe Brendan would have been exonerated. But no, the few people we did wonder about all had watertight alibis.'

Jackman looked at her. 'The man who is killing people connected to the trial is ruthless, cunning, and has no human values whatsoever.'

Sheila shook her head. 'The people who help us are all ferociously loyal, but we've always done everything by the book. We've used the media, organised vigils and protests and written more letters than there are chapters in the bible.' She smoothed the bedcover with stiff, knobbly fingers. 'Liam has sometimes been confrontational, and he's had a few fights, but no one I know of would stoop to anything like murder.' She gave him a searching look. 'It was murder that brought us to where we are now. Can you honestly see us falling that low?'

'No, I can't,' Jackman said. 'But someone has, so we need to talk to everyone who either knew Lyndsay or Brendan, or had a connection with the outcome of the murder trial. Has anyone you've come across during your campaign ever seemed overzealous, possibly manic, in the way they've spoken?'

'We were all hot blooded to start with. We fought hard for Brendan and we believed we'd win.' Tears welled up in her eyes. 'Who would have dreamed it would go on this long? And we're no nearer than we were at the start.'

Jackman handed her a box of tissues from the bedside table. 'That is why we now have to investigate everything again, to try to discover who this killer is. If it's any consolation, I believe the truth *will* come out this time, although it may not be exactly what you want to hear.'

For a moment Sheila didn't answer. Then she said, 'If the truth comes out, then you'll find that my son was not guilty. I couldn't have gone on for so long if I didn't believe that.'

'Whatever the outcome, I promise to tell you everything we uncover, and I truly hope we can give you closure.'

'I hope that happens. It may come too late for me, but it would mean my children could finally be allowed to live their lives, without committing so much of them to their dead brother.'

'They seem very different from each other, your children. In looks and temperament.'

'Oh, they are! But then they are all adopted. My husband and I fostered dozens of abandoned and damaged children, and these are the ones I couldn't let go. Brendan was my only natural child.'

'I see.' This struck Jackman as important, but he couldn't say why. 'Finally, Mrs Symons, is there anyone in your group of supporters that bothers or worries you in any way?'

She was silent for a while. 'There were a few people who didn't exactly bother me, but I never quite took to them. We had a young man called Jeremy Shaw, an intelligent chap, but I was never truly certain about his motivations. I was told that he studied theology and had gone into the church, but had suffered a crisis of faith and left. I wondered if taking up our cause was a substitute for what he'd lost.' She paused again. 'And although I should never criticise Mark — that's Mark Courtney, he's been my spokesman for years — I still find him puzzling. He practically took over the whole thing at one point, but I always wondered why. He never even knew Brendan.'

Sheila was starting to look tired, and Jackman brought the meeting to a close.

As he got to the door, she said, 'You're different, aren't you?'

He stopped and smiled back at her. 'I hope so.'

'So do I.' Sheila lay back and closed her eyes. 'I believe you're our last hope.'

* * *

'How's Rosie?' Robbie asked Max.

'Pretty grim, mate, if I'm honest.' Max flopped down into a chair in the CID room and yawned. 'I've been up half the night with her.'

'I thought the doc gave her something to help her sleep?'

'She wouldn't take it, the stubborn little mare! I told her she really needed help, but she'd have none of it.' He shook his head. 'She hates taking tablets. Said she'd seen too much of what drugs do to people.'

'I can understand that, but a mild sedative would hardly have her hooked for life.' Robbie smiled. 'But she is stubborn, I'll give you that.'

'Immovable! One good thing, her eldest sister has come over to keep an eye on her. She's a force of nature, and Rosie adores her, so, hopefully . . . ?'

'Try not to worry, Max. Rosie will come through this, I'm convinced of it. I did, when I had a really bad time, and to be honest, I don't think I have nearly as much strength of character as Rosie. So hang on in there, my friend.'

Max swallowed and sighed heavily. 'It kind of puts things into perspective.'

'Like, how much you really care for someone?' asked Robbie gently.

'Bang on target. I mean, I knew I was pretty smitten, but hell . . .'

'Dare I mention the word *love*?' Robbie grinned.

'With bells on!'

'Then you'll see her through.' Robbie leaned forward and grasped his friend's shoulder. 'And if I can help, just let me know. I'm here for you, both of you.'

For a minute Robbie thought the tough Cockney was going to burst into tears. Then Max shook himself. 'Ta, mate. Appreciate it. And now I guess we better get some work done, huh?'

'Fancy interviewing some suspects for our DIY killer?' Robbie asked.

Max winced. 'DIY killer. Gross, man. Don't tell me you came up with that one?'

Robbie held up his hands. 'No way! It's what the mess room are calling him. So, are you in? Because I've got a couple of names here that the boss wants us to talk to.'

Max looked at the names on the memo Robbie showed him. 'Christian Ventnor and Shaun Cooper? Who are they?'

'Ventnor is one of Sheila Symons's crusaders, and Cooper is a local guy who never joined the protest group, but he had a lot to say to the media. Very much an activist, but more of a loner by the sound of it.'

Max rubbed his hands together. 'Right. Then we better go talk to them, I guess.'

It took fifteen minutes to reach the village of Saltville and Christian Ventnor's house.

Max whistled. 'Nice pad. Wonder what this guy does for a living?'

Robbie glanced at his notes. 'Architect, I think.' He looked up at the Georgian house. 'But he sure didn't design this.' The house was a beautiful example of the middle-class homes of that era. Robbie reconsidered his preference for modern houses.

'Are you thinking of just memorising this property, mate, or shall we ring the bell?'

Robbie laughed. 'Sorry, daydreaming.' He rang the bell and stepped back.

Christian Ventnor took a while to answer, but when he did, he merely glanced at their ID and swung the door wide. 'Come in! Come in! This way, gentlemen.'

He ushered Robbie and Max into an elegant sitting room. The focal point was an arched cast-iron fireplace set in an intricately carved wooden surround. Robbie liked it. 'Lovely house, sir.'

'Family home, Officer. But even though it's just me left, I can't part with it.'

Ventnor was a tall, thin man. He wore his hair rather too long for someone in their mid-forties. His skin was pale, his eyes a washed-out blue, but he radiated energy.

'Please sit and tell me why you are here.' He indicated two armchairs, while he sat on the arm of the sofa, obliging them to look up to him.

Robbie wondered if this was intentional. 'We need to speak to you about your involvement with the people trying to clear Brendan Symons's name.'

Ventnor frowned. 'What have they done now? Has that damn fool Liam got himself into trouble?'

Max shook his head. 'They've done nothing, sir, but there have been some incidents recently that seem to be related to the Ashcroft murder trial.'

'Incidents?' His pale eyes flashed.

'Sorry, sir, we can't say more at this stage in our investigation,' Robbie interposed, 'but if you could just tell us why you joined the campaign?'

'I strongly believe in fair play, Detective, and I don't like to think of an innocent man suffering for something he didn't do. Like Brendan suffered — to the point of taking his own life.'

'This campaign has run for years, sir. Even though it's got nowhere, you still keep trying?' Robbie looked at him.

Ventnor sat up straight. 'Of course! When you believe in something — really believe in it, you don't give up. Wars were not won by throwing in the towel, young man.'

This sounded pompous and very patronising to Robbie.

'Have you always lived here, sir?' asked Max, 'In the family home?'

'Oh no. I travelled a lot when I was younger. I worked all over the country. I only settled back here when my father died. I supported my mother through a long illness, until she passed away. Now here I am.' He looked around the room. 'Home alone.'

'No brothers or sisters?'

'One sister, but she was killed on a backpackers' holiday in Asia. As I said, there is only me now.' He shifted on the arm of the sofa. 'Forgive me for asking, but it seems I'm being interviewed, and I have no idea why. Is this normal procedure?'

'We appreciate your assistance, sir. I'm sorry we can't say much at present, but I can assure you it's a serious matter.'

'Two detectives? It sounds like murder to me.' He looked from Max to Robbie, who both returned his gaze impassively. 'But as you say, you can't tell me anything.'

'You are an architect, sir?'

'A project architect. I'm self-employed now, but I work with a company that designs homes in the fusion style.' The two detectives looked blank. 'It combines art with nature and science. It's interesting and quite challenging work.'

'Why do you believe that Brendan Symons was innocent?' Robbie asked abruptly.

The question seemed to disconcert Ventnor. He answered almost angrily. 'Because it was clearly a travesty of

169

justice. Any fool could see that. There wasn't nearly enough evidence, and what *was* presented was questionable.'

'The jury clearly didn't agree with you there. So you followed the case from day one?' Robbie's tone was harder now.

Ventnor shifted again. 'I suppose I did.'

'Why? Why were you so interested in it? Did you know Brendan personally? Or maybe you knew Lyndsay Ashcroft?' Robbie persisted.

'No, I didn't! And I object to this kind of questioning!' Ventnor stood up. 'I think you should leave now. If you need to come back, make an appointment and I'll have my solicitor with me.'

After the door slammed shut behind them, Max began to chuckle. 'Nice one, Robbo! That got him miffed!'

'So, what did you think of him?' Robbie asked.

'Pompous prat. He's clearly twitchy, but I wonder why.'

'I'd say he was personally involved,' Robbie said. 'Why so much interest, right from the beginning, and then keep at it all this time? He knew one or both of them, I'm certain.' He shrugged. 'But I can't see him as our DIY man, can you?'

Max looked back at the house. 'I can't. I didn't like him, but that doesn't make him a killer.'

'So,' Robbie started the car, 'on to check out Mr Shaun Cooper.'

'Can hardly wait. Hope he's not like that one. "Wars weren't won by throwing in the towel, young man!" Supercilious old git.'

* * *

Marie and Gary were combing through the past, their desks scattered with printouts and copies of old newspaper articles.

'I'm starting to get a feel for what life was like in that small village back in those days,' Gary said.

'Me too, and boy was it claustrophobic!' Marie grimaced.

Gary grinned at her. 'Incestuous even. Such a small community, and everyone related to everyone else.'

170

'It was much worse a couple of generations ago, when few people travelled outside the village.' Marie was looking at her screen. 'Finally! I've found something on Lyndsay Ashcroft. There's a background report here, done at the time of her death, along with a short bio from her class teacher.' She printed them out and handed copies to Gary.

They read in silence. Marie said, 'Nothing screams out at me.'

'Mmm. This bio is a bit, what's the word, sterile, isn't it? I mean, this poor young girl has just been horribly murdered, and whoever wrote this might have been copying out the shipping forecast. You'd think a bit of emotion might have trickled through, wouldn't you?'

'Maybe the teacher who wrote it *was* affected, and was trying to keep to the facts. It's not supposed to win the Booker Prize.'

Gary snorted. 'You know what I mean. "Good at sport. Liked animals." I don't think this teacher liked Lyndsay Ashcroft much.'

Marie read it again. 'I see what you mean. It isn't exactly warm and friendly, is it?'

Gary skimmed the police report. 'I get the feeling this lass was a bit of a Billy No-Mates. I wonder why that was?'

Marie shrugged. 'Crap family? Crap house? Too ashamed to bring friends home?'

'Or she could have been a bully, and the other kids steered clear.' Gary looked up. 'We need to find out. It could have a bearing on the case.'

'Okay, let's get phoning and see if we can trace someone who remembers her.'

Ten minutes later, Marie put down the receiver. 'Got one! The local post office put me in touch with an old neighbour. I've rung her, and she'll talk to us.'

'Excellent. When?'

'Now. Well, as soon as we can get there.' Marie stood up. 'Let's go. I'm dying to find out what Lyndsay was really like.'

* * *

Mrs Beatrice Harper's home was a small, neat bungalow set in a large corner plot. Gary looked around, lost in admiration.

Beatrice met them at the gate and greeted them cheerfully. She was dressed for gardening in green corduroy trousers, a check shirt and a quilted half-jacket with more pockets than a fishing gilet. 'Let me get these boots off and we'll go inside.'

Inside the back door, she hauled off her wellies with a grunt. 'I do love my garden, but at eighty-three it's beginning to get the better of me, I must admit.'

Gary was amazed. 'Your garden is a picture. You put me to shame.'

'You're a working man. I have all the time in the world, except for my craft classes, oh, and the film club.' Beatrice bustled into the kitchen and put the kettle on. 'I'll get us some tea. You are "proper" police officers, I take it? You do like a brew?'

They nodded vigorously. 'Nothing like it,' said Marie.

'You two go through to the conservatory and make yourselves at home. I'll bring the tea.'

Gary followed Marie into the garden room through a lounge/diner, vastly impressed by how clean it all was. Plenty of older folk lacked the energy for dusting or hoovering, he knew, but evidently not Beatrice. They sat in cane chairs and looked out at the garden. Surely it was too big for an eighty-three-year-old to cope with? Yet somehow she seemed to be managing, and very well. Gary just hoped her memory was in as good nick.

Beatrice arrived with a tray of tea and chocolate digestive biscuits. 'Dig in, and tell me what you want to know.'

Marie helped herself to a mug of tea and a biscuit. 'We need to get a clear picture of what Lyndsay Ashcroft was like. Do you think you can help us, Mrs Harper?'

'I certainly can! And it's Beatrice, please. I've only lived here for, oh, around five years I suppose. Before that, when my husband was alive, we lived next door to the Ashcrofts. Ash Grange, it was called. Rather ostentatious, but it was a big property.'

'They were well off?' asked Marie.

'Charles Ashcroft was a businessman, something in the building trade I think. Not a friendly man at all.' Beatrice's bright face clouded over. 'My husband fell out with him, I'm afraid.'

'What was the wife like? Lyndsay's mother?' asked Gary, nibbling a digestive.

'We never really knew her. She ran off one day. Never came back.' 'Not that we blamed her really. All the shouting and screaming that used to come from that house, it was terrible.' Beatrice shook her head. 'We worried about the children.'

Gary stared at her, surprised. 'Children?'

'Yes. Lyndsay and her little brother, Alistair.'

Marie gave Gary a puzzled glance. 'None of the reports mentioned a brother.'

Beatrice put her mug down. 'No wonder! Poor little thing. They said he was autistic. He had behavioural problems. He was treated really badly by the other children at school, and if Lyndsay hadn't looked out for him, I dread to think what would have happened.'

'I wonder what did happen to him?' Gary mused.

Beatrice shrugged. 'I have no idea. After Lyndsay died, Charles put him in a special school. We never saw him again.'

The alarm bells were clanging in Gary's head, and from the look on her face, Marie heard them too.

'Lyndsay . . .' Beatrice hesitated. 'I know I shouldn't speak ill of the dead, but she was a bit of a wild child. She did her best for Alistair, I know, but she bullied him too. He was a strange little thing, and he idolised her, but she rarely had a good word to say to him. Ali was the reason my husband argued with Charles. We knew he sometimes took his belt to the boy but we didn't want to make it worse for the poor little mite. Eventually Harry read Charles the riot act, but it did no good. We were about to go to the authorities when . . . when Lyndsay was murdered.'

Marie leaned forward. 'You said the girl was wild. In what way, Beatrice?'

'Boys mostly. She would sneak out at night. We could see her go from our bedroom window. What she never knew, or so we believed, was that little Ali would follow her. God knows what hanky-panky that poor child witnessed.'

'The reports say that the night she went with Brendan Symons, it was her first time. Does that sound right to you? Given her behaviour?' Gary asked.

'When I said she liked the boys, I meant she was a terrible flirt and an awful tease, not that she went any further. I saw the statements and I thought they were probably the truth. She was little more than a child.'

'Did you know Brendan?' Marie asked.

'Yes. Not well, but he did odd jobs for us once or twice. We liked him.'

'What did you think of the verdict?'

Beatrice sighed. 'Heartbreaking. Brendan had always seemed such a fun-loving boy. He did like Lyndsay — he told us that much himself — but kill her? I don't know, I really don't. I would never have believed it, but the two girls who witnessed it were good honest children. Why would they lie?'

'You knew them too?' Marie was surprised.

'I knew Pauline's parents well, and Heather was always in and out of our house as a little one. I sometimes wonder how she is. I know why they ran away, but I would love to hear from her again.'

Gary bit his lip. They couldn't tell the old lady that Heather and Pauline had both been driven to suicide. It would be too cruel.

After a quick glance at Gary, Marie said, 'Beatrice? What happened to Charles Ashcroft?'

'Oh, he's dead, dear, not long after Lyndsay was killed. Got drunk and drove off the road at speed. Went nose down in a deep drainage ditch and broke his neck.' There was no sadness in her voice this time.

Gary thought of the mysterious younger brother. Where was he now? 'You said that Alistair used to follow Lyndsay? Did you see him follow her on the night she was attacked?'

'We weren't here that night, I'm afraid. We had gone to our daughter's for the evening.' She gasped. 'Are you saying that little Ali might have witnessed . . . ? Oh, that's too awful!'

'Please don't upset yourself. It's just that he might have seen her with someone.'

'Why did I never think about that before? That poor child!'

Marie leaned forward. 'Beatrice, we need your help. Do you know anyone who could tell us where we could find Alistair Ashcroft?'

The old lady frowned. 'You could talk to the vicar. He had a friend, another clergyman, who was covering this parish at the time of the murder. He spent a lot of time with the people of Nettleby, and Nettleby Oaks. Everyone was in shock and he was a tower of strength. He did go up to Ash Grange to try and help Charles, but I don't think he was made to feel very welcome, But he might have heard something about where the boy was sent.'

They thanked Beatrice and apologised for upsetting her. 'You've been a great help,' Marie said. 'Now we have something concrete to work on. We do appreciate it.'

'I can't think why I never asked myself that question before. I suppose hearing what happened to Lyndsay just pushed it out of my mind. Ali didn't *always* follow her, but he very often did.'

'And then his father suddenly sent him away,' Gary breathed. 'What *did* that boy see?'

'I dread to think,' Beatrice said sombrely. 'But if you do find him, he might not be the most reliable of witnesses, you know. He was a strange child, so he could well be a very disturbed adult.'

Marie smiled. 'We must go. Thank you again for all your help, and for the tea and biscuits.'

'Any time you're passing. I'm nearly always here.' Beatrice looked at each of them and her voice fell to a whisper. 'Something terrible has happened, hasn't it? That's why you're here. The blight that set in all those years ago . . . it's back, isn't it?'

Gary badly wanted to explain, but knew he mustn't. 'You look after yourself, Beatrice. And if you ever want a job as a gardener, I've got a vacancy at my place.'

She smiled sadly. 'Good luck, Officers. I hope you find him.'

* * *

Marie drove back in record time. At the station, they practically threw themselves at their computers and began searching for Alister Ashcroft.

The rest of the team were out, apart from Charlie Button, who was eager to help.

'What a stroke of luck, Sarge! You might have identified the killer in one hit! I mean, if the kid did witness his sister's death and knew it wasn't Brendan — bingo! When he grows up, he goes all out for vengeance.'

Gary held up his hand. 'Wait! Think about it, Charlie. If he knew Brendan didn't do it he'd have told someone, hopefully the police. He wouldn't let Brendan go to prison, then wait donkey's years for revenge, would he?'

'Maybe he would if he was traumatised.'

'Or maybe he told his father,' said Marie slowly. 'But Daddy didn't believe him and decided to magic him away before his crazy ideas got someone into trouble.'

Gary dropped into a chair. 'Too many possibilities.'

'What do we know for sure?' Marie cleaned one of the whiteboards and picked up a marker.

'Alister Ashcroft had learning difficulties, possibly autistic,' Gary stated. 'And he had a habit of following his wayward sister when she went out of an evening.'

Marie wrote it down. 'Plus his father ill-treated him.'

'His mother ran out on him. The kids at school gave him a hard time,' Gary continued.

Marie nodded. 'And even his sister, who was the only one to care for him, bullied him sometimes.'

'Didn't have much going for him, did he? Poor little sod!' Charlie exclaimed. 'Then, according to rumour, he got stuck in a special school. What a life!'

'And since the father, Charles Ashcroft, is brown bread, we need to do some digging.' Marie stared pensively at the board. 'Do we honestly think that someone as mentally challenged as Alistair was could possibly be our clever and calculating killer?'

'It's a big stretch of the imagination, that's for sure.' Gary sighed.

'Not really.'

Marie and Gary stared at Charlie.

'It's only hearsay that he was autistic *or* had learning difficulties. It also might be something his father put around to cover up the fact that the kid was a mess after his mother left. What if he was clever and cunning even at that age? There was a kid at my school who was treated like a total idiot, but he turned out to be a genius. Fine line, and all that?'

Gary nodded thoughtfully. 'He has a point.'

Marie stared at the name. Was this the man they were looking for? Or was he just a screwed-up kid, deserted and abandoned by the very people who should have loved him? 'Time to do some detecting, folks! Gary, chase up that vicar, and see what he remembers about the boy. And Charlie, try to unearth his school records and also his medical records. He must have had some sort of mental health evaluation. I'm going to ring Jackman. He needs to hear this.'

CHAPTER TWENTY-TWO

Kenny Symons was surprisingly easy to talk to. Jackman had envisaged a difficult interview, but after he'd made sure that his mother was asleep, he took Jackman into the lounge, closed the door and sat back on one of the sofas.

'I don't ever remember a time when things were just simple. All our lives, the family seems to have spent time fighting for something or other. Even when Mum and Dad wanted to adopt the younger ones, they had to battle for them. And then our Brendan was accused of that terrible crime . . .' Kenny shook his head. 'It was the start of a night-mare that we never woke up from.'

'I can only imagine,' said Jackman calmly. 'I'm sorry to have to rake everything up again. If there was any other way, I wouldn't be worrying your mother at this stage in her life.'

'More like this stage in her death, Inspector.'

Kenny sounded tired, as if he were doing everything on automatic. Maybe it was like that when you were waiting for someone you loved to die. Jackman could not imagine life without his mother. His father was a different story. His dad had always been more of a figurehead than a hands-on parent. He would hate to lose him — after all, you only had one father. But miss him? How could you miss someone who was never there in the first place?

'Are you married, Kenny?'

Kenny nodded. 'Jennifer. She's a really lovely human being. Patient, too. She knows that I have to support Mum, and she's taken on everything until I get home again.'

'That's good. You need someone like that when things get difficult.' Jackman paused. 'Kenny, I need to get a picture of the real Brendan. I've had your mum's version, now can I have yours? Please be as candid as you can.'

Kenny was silent for a while. 'We were close, but I always felt there was part of him I didn't know. He was funny, easy-going. He liked people to think of him as a bit of a bad boy, but he was really very sweet.' He stared down at his hands, clasped tight. 'I knew what he had in mind that night.'

Jackman tensed. He remained silent.

'He borrowed a condom from me. He said he and Lyndsay had decided that they wanted to . . . to do it, but he was worried about getting her pregnant.'

Kenny looked thoroughly miserable.

'I told him to wait, but he said she was really up for it, and he didn't want to let her down.' He sniffed. 'Jesus, how I wish he had! Stupid sod. For all his bravado, it was his first time too.'

'Did Brendan have a temper? Is there any chance that he got carried away in the heat of the moment? Wanted more, maybe?' Jackman asked.

Kenny looked up at Jackman. 'Brendan was the peacemaker in our family, Inspector. I never saw him lose his temper, never once.'

They sat in silence for a moment, then Jackman said, 'Is there anyone in your group of supporters who you believe is capable of taking the law into his own hands, of committing terrible crimes to right a perceived wrong?'

'How can I answer that? Everyone was fired up at one point. There was a time when I could have named quite a few like that, but now the flames burn low, and with a few exceptions we're running out of steam.'

'And those exceptions?'

'Mark Courtney seems as passionate as he ever was. And Art Pullen, well, he's just a constant. Reliable Art, the girls call him. Every meeting, every rally, every protest, Art's there.'

Jackman hadn't heard that name before.

'And let's not forget my brothers.' Kenny's tone was sombre. 'The girls and I agree that as we run out of steam, the more enthusiastic Dale and Liam get.'

'What do you think will happen when your mother passes?'

'I've thought about that long and hard. I believe the family will disintegrate, Inspector. Mother is the glue that holds us together. Unless she gives some deathbed edict that we have to obey, we'll all just fade away like the pearled dew of May.'

'What did you study at university, if I might ask?' Jackman made a bet with himself.

'English Literature.'

'I thought so,' Jackman said. 'It explains your evocative language.'

Kenny raised an eyebrow. 'Purple prose? It's the mood I'm in at present.'

Jackman stood up. 'I'm sorry, this is an awful time for you. But please, if you think of anything, or hear anything that could help us, just ring me.'

Kenny stood up and looked thoughtfully at Jackman. 'Mother trusts you. She's never trusted a copper before, and she's got good reason. Can I ask? Do you know something about our Brendan? Could there be some new evidence that would prove his innocence?'

Jackman had to remind himself that this man was still a possible suspect, despite his educated and pleasant manner. 'Sorry, Kenny, not yet. But as I said to your mother, we are going to take this whole case apart, so who knows what we might uncover?'

Jackman left Kenny at the door, staring after him.

As he got into his car, his phone rang. 'Marie?'

He listened and broke into a smile. 'Brilliant! I'm on my way back. This could be what we've been waiting for! Well done!'

* * *

It was lunchtime when Jackman got back. Even so, the CID room was full of officers.

'How about an impromptu meeting, just to bring each other up to speed on where we are?'

Everyone agreed.

Jackman began with his opinions on Sheila and Kenny Symons, 'Dale, Liam and Susie were out when I called, so they are next in line for a chat. What luck did you have, Robbie?'

In glorious technicolour, Robbie and Max described the pompous Christian Ventnor. Max added that they had had no luck with tracking down Shaun Cooper. 'The neighbour said he was often around in the afternoons, so we'll try again.'

Marie reported on their meeting with Beatrice Harper. 'We're doing all we can to find out what happened to Lyndsay's brother. If nothing else, he might have been a witness to her murder.'

Jackman nodded. 'Nevertheless, keep up the interviews, but the rest of your time, help Marie and Gary find Alistair Ashcroft, okay? And Charlie? Any news from forensics on our double murder?'

'No, sir. Shall I ring the professor?'

'No. If he has anything for us, he'll let us know.'

Marie raised her hand. 'Shall I run this by Orac, sir? She seems to be able to access records that we've never even heard of. Perhaps she could help track down Alistair.'

'Good idea. You liaise.'

Marie grinned.

'Okay, folks. Back to work.'

'DI Jackman?' Jackman turned and saw the drawn face of Annie, the supervisor of the cleaning team. 'Sorry to bother you, but could we clean the offices early today? We've had a bit of a week with illness and staffing problems and I'm left with only Eric to do the whole station.'

Jackman nodded. 'No problem. Just let us know where you need to go.' He liked Annie. She was reliable and a hard worker. He couldn't say the same for Eric. He didn't even know the man, but he didn't appreciate people who went off and left their fellow workers to mop up their mess. 'It's not like Stefan to be sick.'

'Poor lad, he's not sick, but his little kiddie is. She has some sort of congenital illness and apparently she's quite poorly this time.'

'I never knew,' said Jackman.

'Not many do. Stefan's not like Eric, who tells anyone who will listen all about his illnesses and his problems.' She lowered her voice. 'Actually, sir, I've requested that Eric be moved from my team. He spends far too long chatting to the women. He's not a team player, sir, and I've had enough of him.'

'Good for you, Annie. Hope they agree.'

'Me too, and I'll make sure to do your office myself in future. Eric's been doing it, and although he spends a lot of time, he doesn't seem to get much cleaning done.'

'Then it's time he moved on, Annie. Want me to endorse your recommendation?'

'I'm okay, sir. They'll take my word, I'm sure. I've worked for the company since it began, twenty-five years ago.' Annie grinned at him. 'I'll get my own way over this, you'll see.'

* * *

Ella finished her chores early, running on nervous energy. She had phoned the school twice, just to put her mind at rest, even though she knew there was a plainclothes police officer there, disguised as a trainee teaching assistant. What now? There was only so much cooking, tidying up and ironing you could do. She was beginning to understand how terrified Sarah must have felt. She hadn't seen the Bad Man herself — it had been the boys who had spotted him — but she believed them absolutely, and was certain he wasn't imaginary. True, Miles was artistic and sometimes fanciful, but she was sure that his nightmares were based on reality. Ryan was too serious to make up stories.

Ella folded the boy's ironed pyjamas and took them upstairs to the airing cupboard. She was just closing the door when she had an idea. It had been suggested that one of the police officers collect the boys from school. She had protested that she should continue as normal, to give the lads continuity. But what if she agreed to them being picked up? She could go to the school early and find a hidden spot from where she could watch the gates. If their Bad Man really was watching them, she might just see him for herself.

She went back downstairs and thought it over. There was nothing to lose, and it was better than pacing the house and worrying herself sick. Should she tell Jackman? She pulled a face. He had more important things on his mind. She just hoped one of them wasn't Laura Archer. Ella flopped down into an armchair. She was sure there had been a spark of electricity between Jackman and Laura last night. The trouble was, she really liked Laura, which made it much worse.

She jumped up again. This was stupid! She hadn't felt like this since the sixth form! Wasn't she a bit old to develop a crush? Action, that's what she needed, something to take her mind off gorgeous detective inspectors.

Ella pulled on a jacket and went to find her car keys. She'd talk to the police officer stationed at the entrance to the school drive, and arrange for Ryan and Miles to have a police escort home. Meanwhile, she would do her own detective work

* * *

Brushing straw from her trousers, Harriet Jackman left the stable. Her newest acquisition, a rescue pony called Sherbet, was showing signs of improvement. Harriet ran a riding and livery stables, but occasionally someone would tell her a sad story of an animal that needed help, and before she knew it, she'd find herself with yet another mouth to feed. Sherbet had been left in a field with no shelter and only a matted old rug for protection. He had developed rainscald, a skin infection caused by persistent saturation, and his back and quarters had been covered in sores. Now the skin was healing and the hair growing back, and Harriet was delighted. Sherbet was a grey Connemara Pony that would be perfect for the boys. Connemaras were good-tempered and intelligent, and Harriet thought that having a pony of their own would be a wonderful way to lift their spirits.

As she walked back across the yard, she saw one of her stablehands, a teenager called Erin, talking to a tall, rather good-looking man in a Barbour wax jacket and beige moleskin trousers.

'Can I help?' she asked.

'This gentleman was enquiring about stabling his horse with us, Mrs Jackman.'

The man held out his hand. 'I'm Edward Craven. I have to go abroad on business in a month's time, and sad to say, I don't trust my daughters to give their horse sufficient care while I'm away. They are not bad girls but their attention seems to be wandering from horses to boys — need I say more?'

Harriet laughed. 'Probably not. What breed is your horse? And how old is it?'

'She's a Snowflake Appaloosa, Mrs Jackman, twelve years old. Her name is Fleur. She's a docile creature and loves being ridden. Do you think you could take her?'

'I'll have to check the diary. Would you like to come across to the office, Mr Craven?'

They strolled over to the stables' office and Harriet opened the diary. 'Do you live round here?' she asked.

'Oh yes, and you came highly recommended.' The man grinned. 'Your son, actually. I met him at a function and we got talking horses. He told me all about his lovely Arabian event horse, Glory.'

Harriet smiled. 'I thought he was never going to get over the death of that horse. She was his world.'

'So he said.'

'So what dates are you looking at?' Harriet looked up at him.

'Let's say exactly one month from now, then even if my trip is delayed, I'll know she's settled in.'

Harriet found herself thinking that he would make a brilliant narrator for audiobooks. His voice was quite mesmerising. 'Yes, we can do that. I suggest we work on a weekly rate, then if your trip is extended, or shortened, you won't be paying more than you have to. Naturally, we will provide a contract. All the usual things — vets, farriers, insurance, stable rules and so on.'

'Of course. I have transport, so I'll bring her myself.' He glanced at his watch. 'Oh, is that the time? Lord, I have an appointment. Can you pencil me in, and I'll ring you later with all my details?'

He gave Harriet a mobile number.

'We'll be pleased to look after her for you,' Harriet said.

'Thank you so much and forgive me for being so rude, Mrs Jackman. Give my best to your son. I'll ring tonight. Around seven?'

'Perfect. Hear from you then.'

Harriet scribbled a note to remind herself to expect his call, then went to the pharmacy cupboard to work out Sherbet's next course of treatment. If he kept up this rate of recovery, in a few weeks' time her lovely grandsons would have a pony of their own.

* * *

Once she had notified the police and the school of the temporary change of routine, Ella felt quite excited to be doing something positive. Part of her missed her old job as a scene-of-crime officer. It was something that made a difference.

Prior to Harriet Jackman's request for her help, Ella had been dangerously close to a serious breakdown. The plight of the Jackman boys had spurred her into action and given purpose to her life, and she knew that by the time the family no longer needed her, she would be capable of moving forward again.

The school was situated at the bottom of a leafy, tree-lined avenue. The parents parked along the avenue, and then gathered at the gates to wait for their chattering offspring to be released back into their care. Ella walked towards the school, looking for suitable places to conceal herself.

She chose a spot a little to the left of the gates, on a grassy mound that housed a seat, a litter bin and a few straggly bushes. Some parents would sit there and wait if they had arrived early, so she didn't feel too conspicuous. After all, she could hardly lurk behind a tree, could she? Better to just act naturally.

Her view of the gates was about as good as it got, so she settled down with a book open on her lap, and kept a careful eye on the gathering throng of parents.

Some of them she knew by sight, a few she occasionally spoke to, and there were a couple of local women she remembered from her own schooldays.

There were very few men in the company, and she recognised those from when she collected Ryan and Miles. She sat on, beginning to feel very silly. There was very little chance of Miles's Bad Man turning up every day. How often would she have to come here?

And then she saw someone she didn't recognise.

A man stood at the back of the group. He was tall, wearing a black leather bomber jacket and black jeans. He wasn't watching the school gates.

He was watching her.

Ella realised that she'd stopped breathing.

Then he made a small gesture, and it froze the blood in her veins. The man pointed to himself, lifted his hand and directed two fingers at his eyes, then aimed a finger at her.

The message was as clear as it could possibly be: *I'm watching you.*

Ella sat, unable to move. She watched, rigid with fear, as he moved away from the crowd of waiting parents. Then all she could see was his back, disappearing between the parked cars.

For a moment she had no idea what to do, then she pulled out her phone, rang Jackman, and sprinted towards the school gates just as they opened. All she could think of was that she wanted the boys in her arms.

CHAPTER TWENTY-THREE

When Marie arrived in Orac's basement underworld, she was surprised to see a whole group of technicians hard at work. Generally Orac worked alone, or with just one or two assistants.

'Bad time?' she asked.

'No, no. Come in, Marie.' Orac smiled at her, those disturbing eyes glinting in the half darkness. 'Housekeeping. I'm cleaning.'

Marie frowned. There were no dusters or polish in evidence.

'Cleaning out the crap that builds up in the systems. We can't afford to leave the smallest bit of info hanging around for some hacker to grab hold of. I run a tight ship, my friend.'

Marie didn't doubt that for one second. 'I need your help.'

'You? Or Jackman?' There was a hint of amusement in Orac's voice.

'Well, both really. We wondered if you could trace a boy who went missing in 1995. It was assumed that he was sent to a special school, for autistic children. He's never been seen since.'

Orac ran the tip of her tongue across her lips. 'Sounds interesting. Give me what you have.'

'His name is Alistair Ashcroft and his address was Ash Grange, Nettleby. Father, Charles, mother unknown. One sibling, named Lyndsay. Aged around nine when he was sent away. Said to have learning difficulties, possibly autism. And that is all we have.'

'That's plenty to be getting on with.' Orac spun her chair to face Marie. 'Can I ask why you are interested in him?'

'He might have witnessed the murder of his sister, Lyndsay Ashcroft.'

She raised her eyebrows. 'That's a good reason to want to find him.'

'There is also an outside chance that he is our killer.'

'Then I'd better start work immediately, hadn't I?' Orac picked up a folder. 'Before I forget, these are for you. The results of the checks I ran on Sarah's laptop. It's basically a string of locations, but what it comes down to is that Sarah's nemesis made the calls and sent the emails from here in Saltern. We will never find the caller ID but I'm guessing it doesn't even exist anymore. It's the best we can do.' Orac turned back to her screen. Still facing it she said, 'Something really bothers me about those two women's deaths.'

Marie waited.

'Why London? Why not throw yourself in the Westland River? Jump from the local hospital roof? That's the tallest building round here. Why go all the way to London to kill yourself?'

Marie had been wondering the same thing. 'The only thing we can think of is that it was part of the killer's mind-control scheme, something else he threw in to screw their heads up even more.'

'As in, "You must go London and do exactly what I tell you, only then will I spare your children?"'

'Something like that. I'm guessing we'll only discover the real reason when we have the bastard sitting in an interview room.'

'*If* he decides to tell you.'

'He'd bloody well better,' growled Marie. She opened her mouth to continue but a voice behind her called out, 'Marie! The boss wants you right now!'

Robbie met her at the door. 'His nephews' nanny called him in a right panic. She reckons the killer was at the school gates at going home time.'

Marie strode after him down the corridor. 'How would she know it was the killer?'

'He didn't say anything else. He wants you to go to the school with him.'

'Of course I will. Oh hell, this is all he needs — another threat to his family.' She wondered to herself how Ruth Crooke would see this latest development.

She caught up with Jackman at the door. 'Want me to drive, sir?'

He handed her the keys. 'Please, Marie. I want to ring Ella back, make sure nothing else has happened. And put your foot down, huh?'

They reached the school in record time. Jackman was out of the car and running before Marie had put on the handbrake. She parked up and hurried in behind him.

Ella was waiting in the head's office, along with Ryan, Miles, and two plainclothes officers.

Jackman asked whether there was CCTV.

One of the officers, a PC named Chris Bourne, said he'd already requested the footage. 'They've just installed cameras to check on illegal parking. They are trying to get the parents to park further away from the gates.'

Jackman turned to Ella. 'Maybe they've captured something then — if, as you say, he was right there at the gates.'

'He was, Jackman.' Ella looked more angry than shaken. 'With all the parents. Then he ran down the avenue. He *must* have been caught on camera!'

'I need you to look at the footage, Ella.' He glanced over to where the boys were sitting quietly, looking at some books. He lowered his voice. 'Miles mustn't see it. Marie? Would you stay here with Chris and Don and watch the children?'

Marie nodded, and he and Ella left the room.

Marie introduced herself to the brothers.

189

'Oh, you're the sarge!' Ryan looked at her with interest. 'My uncle has told us about you.'

Marie wondered what was going to come next. 'Nice things, I hope.'

'Well,' Miles looked at her critically, 'We're not sure if he's telling porkies.'

'Try me, and I'll tell you.'

'He says you ride a huge motorcycle.'

'True. Next question?'

'How huge?'

'Pretty big. You should get him to bring you to the police station one day and you can see for yourself. You can sit on it if you want.'

Miles's face clouded over. 'Mummy says they're dangerous.'

Oh dear. 'Mummy was right, they can be. But not if you ride them carefully and know what you're doing. I would never let any harm come to you. My bike's name is Harvey.'

'That's a silly name for a motorbike.' Ryan sounded rather superior.

'It's named after someone I know, and it reminds me of him.' She refrained from telling them exactly why — that Harvey Cash's thunderous farts had reminded her of someone kick-starting an old 650cc Triton.

'Uncle also said you were on Amazon, but we looked and looked and we couldn't find you.'

Marie could cheerfully have throttled Jackman. How would she explain that one? Luckily she was saved by a broadly grinning Chris Bourne. 'No, kids, you got it wrong! Your uncle said the sarge *was* an Amazon. They were warrior princesses in Greek mythology, tall and strong and fearless. Your uncle reckons that when Marie rides her bike, she's like an Amazon warrior queen.'

Marie glowered at him. 'What rubbish! Shut up, Chris!'

But Miles was clearly impressed. 'Wow!'

Ryan just nodded sagely, evidently well versed in the myths and legends of ancient Greece.

Chris, who had three children of his own, steered the conversation to superheroes. Marie breathed a sigh of relief.

Soon, a stony-faced Jackman appeared in the doorway and beckoned to her. Outside, he whispered, 'Ella has pointed him out. He's there alright, and he obviously didn't give a toss about the cameras.'

'Any full-face shots?'

'No. He knew exactly where they were, and kept his face turned away. All we can do is get the pictures enhanced and try to pick out anything that could identify him.'

'IT will be able to estimate his age, won't they? From the way he moves, and his general physique?'

'It won't be very accurate, but yes, and it will all help to build up a picture. Shame there are no more cameras in the area. He'll have had a car somewhere nearby.'

'Are you okay?' she asked quietly.

Jackman sighed. 'Yes. I daren't read too much into this, although it's hard not to. It could have been anyone, not necessarily Miles's Bad Man. Ella is as uptight as hell with worry about the boys. She could have blown it out of proportion. She's a good-looking woman, maybe what she saw was a guy who was interested in her.'

Marie doubted that. Ella was sensible, and she certainly wouldn't have imagined or misconstrued that pointed gesture.

'I know what you are thinking, Marie, but right now I have to have hard evidence before I go into panic mode.' Jackman took her arm and pulled her a little closer. 'I'm considering ditching the home protection and getting them into a safe house. What do you think? Am I over-reacting?'

She shook her head. 'No way. I'd do it immediately. Even if it's just until we get a better handle on this.'

'Then I'll notify the superintendent.' He pulled out his phone, which showed an incoming call. 'Mum? Is everything alright?'

Marie saw Jackman's face darken. 'Look, don't worry,' he said. 'I have something to sort out here, and then I'll be straight over.'

He hung up and stared at Marie. 'Something odd happened at Mother's stable. Some man came and asked her to stable his horse. He claims to be an old friend, but I've never heard of an Edward Craven.'

Marie felt a chill of apprehension. 'I'll go with you to your mother's. Is she worried about this man?'

'No, not at all. She just wanted to know if I'd vouch for him before she accepted his horse for livery.'

She frowned. 'Could be a bona fide misunderstanding, I suppose, but we should check it out.'

'I must tell Ella what we're doing,' said Jackman. 'She'll need to collect stuff for the boys — clothes, games, toiletries. I'll get Chris and Don to escort her home, then a protection officer will take it from there.'

They heard Ella's voice behind them. 'Do I get a say in this?'

'It's only for your safety — all of you,' Jackman said softly. 'And it won't be for long.'

'You don't know that, Jackman. Actually, I think I'd rather stay at Rainham Lodge, as long as we have those police officers with us.' She looked at Jackman. 'It will be almost impossible to keep two recently bereaved youngsters occupied and happy in a safe house. Don't you think they're confused enough? What would that do to them? They need stability. They certainly don't need to be bundled off to some hotel room for an indefinite period of time.'

Marie nodded slowly. 'She has a point, doesn't she? I don't think I'd looked further than the safety issue.'

Jackman held up his hands. 'Alright. But do *not* go charging round town on your own. Understood?'

'Promise. Once was enough, thanks.' Ella gave them a rueful smile. 'I'll leave the detective stuff to you from now on.'

Marie grinned at her. 'Too right! But at least you got us a description of him.'

Ella grimaced. 'Fat lot of good it was too. Thick dark wavy hair, tall, dark clothing, and a neat line in scary gestures.'

'It could be worse,' said Marie. 'At least we can rule out short fat blond men and chubby redheads.' She looked at Jackman but he seemed to be miles away. 'Jackman? We should get over to your mother's stables.'

'Sorry? Oh, yes. Ella? Are you absolutely certain about this?'

Her look said it all.

'Then let's fetch the boys, put Chris and Don in the picture, and get you out of here.'

* * *

Harriet rolled up a lunge rein and put it in a drawer in the tack room. 'He seemed, well, so *plausible*. Then after I'd spoken to you, I thought the way he dashed off for an appointment *before* he gave me all his details was a bit suspicious.' She looked at Jackman, her face etched with concern. 'Do you think he's the man who hurt Sarah?'

He'd already rung the number the man had given her. It was unobtainable, but he didn't tell his mother that. 'Mum, this could be nothing, and we have no idea who he is. Tell me again what he looked like.'

Harriet busied herself hanging up bridles and straightening out reins, as if keeping her hands occupied would make her think more clearly.

'He was very well dressed — smart, in that county manner. Moleskin trousers in a stone colour, a navy-and-cream check shirt, and a well-worn Barbour. He had thick wavy dark brown hair and dark eyes. He looked like a rider and he seemed to know his horses. That was why I thought no more about him.' She looked apologetically from Jackman to Marie, 'I'm so sorry. Knowing what is going on at the moment I should have been on my guard, shouldn't I?'

Jackman hugged his mother. 'Oh, Mum! You weren't to know. Maybe he is kosher and I've just forgotten him. I meet a hell of a lot of people at functions.' He didn't really believe his own words, and suspected that the horse knowledge came from the University of Google, but his mother was looking uncharacteristically unsure of herself and until he had proof, he needed to reassure her.

She finally extricated herself from his bear hug and said, 'What on earth should I say if he does phone back?'

'Nothing, because if the phone rings at seven, I'll answer it. That should tell us all we want to know, shouldn't it?' He looked at his watch. 'Not long to wait now.'

To pass the time, Harriet walked Marie around the stables and introduced her to some of her favourite horses.

'Oh, I love this little guy!' Marie exclaimed, stroking the muzzle of a little grey pony.

Harriet beamed. 'That's Sherbet. I rescued him and I'm getting him back to full health as a present for Ryan and Miles.'

'He's gorgeous! The boys will be over the moon.' Marie sighed. 'I've never ridden a horse, only motorcycles.'

'Come down on your next day off, and I'll show you what you're missing,' Harriet offered. 'She'd love it, wouldn't she, Rowan?'

'Do you know, I'm going to take you up on that! I'd love to.' Marie grinned at him. 'Think I'll make a horsewoman?'

Jackman smiled. 'If you ride a horse like you ride that bike, I'd say it's a given.'

'Excellent, that's a date.' Harriet looked more like her old self. 'Rowan's right, I have a feeling you'll be a natural. You clearly have a fondness for them, and Sherbet loves you!'

Jackman watched Marie tickle the pony's ears and checked his watch again.

'Nearly time?' Marie asked.

'*If* he phones.'

At seven o'clock precisely, the phone rang.

'Jackman. Who is this, please?'

For a moment there was silence.

'Ah, an astute woman, your mother. But I'm pleased you answered.'

Jackman let him speak.

'You know who I am, Detective Inspector. Or should I say, you know who I *was*. The thing is, who am I now?' He gave a sharp laugh.

'Alistair Ashcroft?'

'If you say so, but I rather think he doesn't exist anymore, Rowan.'

'No one calls me that!' snapped Jackman, unable to stop himself.

'Except your mother — oh, and your boss.'

Jackman held his tongue. Out of the corner of his eye he could see Marie talking urgently to someone on her own phone, and knew she was trying get a trace on the man's number.

'I'm a very patient man, Jackman. With patience, there is nothing you can't find out.'

What did he mean? 'What do you want from me? Haven't you done enough already?'

'But, Detective, I want nothing from *you*, other than your attention.'

'Well, you've got that. What now?'

'Don't patronise me!'

It seemed to Jackman that all his training, all the years spent studying the psychology of the criminal mind, had been useless. He had absolutely no idea how to handle this man.

'I'm sorry.' He tried to sound sincere, and to keep the man on the phone for as long as possible. 'But you must understand. I know what you've done, and I'm scared for the people closest to me. I have to know what you want.'

'You're right to be scared. Just consider this. "Until justice rolls down like waters, and righteousness like a mighty stream." I'll be in touch, Jackman. Goodbye.'

Jackman closed his eyes. He knew those words. Taken from *The Book of Amos*, Martin Luther King Jr used them in his "I Have a Dream" speech. Alistair Ashcroft was telling him that he hadn't yet finished his quest for vengeance. There would be more deaths.

Marie was staring at him, shaking her head. 'They tracked it, and it's a local call, but an unregistered SIM card.'

What else did he expect? At least he knew now who they were looking for, even if — in his words — he no longer existed.

Jackman had lost his fear.

CHAPTER TWENTY-FOUR

Jackman had never been much interested in his father's frenetic business ventures. He left all that to his brother James. Now Jackman wondered if he should have looked closer. His father had taken charge.

Thirty minutes after hearing that his wife had been eye to eye with a killer, a van containing four security guards arrived at Lawrence Jackman's home. When Jackman asked his father what was going on, he merely said, 'Trust me, Rowan. I know what I'm doing.' Then he gripped Jackman's shoulder in a most uncharacteristic gesture. 'I may not have said so, son, but I know you are a damned good police officer. Go and do what you are best at, my boy. We are safe here. I suggest you consider bringing James, Ella and the boys here too.'

Speechless, Jackman nodded. From what he had seen of those granite-faced guards, it was a viable option. Tomorrow he would put it to Ella and James and see what they thought.

* * *

At around eight o'clock in the evening, Jackman and Marie were on their way back to the station when Jackman's mobile made them both jump.

'Jackman.'

'Orla Cracken here, Inspector.'

Jackman almost asked, "Who?" Orac never used that name. Orac never phoned him. She always used Marie as a go-between.

'I'm sorry, but I really need you to come to the lab immediately,' Orac said.

He had never heard her sound so serious. 'Marie and I are on our way. Can I ask what it's about?'

'I'd prefer to explain when you get here, if that's alright.'

'We'll be with you in ten.' He ended the call and turned to Marie. 'Orac.'

'I asked her to trace the little brother.'

Marie accelerated, and they arrived at Orac's lab in precisely ten minutes.

Orac was alone, and Jackman felt a little of his old discomfort return. But this was urgent, so he pushed it aside.

Orac asked them to take a seat. 'Two things. First, a little earlier, I had to sort out a problem with Laura Archer's laptop. When she collected it, she left this for you.' She handed him an envelope. 'She was going on to another appointment, and when I told her I was going to ask you to call here tonight, she asked me to pass it on. She said to say it was a simplified outline of her thoughts about a man who has that level of control over others.'

'Thank you. I appreciate it.' Jackman took the envelope from her. 'And the second thing?'

Orac turned those metallic eyes on him. 'Now we move to hard facts, which is probably more to your liking right now. The Ashcroft family, God help them. With his high-profile business, Charles, the father, was easy to trace.' She handed Jackman several printouts from old newspaper articles and interviews on Ashcroft's self-made building empire. 'He had dragged himself up from the gutter, and was keen to tell anyone and everyone about his abusive background and how he rose above it. He admits openly that his father was a violent man and domestic violence was a regular occurrence in

197

their home.' Orac picked up another file. 'Working on the assumption that Charles had possibly inherited some of his father's traits, I searched old police files for the Nettleby area, covering the years after he married his wife, Louisa. And I found these.' She passed him the reports. 'Police were called on several occasions by neighbours to disturbances at Ash Grange. The police knew exactly what was happening, but as no allegations were made by the wife, no action was taken.'

'So, he was an abusive bully,' Jackman said.

'As his old neighbour told us,' added Marie. 'And I should think a very nasty one, considering the wife finally ran away and left the children. That takes some doing, leaving your kids.'

'Now,' Orac continued, 'you know what finally happened to poor Lyndsay, and you also know that her brother Alistair dropped off the radar at the same time. What you didn't know, is that there were three Ashcroft children, not two.'

Jackman and Marie exchanged glances, then Jackman said, 'Three kids?'

'Yes, a boy, one year younger than Alistair. But then nothing, no medical records for the child and no primary school registration. I assumed he must have died, but I didn't find a death certificate. The other two children were correctly registered with doctors and schools, so why not the third? I was beginning to think that unless he was given away, or stolen by the fairies, I'd reached a dead end.' She flashed them her strange smile. 'But not for long. His name suddenly resurfaced into the system at exactly the same time as Alistair's disappeared.'

'What was this mysterious third sibling called?' asked Marie.

'Richard Stephan Ashcroft. Stephan spelt with an "a."'

'And in what way did he reappear?' Jackman asked.

'Charles Ashcroft enrolled him into a special school, privately run and expensive.'

'But surely he enrolled Alistair?'

'Nope. He enrolled Richard.'

'What the . . . ?' Jackman puffed his cheeks out and exhaled.

Orac sat back. 'I've had a little more time to think about this than you, DI Jackman, so please allow me to put forward my hypothesis, and it's the only thing that makes sense considering the facts I have here.' She paused, then said, 'If Richard died young, as I suspect he did, and for some reason his death wasn't registered, I'm guessing that Charles Ashcroft took Alistair to that school and enrolled him under his dead brother's name.'

'How on earth would he get away with that?' Marie asked.

'If he had money, and we know he did, Richard's birth certificate and some kind of credible history, what was there to question?'

'It's possible,' Jackman murmured, 'and it would fit in with what we've heard about Alistair being sent away to some kind of boarding school.'

'You'll need to do some work on that though, as the school closed down quite a few years ago, and I haven't had to time to chase it up further,' Orac added.

'I guess if they were only a year apart, then the difference in age wouldn't be noticed,' Marie said. 'And his old neighbour kept calling him a "funny little thing." Maybe he was small for his age?'

'Quite possibly.' Orac frowned. 'I'm certain this is what happened, but I have no idea why the father would want to do such a thing.'

'And if the child died, why was his death never reported?' Jackman stared at Orac. 'You're sure that neither parent reported an infant's death?'

'There is no record of it anywhere. But, what I have found is that his wife's maiden name was Tasker.' She placed a telephone number in front of him, 'And I've traced her mother. She lives near Maldon in Essex. That's Liz Tasker's phone number. If she'll talk, you could have the answer to a lot of questions. I was dying to phone her myself, but I think that is something you must do.' She smiled at him and pointed to the end of her desk. 'There's the phone. Please, be my guest.'

Jackman talked to the woman for around ten minutes, then replaced the receiver and exhaled loudly. 'That was one angry lady! She's given me the background, but we have a problem . . . the daughter suffered a severe mental breakdown and is now in a psychiatric unit. There is no easy way she can be questioned about her life with Charles Ashcroft.'

'Okay, but what did the mother tell you?' Marie asked impatiently.

'Your assumption was correct, Orac. Apparently Charles knocked his wife senseless when she wanted to register the death. He swore it wasn't even his baby in the first place, even though it undoubtedly was. Her mother swears her daughter was too terrified of him to go with anyone else! In the end, Louisa stopped fighting him and allowed him to have his way. She never tried to register the death.' Jackman gritted his teeth. 'Liz Tasker says if we excavate the garden at Ash Grange, we will find a baby's remains.'

'My God!' Marie exclaimed. 'But why? Why hide the death? Did it have something to do with Charles?'

'No, apparently the baby died after a seizure of some kind. And Mrs Tasker says the reason the death was never reported was control, plain and simple. Complete control over Louisa, and the denigration of her personal wishes. Her child was never even given a proper funeral, so the poor woman had no closure. Charles was an abusive bully of the first order, and finally things got so bad for Louisa that she ran away, leaving him and her two other children.'

'Left them, with a bully like that?' Marie shook her head.

'In fairness, she told her mother his anger was only ever directed at her, not the kids.' He shrugged. 'We now know that wasn't the case later on, but maybe she was right at the time, or maybe she just never saw it. What we do know, is that by that time, Louisa was psychologically damaged, and she never made it to a better life halfway around the world. She finished up in a psychiatric unit, heavily medicated.' Jackman turned back to Orac. 'This is a real step forward, incredible stuff, Orac. Thank you.'

Orac inclined her head. 'All in a day's work, albeit a pretty long one. Don't forget Laura's notes.'

'I won't, and thank you again.' For once Jackman didn't feel like fleeing Orac's presence. He saw her better now, a valued and extremely talented colleague. 'I really do appreciate your help.'

'Anytime. I'm always here. Now you know where to find me.' Orac gave Marie a sly metallic wink and turned back to her screens.

Back in the CID room, DCI Cameron Walker was still beavering away at a computer.

'What's this, Cam? Doing night duty?'

'I could ask the same of you two.' He grinned. 'Kaye is away at a seminar in Cambridge, so I thought I'd dig deeper into some of the Symons family camp followers.'

'And we now know that Lyndsay Ashcroft's little brother Alistair is our killer!' Marie announced.

Cameron gaped at them. 'How on earth did you find that out?'

'Oh, he rang Jackman and told him.'

Jackman grinned. 'She's not joking either.'

Cameron sat back in his chair. 'I think this needs some explanation, don't you?'

'Let's go to my office and we'll fill you in.'

'I'll just put the name Richard Stephan Ashcroft into the PNC, then go grab some strong coffees,' Marie said. 'Cam looks as if he could do with one.'

'Three sugars please, Marie, for shock, but don't tell Kaye if you see her.'

'As if!'

Jackman sat in silence for a while, putting the sequence of events in order. Finally he related the whole story, from Ella Jarvis spying on the man who had been watching the children, to his mother's visitor, and then the killer's chilling phone call.

Marie added, 'And Orac has confirmed that Charles Ashcroft did place his son in a special school, but under his dead brother's name. Right now we can only surmise that little Alistair told his father something about Lyndsay's death that he didn't want anyone else to hear, so he got him out of the way, fast.'

'So we were right to think that Alistair might have witnessed something that night and it never came out at the trial?' Cam asked.

Jackman nodded. 'Looks that way. And whatever it was, it seems to have sent her little brother on a vengeful killing spree.'

Cameron sipped his coffee. 'I'm still not sure how Charles Ashcroft got away with switching his sons' identities. Surely he would have needed medical reports to get the boy into the school?'

'It would seem that young Alistair was never assessed. In fact, although he was registered with a local GP, he was only ever seen for a few inoculations. His school reports mention only that he was a very quiet child and not a good mixer.' Marie shrugged. 'I think Charles flashed a lot of cash, turned on the charm and the crocodile tears, and spun a yarn about the family trying to manage the boy's behavioural problems until they realised he needed specialist help that they were prepared to pay for.'

'And an assessment will have been done then, in the name of Richard.' Jackman scribbled some notes on a memo pad. 'First thing tomorrow we need to find out more about that school and talk to someone.'

Cam nodded. Then he frowned. 'Okay, so Dad bundles the problem child into a private school, but surely the boy wouldn't have answered to Richard when his name was Alistair? And why didn't he simply tell the truth about himself?'

'Fear,' chorused Jackman and Marie.

'His father was a violent bully. We know that from two sources already, and we've not even started asking proper questions yet. The child was most likely threatened, and witnessing his sister's murder must have traumatised him. He would have been pleased to get away and hide.' Jackman shook his head. 'We can only guess what those two kids suffered after the mother ran off.'

'Ah, I see.' Cam folded his arms and exhaled.

'After his sister's murder his mental condition must have been one of total shock. He could even have had some sort of dissociative amnesia,' Jackman added.

Cam nodded. 'Maybe that's what sent him on his terrible journey of revenge.'

Jackman leaned back in his chair and stretched his arms above his head. 'What a bloody awful day! I'm exhausted.'

Marie smiled at him. 'I'm not surprised after what you've had to cope with in the last twenty-four hours.' She finished her drink. 'Still, we are so much further forward than we were.'

'Yes and no.' Jackman ached all over. 'We know *who* the killer is, but we have no clue as to what bogus identity he's now hiding behind. How's that for a conundrum?'

Cam stood up. 'Whatever, my friend, it's a puzzle for tomorrow. You need some rest.'

'I'm not arguing, Cam, believe me.' Jackman sighed. 'However, there is one thing I can't ignore.' He waved the notes that Laura had sent them. 'We need to read this.'

Marie took it from him, saying, 'Photocopier. A copy each. Take it home, read it before we come in tomorrow, and then we can discuss it. Cam is right. It's something for tomorrow, not tonight. And that, sir, is an order!'

* * *

Marie sat up in bed and for a second time, went through Laura's notes. They had dealt with some terrible people in their time, but this man had to be the worst.

203

She pulled the duvet up around her and slid down into its warmth.

She couldn't begin to imagine the workings of his brain, but what really scared her was his utter self-possession. The school's CCTV footage showed the casual way he skipped between the parked cars, twisting aside to avoid the cameras. It was almost a dance. He was enjoying himself.

Laura described the killer as devious, deceptive, exploitative — a master of manipulation. His power resided in his knowledge of his victims' vulnerabilities, and his ability to make use of them. He was totally ruthless, caring nothing for his victims. It is probable that he led Sarah and Suri to believe that they were guilty of complicity in a terrible miscarriage of justice. He then escalated his accusations until the women were so confused that they doubted their recollections of what really happened. And when they were ready, he used threats to their children's lives to push them into total submission and finally, death.

Marie wondered how this "poor little thing," as Beatrice had called him, had turned into such an intelligent, calculating avenger.

It seemed that Laura had brought Sam in on it, and the two psychologists had discussed multiple kinds of complex personality disorders, but she had simplified it to say they believed that the killer exhibited traits of what was known as the "dark triad," a trio of psychoses. Anyone who exhibited all three of these traits would have a severely malevolent nature and would be a danger to the mental health of those around them. These people were usually extremely intelligent and highly functioning, but their self-image was unstable and illusory. They concluded that the killer was an extraordinarily evolved version of this particular disorder.

Marie put down the paper and turned out the light. She hoped that Jackman was asleep, and not poring over Laura's notes as she had been. He had looked drained. But she knew him very well. He wouldn't give up until he found the killer.

CHAPTER TWENTY-FIVE

Jackman started awake at around five a.m. Laura's notes lay unopened beside his bed, where he had dropped them the night before. He had intended to read them before going to sleep, but had succumbed to exhaustion and fallen into a deep slumber. He stretched. Well, the sleep seemed to have done the trick. His old fervour burned like a torch in the cold darkness.

He picked up the pages and began to read.

Laura referred to studies that found that people with a controlling megalomania such as their killer exhibited often believed that they were far more omniscient and powerful than they really were. This could be a way to bring him down. She had added, '*Try to see things as they are, Jackman, not how he wants you to see them. He is not all-powerful, no human being is. Remember what happened to Machiavelli? He was tortured, imprisoned, alienated from the society he had devoted his life to, and he died a bitter man.*'

Jackman wondered if that were really true. He liked to think that evil people paid dearly for their transgressions, but he knew that wasn't always the case. At university, he and his fellow students sometimes debated whether Stalin or Hitler had been the world's worst mass murderer. Jackman had voted for Stalin. That man had overseen the deaths of millions of his own people, and instead of being brought to justice, he died of a heart attack while still in power.

Jackman shook off these negative thoughts. He had to catch this man. He *would* catch him.

* * *

The morning passed in a frenetic blur. The CID office was alive with the sound of phones, printers, voices, and the feet of staff coming and going.

Jackman spent the whole morning in his office, fielding questions, delegating tasks and overseeing progress.

At around twelve, Cameron knocked on his door. 'We've found the special school!'

Jackman almost punched the air. It was a massive step forward. 'Where?'

'It's just outside Spalding. The name has changed from the one Orac tracked, and it no longer functions as it did back then, it's now part of a group of schools that specialise in children with learning difficulties. The good thing is, I've tracked down the name of the head that was in charge in the nineties, and he lives here in Saltern-le-Fen. I've phoned him and he's in all day. Would you like to go and see him, or shall I?'

'You go, Cam. And take Marie with you.' He glanced at his desk and the mountain of paperwork, on top of which was a memo written in thick black felt pen: *Ruth Crooke, meeting 12.30*. 'I'm a bit tied up until after lunch.'

Cameron nodded. 'We'll go right away.'

Cameron opened the door to Robbie Melton. 'Sir, I've been to see one of the men who support Sheila Symons's cause. Jeremy Shaw?'

Jackman had to think for a moment. Ah, Shaw. A well-known radical but a loner, according to the sources. 'And?'

'He's certainly motivated. There are giant posters of Che Guevara on his walls and he probably has every newspaper article ever printed about the trial of Brendan Symons. Seems to attach himself to lost causes. He lectured me for several minutes before he realised I was a copper, then he got really bolshie.'

'Description?'

'As far as looks go, he fits the bill. He's dark, tall, and around forty, I guess.' Robbie looked at Jackman. 'But the only vibes I picked up were a particular dislike of the police, plus he loves the sound of his own voice — so nothing significant.'

'Can we take him off the list, do you think?'

Robbie frowned. 'Unless he's a consummate actor, he doesn't seem to fit the profile for Alistair Ashcroft.'

'So who've you got next?'

Robbie glanced at his notebook. 'Well, we were hoping to tackle either Dale or Liam Symons, but we can't pin them down. So Max and I are just off to see Art Pullen. Reliable Art, according to your notes.'

Jackman remembered Kenny saying how Art *always* turned out for a meeting, a protest, a march — anything and everything. 'Okay, but if you think he's simply another enthusiastic camp follower, don't spend too much time on him, will you?'

'No, boss. We'll give him the once over and report back.'

When Robbie had gone, Jackman looked at the memo again. He was pretty certain he was on borrowed time. His close family were involved now, so it wouldn't be long before Ruth was obliged to ask him to hand the investigation to someone else. He couldn't let that happen. He couldn't. From the moment he'd heard Alistair's voice on his mother's phone, the case had become truly personal. He drew in a long breath. This investigation had started with Sarah Jackman. Rowan Jackman would finish it.

* * *

It felt odd to be out with a different senior officer, but Marie had liked Cameron from the very beginning. For a DCI, he really was a breath of fresh air.

They found the old headmaster in a flat in a very nice retirement village on the outskirts of town. After the introductions, Ralph Burgess invited them in and disappeared into the small galley kitchen to make tea.

Marie looked around the room. As old people's residences went, this was the best she'd seen. It had a lounge and a separate bedroom, along with a shower room and the narrow kitchen, but it didn't feel cramped or claustrophobic. Ralph had kept several good pieces of furniture, including an oak bookcase that groaned with books. A panorama of school photographs covered one wall from floor to ceiling.

Marie's hopes rose.

When tea had been poured, Ralph asked, 'Was it Richard Ashcroft that you wanted to know about?'

'Yes, sir,' said Cameron. 'Only we have recently discovered that he was enrolled with you under a false name, that of his dead brother. His real name was Alistair Ashcroft.'

Ralph Burgess digested this information. Then he nodded slowly. 'That could explain a lot of questions we had about that boy.'

'You remember him clearly, sir?' asked Marie.

The man gave a tight little laugh. 'Oh yes. There are some children you never forget.' He stood up and went to his photo display. After searching for a moment, he removed two framed photographs and returned to his chair. From a side table, he took a handsome magnifying glass with a carved handle, and examined the pictures.

'Here he is. The year he came to us.' He handed the picture to Cameron. 'Second row from the front, in the centre.' He then showed them the second photograph. 'And this was the year he left. Rather a change, isn't there?'

Marie looked at the pictures. The child in the first image was small, hunched, with feral eyes, but in the second picture, he was standing in the back row, a head above his classmates, tall, strong and with a clear, intelligent gaze.

'That's the same boy?' asked Cam incredulously.

'Hard to believe, isn't it? Mind you, we had a whole year of hell with him, and then something just clicked. He started to thrive and never looked back.' Ralph looked proud of the transformation. 'He was a real success story.'

'Tell us about his first year, especially when he first arrived. Did you meet the father?' Cameron had his notebook and pen ready.

Ralph frowned. 'I did, and I saw through him immediately. Oh, he said all the right things, declared that his wife was on the verge of a breakdown over the child, how he'd done all that was humanly possible to keep Richard at home, but after his sister's demise things had become intolerable, et cetera, et cetera.'

Marie smiled wryly. 'But you still took him?'

'I decided, after a very short conversation, that it was in the child's best interests to get him away from his home. I didn't know exactly what was going on, but the father wanted full board, so, yes, we took him in.' His face darkened. 'I never saw the father again. His fees were paid through a solicitor, and the payments continued after the father died in a car crash.'

'And prior to his death, he never visited his son?' Cameron asked.

'Never. It was as if he was glad to be shot of the boy.'

'Nice man,' muttered Marie. 'So what was the boy like?'

'For a long time he never spoke at all. He seemed unable to interact with others, and suffered from extreme anxiety. Because we'd been given no medical history, we really struggled.'

He picked up his mug of tea and drank thoughtfully. 'We ruled out autism, Asperger's syndrome and a dozen different learning difficulties. One of our very experienced staff was certain he suffered from Fragile X Syndrome, and for a time I agreed.'

Cameron tilted his head. 'Fragile X? I've never heard of that.'

'Not well known, I agree,' Ralph said, 'but it's actually the most common cause of learning disabilities. It's a genetic condition that is found more often in boys than girls, and girls often have milder disabilities. The thing was, there are often physical features associated with Fragile X — a long narrow face with prominent jaw and ears, and Richard did seem to have those.'

Marie recalled Miles's drawing of the Bad Man. That pointed chin and dark, almond shaped eyes. She had never been able to fathom who or what it reminded her of.

'It took a long while to understand that it wasn't a genetic disorder at all. Richard was simply a damaged child. Emotional and physical abuse had made him what he was.' Ralph's face brightened. 'But when we understood that, we had something to work on, and my staff and I began to find ways to bring him out of himself.' He laughed softly. 'The best thing we ever did was take him to our school playhouse. Richard suddenly began to talk, but only when he was acting a role. As Richard Ashcroft, he seemed incapable of thought or action.'

'How long did he remain with you, sir?' Cameron asked.

'Until he was seventeen.'

'And where did he go from there?' Marie wondered.

Ralph shook his head. 'We never heard from him again.'

'Did he give any indication what career he wanted to take up? I suppose he was employable by that time?' Cameron asked.

'Oh, Richard was *highly* intelligent. His IQ was around 140, as I recall. Around genius level.'

'What is normal?' Marie enquired, recalling Charlie Button's words. There is a fine line between idiocy and genius.

'Between ninety and a hundred and ten.'

Marie's heart sank. So not only were they chasing a meg-alomaniac psychopath, he was a bloody genius to boot!

Ralph raised a finger. 'But that can sometimes come at a price. Mental illness and very high intelligence are some-times linked. And when you consider the boy's background, I would be very surprised if he made it to maturity without suffering a serious psychiatric condition at some stage.'

You don't know how right you are, Marie added silently.

'In answer to your question regarding a career, Richard could have done anything he wanted, and whatever that was, he would excel at it.' Ralph nodded, as if to himself.

Marie glanced to Cameron. 'We're sorry to take up more of your time, sir, but I was wondering if there was any way you could find the name of the Ashcroft family solicitor for us?'

'That's easy. Ashcroft senior used the same solicitor as I do, and they are still operating from their head office in Greenborough. I'll give you their number.' Ralph went to the bookcase and took down an old, well-used address book. 'Bell and Murchison, 14 Old Cask Yard, Greenborough.' He gave them the phone number, then stopped and looked at them. 'Is he in trouble, officers?'

Marie nodded. 'He could be, sir. Serious trouble.'

Ralph looked deeply saddened. 'And I had such high hopes for him. I honestly believed that one day I'd read about him in the papers, work that he'd done, or that he'd achieved something truly amazing.' He sighed.

Marie felt very sad. Ralph Burgess had spent years putting a broken boy back together again, and when the truth came out, he would know it had all been for nothing. There was indeed a very good chance that his pupil would make the papers, though not in the way his old mentor would have liked.

CHAPTER TWENTY-SIX

At precisely twelve thirty, Jackman knocked on the door of the superintendent's office.

'Ah, good, Rowan. Come in and sit down,' Ruth said.

His heart sank. She was being nice. Never a good sign.

Ruth looked at him in silence for a while, and then shook her head. 'I know what you were expecting. Well, you've been given a stay of execution. As the details of this investigation haven't yet been made public, the deputy chief constable has instructed me to allow you to carry on for the time being, so long as you show no sign of undue emotional stress. You will check in regularly with the FMO and Laura Archer, and they will in turn report their findings directly to me. Are we clear?'

Jackman nodded mutely, trying to understand why on earth the DCC had interceded on his behalf.

'And having got that over with, thank you for keeping me up to speed on what is going on.' She rested her chin on a cupped hand. 'Discovering that Alistair Ashcroft is behind it all is quite remarkable progress.'

Jackman dared a smile. 'The team, with DCI Cameron Walker's help, have been working flat out, ma'am.'

'And it hasn't gone unnoticed. Tell me, do you really believe this man is now directly targeting you and your family? Only I have a theory — from a complete outsider's point of view of course.'

Jackman chose his words carefully. 'He has put the frighteners on us, certainly, and from his threat to my sister-in-law, Sarah — his use of the phrase *dashing your little ones against the rocks* — my biggest fear is that he will carry out this threat, even if Sarah herself is dead.'

Ruth Crooke inclined her head slightly. 'That's a reasonable fear to have, Rowan, but I don't think he will do that.'

Jackman leaned forward. 'Why, Ruth?'

'I'm not sure, but I think he is after your undivided attention. I think he wants — no, *needs* you to know who he is and what he is capable of. I think you are his chosen duelling opponent, a Sherlock to his Moriarty, if you will.'

'Why? Why me? I know some serial killers crave attention, but usually it's to get their names in the media. They want fame.'

Ruth raised her hands. 'It's just a theory. Let's gather everything we can on Alistair, then we'll look at his profile together with Laura, and maybe Professor Sam Page as well. She tells me he is assisting with your nephews?'

Jackman nodded. 'Sam's a good man. We could certainly use his input.'

'Okay, well, every man and woman available is ready and willing to help you. I suggest you get back out there and find Ashcroft.'

Jackman returned to the CID room, still wondering why the DCC should have intervened. Moreover, why had he taken his side? After all, the most natural reaction would have been to take him off the case. He gave a relieved sigh. What mattered most was that he was still in the game.

* * *

At one o'clock, the man who had once been Alistair Ashcroft made ready to go to work. His father, a successful businessman and asshole, had amassed a fortune, and when he obligingly did away with himself, Alistair's future was assured. He was the only heir, and there was money aplenty. He didn't have to work at all, but it was part of his new persona.

He looked around his home to check that everything was in order. Attention to detail was vital. He would never have succeeded so well had he not been meticulous in everything he did.

He took his jacket from the hall cupboard. He would leave his motorbike and walk to work today, perhaps calling in at the church on the way. He had the beginnings of a new idea, and the quiet would help him formulate a plan.

He locked the door and strolled beneath the bare-limbed trees. By now Jackman would be interviewing everyone involved in the murder trial. He supposed that the Symons family and their supporters would be first in line. Well, it would keep "his" detective busy, though it would soon be time for them to meet. The church tower rose before him. He would calculate his next move, and then he'd set the stage for their confrontation. It was time Jackman realised just who he was up against.

* * *

Harriet sounded like her old self again. 'Son, I've been wondering if you've given any more thought to your father's idea of bringing Ella, James and the boys to stay with us?'

'I haven't had a minute to spare, Mum. I was going to speak to Ella first.'

'I've spoken to her, Rowan, and she thinks it would do the boys good. They can't go to school, and they'll soon be bored. There is plenty here to keep them entertained, and they'd be watched over like royalty.'

Jackman thought of those security guards. 'Okay, that's fine with me if they want to. What does James think?'

There was a short silence. 'He's busy working, Rowan. He told Ella he'd agree to whatever she wanted to do.'

'Hell, Mum! Couldn't he, just for once—?'

She spread her hands. 'I know, I know! But it's the only way he can cope at the moment. Give him some time. Please?'

He bit back his retort. 'I'll tell the superintendent and arrange transport for Ella and the boys. As long as you are sure?'

'We are, son. We'd feel much happier if we were all together.'

Sitting ducks. Jackman wasn't convinced. 'Okay, Mum. I'll ring Ella and ask her to get ready.'

'Before you go, Rowan, don't be angry with him, but your father had a quiet word with a golfing friend of his,' she looked at him rather sheepishly, 'who I believe might just have been a deputy chief constable.'

'Mum! I don't need my father's help to hold on to my job!'

'He meant it for the best, Rowan, and did it because he believes that you, of all people, can get to the bottom of all this. He did it because he trusts you, and he didn't want this conflict of interest thing holding you back. So, as I said, don't be cross, dear.'

Jackman gritted his teeth, then suddenly felt quite emotional. To hear that his father trusted him and thought he was the best man for the job was extraordinary. 'Don't worry, Mum, it's fine.'

Ella had already begun to pack when he rang. 'Your parents are right, Jackman, and it's also one less worry for you. Your mum says the security men are highly trained ex-military men, used to protecting VIPs and government ministers. I reckon we will be safer there than anywhere, don't you?'

Keeping his reservations to himself, Jackman agreed. 'I've seen those goons, Mum's right about them. But even so, keep your wits about you, won't you, Ella? I've just learned that the man we are up against has an extremely high IQ.'

Ella laughed. 'Good. It's been my experience that highly intelligent people have little or no common sense.'

Jackman chuckled. 'Nevertheless, I'm not going to underestimate this man.'

'Nor are we.' Her tone was serious now. 'I'm not letting those two lads out of my sight for one minute, police protection or not.'

'Thank you, Ella. And I mean that. It means such a lot to me, and to Mum too, knowing that you are looking out for them.'

'I'm glad I can help. I wish the circumstances had been different, that's all. They are lovely children.' Ella paused. 'They are Sarah's children, and I think she was a lovely person too. More than anyone, I'm doing it for her.'

'Hang on in there, Ella. We have half the Fenland constabulary working on catching him.'

'Maybe you could use the other half too? I could do with a night's sleep.'

'You and me both.'

Jackman ended the call. How easy Ella was to talk to! It was just such a shame that she had chosen to leave a job she was so good at. Still, if she hadn't left, where would they be now? Jackman wondered what Ella would do when all this was over, and Ryan and Miles no longer needed her. Jackman worried that she might grow too attached to his nephews, and then her cycle of depression could begin all over again.

He straightened up and took hold of his wandering thoughts. It was ridiculously early to be thinking about what might happen years down the line. What was he doing, wool-gathering like this? He should be working.

It was a relief to see Marie.

'I've spoken to the firm of solicitors that dealt with the Ashcroft estate. They assured me that they did deal with Charles's will and that his son, Richard, inherited the whole estate.' Marie sat down facing Jackman. 'That part is fine, it backs up what Ralph Burgess told us. The next bit, however . . .' Marie sighed.

'Is not so good?' Jackman said.

'It's crap, actually.' Marie pulled a face. 'As soon as he was "of age," as they say, Richard took every penny out of the investments and banks, sold the properties — of which there were three — and did a disappearing act. It's anyone's guess where the money went.'

'Would that "anyone" include Orac?' Jackman said. 'I'm sure I heard you say that one of her specialities was tracing money?'

Marie smiled. 'Of course! I'll go and see her.'

'How are the others doing? Anything interesting come out of the interviews yet?' Jackman asked.

'Not a thing. In fact, none of the interviewing teams have had the slightest suspicion about any of them. The two big problems are Liam and Dale Symons. No matter how hard we try, we never catch them in.'

Jackman shrugged. 'It won't be Dale anyhow. We've seen him, remember? He's tall and fairly dark haired, but you saw him — he's big, a bit of a tank really, and the man in the school CCTV footage was slim. Dale doesn't fit at all.'

'I agree, but why is he avoiding us?'

'To piss us off. He hates us, Marie.'

Marie stood up. 'Oh well, there are a few more people to talk to, then we'll have to look further afield, I guess.'

'What's Cam doing at the moment?' asked Jackman.

'He and his DC Penny are trawling through the PNC and local intelligence to look for any mention of a Richard Stephan Ashcroft. We're pretty sure he won't be known to us for any criminal offences, but Cam wants to see if the name pops up in relation to some other matter.'

'I don't think they'll find him, but we have to check.' Jackman was certain they wouldn't find Ashcroft. He was far too smart. 'Go talk to Orac. She's our best bet.'

He grinned. 'And send her my regards.'

Marie laughed. 'Oh, I will, don't worry.'

* * *

James Jackman finished the conference call with his counterparts across the country and heaved a sigh of relief. Another lucrative deal pulled off. He pushed back his chair and stood up. He went over to the window and stared out. Every time his mind was freed from work, the terrible pain flooded in and threatened to drown him.

James knew how his continuing to work looked to others, but it was the only thing holding him together.

Swallowing back a sob, James pulled out his smartphone and rang his brother.

'Rowan?' He fought to control the tears. 'If you have a minute?'

'James? Of course, what's the matter?'

'I need to explain, I need to tell you why I'm here, and not with my children.' For several minutes he poured his heart out to his brother; told him of the dread of having too much thinking time, and his horrible fear of losing control of everything.

Then it was Rowan's turn, and James found his brother's voice incredibly calming. He said *he* understood, but that somehow he had to find time to make Miles and Ryan understand too, because right now they didn't, and he could see them starting to think that their father was not there because of something they'd done. 'Find some downtime with them, James. They love you, and you're all they have now.'

They talked for a while longer and James came off the phone believing that he had said enough to make his brother really understand. The outpouring had done him good, and it also made him realise how little time he and Rowan spent together. He wondered if they'd ever talked this openly before.

He walked back to his desk and sat down. A new resolve coursed through him. He picked up the phone and asked for his secretary to come in.

'Sonia? No more calls. And I'll be leaving early.' He stopped, then added, 'And any emergencies, refer them to one of the team, okay? I want to be with my boys.'

* * *

Following yet another inconclusive interview, they were just about to return to the station when Max asked Robbie if they could call into Rosie's house, just to check on her. Robbie was fine with it, and in a few minutes they were pulling up outside a neat terraced house in Kiln Lane.

'You go in, Max. I'll wait in the car. Give her my best, won't you?'

As his colleague disappeared into the house, Robbie settled back and tried to decide if any of the people they had spoken to could have been a convincing liar. He was sure that they hadn't yet come face to face with the killer.

So who could he be? From several sources, including the CCTV footage and a photo of "Richard" given by his headmaster, IT had produced a passable likeness. No one they had interviewed looked even remotely like it.

Robbie shifted in his seat. He, Jackman and Marie had all agreed that there was something about that image, coupled with Jackman's nephew's drawing of the Bad Man, that rang a bell.

Robbie's thoughts drifted to Marie again. He pushed them away. And yet . . . And yet he decided to speak to Max about cheering up his flat. If anyone could make it work, trendy Max Cohen would.

Ten minutes later, Max heaved himself into the vehicle. His face was drawn. 'Shit! Oh, what am I going to do?'

'Is she no better, mate?'

'No way. Worse, if anything. I'm worried sick about her, Rob.' Max gave a long sigh. 'I should take some time off, be with her. But—'

'Then take it, man! Jackman will understand. We're all really concerned about her, including him.'

Max looked at him. 'What? With a maniac on our bleedin' doorstep? I can't let the team down.'

'But aren't you letting Rosie down? Who's most important?'

'That's not fair,' Max said.

'It is. You told me you love that girl. I think she needs you right now, don't you?'

Max was silent for a while. 'You're right, Robbo. Priorities and all that. I'll talk to the boss as soon as we get back.'

They were about half a mile from the station when the call came in.

Max put the phone on loudspeaker for Robbie to hear. 'DC Cohen. Would you and DC Melton proceed immediately to number Four, Bell Chime Buildings, Belmont Road. PC Stoner is in attendance. We have a report of a suspicious death.'

Robbie swung the car round. 'Reckon it's another one?'

'We'll soon know, won't we, mate?' Max sounded about as miserable as it was possible to be.

Poor sod, thought Robbie. This could well put paid to his request for leave. 'Let's pray it's just a natural sudden death. It could be nothing to do with our Bad Man.'

Neither of them believed that for a minute.

* * *

'Can we come over and talk to you, Jackman?'

Laura sounded slightly on edge. 'We?' Jackman asked.

'Sam's with me. We've been reviewing what we know about your Bad Man.'

'Then come now. We've just had a heads up about another death. Robbie and Max are on their way to evaluate the scene, and if it's our killer, I might have to go out quite soon.' Jackman was still trying to get over his brother's tearful phone call. It had made him appreciate the mental turmoil that James was in. His mother had been right, he needed to give James time.

And now this, another death.

Seated with Laura in his office, Sam sounded more serious than usual. 'This will probably sound strange, Jackman, but we have an idea about how your man operates. We are very concerned that he seems to be fixated on you, your family, and those around you.'

Laura looked intently at Jackman, her eyes glistening with anxiety. 'We believe that his game is reaching its climax. One more death, perhaps, and then his long-running production will be complete. Our concern is that he'll find it impossible to give up killing. His self-belief is most likely increasing, and by now he probably thinks he is omnipotent.'

'And so,' continued Sam, 'he'll need a new cause, a new *raison d'être*.'

'Me.' Jackman looked at the two of them.

Laura nodded. 'It seems that way. We know how well this man is able to prey on his victims' vulnerabilities, so we think you should identify your Achilles heel, and that of everyone around you.'

'We rather knew this, didn't we?' Jackman said. 'From the way he destroyed Sarah and Suri.'

'True,' said Sam. 'But, as you know, serial killers develop in different ways. Some progress and become even more organised, whereas others unravel, become disorganised and finally make terrible mistakes. Whatever the case, they do change with every new killing.'

'And our man?' asked Jackman tentatively.

'This is conjecture, based on case histories, but we think he'll abandon the method of making the target take their own life.' Laura was as serious as Jackman had ever seen her. 'We think he'll continue to identify those closest to the principal victim, and then make the victim watch them suffer.'

'I'm not sure I understand you,' Jackman said. 'You mean, for example, sit my mother down and make her watch as he burns down her stables with the horses inside?'

Sam nodded slowly. 'Exactly. So you really need to identify all the things that you and yours really treasure, and do it quickly, because unless you catch this man soon, he could start to stage some very nasty scenarios.'

Jackman sank back in his chair. 'Marie was right then. I said he was driven by hate, but she said no, it was love that motivated him.'

'More a case of how to manipulate that love,' Sam said. 'But yes, that's quite correct.'

While his imagination took flight, the phone rang. 'Yes? Jackman here.'

It was Robbie. 'I'm sorry to bother you, sir, but you really *have* to come and see this.'

'He's killed again.' It wasn't a question.

Robbie hesitated. 'Yes, sir, but it's different from the other deaths, and this time he's left you a personal account of exactly why he did it.'

'I'm on my way.'

Laura and Sam were staring at him. 'Are you up to coming with me?' he asked. 'I warn you, it won't be pleasant.'

They nodded. 'Maybe it's time we see for ourselves just what this man is capable of.'

Jackman wasn't so certain, but he needed their help. He needed all the help he could get.

CHAPTER TWENTY-SEVEN

'What is this place?' asked Laura in a low voice.

Jackman looked through the car window at the decrepit building's ornate facade. A "For Sale" sign hung drunkenly from a wooden post at the entrance. 'It's the old auction house. It's been on the market for a long time. I'm surprised developers haven't snapped it up by now.'

Robbie was beckoning to him from the doorway. He was already wearing a protective coverall, and around him, police constables had set up a perimeter and were rolling out blue-and-white cordoning tape.

'Uniform are underway, sir. They've set up a log, but you are the first here.' He glanced anxiously to Laura and Sam, waiting in the background. 'Not sure that's a good idea.' He paused. 'With respect, sir.'

'We need them, Robbie. We really do need their professional opinion.'

Robbie shrugged. 'It's pretty awful in there.'

Then Jackman saw Max waiting by the entrance. His face was drawn and pale and his shoulders drooped. Jackman couldn't recall seeing the usually enthusiastic young detective look so withdrawn and miserable.

He exhaled. 'Okay, Robbie. Tell me what's occurred.' Maybe he should take a look before he allowed the other two in.

'A hanging, sir. They're never pretty, are they?'

Hangings were horrible, especially if not carried out correctly. Few were. 'And?'

'It's difficult to work the scene out, sir. We only had a brief look, because we didn't want to compromise it, but he has set up the old auction floor like a courtroom. It looks as though the dead man has been tried, found guilty and then executed.'

Jackman turned to Laura and Sam. 'Wait here for a moment. I need to see how we tackle this.'

Sam looked at him. 'You don't have to spare us, Jackman. We've both seen some pretty horrific things in our time.'

'Fair enough, but I'll still need to check that we won't be contaminating the scene. Meanwhile, you can get suited up. Uniform have brought protective overalls.'

Jackman took one from a pile by the entrance door and pulled it on. Max still hadn't spoken.

'You okay, my friend?' Jackman asked.

Max gave a feeble nod. 'I just wish it was all over, boss. This maniac is tearing us to bits.'

Jackman guessed he was thinking of Rosie. 'Then we need to get him, don't we? Robbie said he left something for me. Hopefully, if he's getting cocky he may have given something away.' He touched the young man's arm. 'Are you up to going back in?'

Max seemed to rally. 'Of course, sir.' He turned and led the way.

What struck him immediately was how "staged" the scene was. Jackman remembered the headmaster saying that Alistair Ashcroft was happiest when acting in school productions.

'Have forensics given us an ETA, Max?'

Max glanced at his watch. 'Should be here shortly, boss.' He looked around the big room. 'This psycho is really something, isn't he, sir?'

Jackman nodded. 'I'll say.'

The judge's bench was placed on the old auctioneer's platform. Behind it, the killer had placed a high-backed carved chair and on the bench rested a gavel, a curled powdered wig and a square of black material. 'The black cap,' whispered Jackman. 'The judge used to place it over his wig to pronounce the death sentence.'

Max grunted.

Jackman turned slowly, noting that the killer had formed a "dock" for his prisoner, out of three heavy bookcases. One formed the front of the dock, and the others formed the sides. In the middle, was a chair with straps over the arms where the accused man would have sat.

Two tables sat on either side of the well of the room, one for the prosecuting team and one for the defence. Each had a neat pile of papers on it. Finally, in the centre were a chair and a smaller table, no doubt for the clerk of the court.

Off to the left of the "courtroom," an area had been curtained off with two tall room dividers and some heavy drapes. It was open at the front, but inside it was shadowy, almost cell-like, which was most likely the intention. Behind this was a flight of stairs leading to a viewing gallery. It was from here that the man had been pushed, so as to drop down into his darkened death chamber.

Jackman steeled himself to look. He noted that the man had been executed without the customary use of a hood, his hands tied behind his back and his ankles bound together. The original design of the auction house had contributed greatly to the assembly of a very simple and effective "gallows." Running the length of the high roof was a series of criss-cross beams and old timber trusses. Alistair had said he had patience, and he hadn't been lying. It must have taken forever to find the perfect place for his trial and execution.

'Who found him, Max?'

'The estate agent who's dealing with the sale of this dump. Poor bloke. Uniform have got him outside in one of their cars. He was shaking like a leaf.'

'Was it a routine property check, do you know?'

'No, boss, someone made an anonymous call saying they thought squatters had got in.'

'Our man, I should think, drawing attention to his handiwork.'

He dragged his eyes back to the dead man.

It was hard to gauge much about him. His mousey hair was almost shoulder length, and the pale face was distorted by the thick purple tongue protruding from his mouth. Jackman stared at his orange clothing.

'Fancy dress hire. Convict costume,' Max said flatly. 'He thought of everything.'

'I wonder.' Jackman was thinking of court records. 'We'd better leave it all for forensics. I should think the photographer will have a field day with this particular crime scene.' He thought of Ella. Rory had often commented that Ella had a natural talent for picking out tiny details. 'I wonder if he's known to us.'

'Not really looking his best, but I can't say I've seen him around, boss.' Max gave a weak smile. 'But you needn't fret over his identity. The killer left full details of who, how, and why. Robbie and I had a brief look at the papers on the desks over there. He's been preparing this for years, I'd say.'

'Wonderful!' Jackman shook his head. 'I can't wait to get my eyes on that.'

'What about your two psychological profilers, boss? Are you going to let them in?'

'As far as Rory will allow, until the scene has been forensically swept. They've seen bad stuff before.'

With a last look at the hanging man, Jackman went to find Sam and Laura.

* * *

Rory Wilkinson spent some thirty minutes in the ersatz courtroom, and almost as long with the dead man. Finally he walked back to the waiting Jackman.

'Remarkable! The attention to detail is quite astounding. If he wasn't an arch criminal, I'd love a long natter over a G&T.' He looked at Jackman's stony expression, and added, 'hypothetically, of course.'

'Sorry, Rory, but after what he's done, I couldn't even imagine meeting him socially,' Jackman said.

'No, it's me that should apologise. That was thoughtless. David is always telling me that I should learn to think before I open my mouth.'

Jackman smiled. Rory looked exactly like his mother's Labrador when he'd been caught chewing a slipper. 'I'm not usually this touchy, but this guy has me wound up tight as a drum.'

'Hardly surprising, is it? But joking apart, the amount of thought that went into this little pantomime is quite amazing. He even tied the perfect hangman's knot, and positioned it in exactly the right place. He managed to successfully fracture the second cervical vertebra, something that is very uncommon indeed, other than in judicial hanging. Plus, he had to calculate the distance of the drop, and to do that he needed the victim's height and weight.' Rory let out a long breath. 'Get it wrong, with too little drop and your condemned man strangles. Too far, and decapitation has been recorded. His preparation was textbook.'

'Some small mercy for the deceased, I suppose.' Jackman said.

'And I'm certain he was sedated. There are needle marks on his right wrist. I'm thinking that was simply to facilitate getting him up the stairs, from where he could be pushed. Prior to that, I'm sure he was very much aware of exactly what was going on.'

Jackman nodded. 'Alistair Ashcroft has clearly waited a long time for this moment, and taken an extraordinary amount of care in its preparation. He is hardly likely to make things easy for his victim. What I want to know is, who is the hanged man? And what did he do to deserve execution?'

Rory glanced at the "prosecutor's" table. 'I'm sure you know already that all those details have been provided for you, by way of some pseudo-legal documents. Not only that, your killer seems to have made a recording, hopefully of the "trial."'

Jackman breathed a sigh of relief. That was exactly what he wanted to know. 'You can guess what I'm going to ask now, can't you?'

Rory smiled. 'The photographer has completed his work, and my team are ready to start bagging the evidence. But if you would like to have a brief glance at the documents? And, although this is very unorthodox, for the sake of your investigation, I'm going to let you listen to the recording before it gets bagged and tagged for continuity. It's evidence, and the killer had to touch it to use it, so we have to follow protocol with this one.'

'You're a diamond, Rory Wilkinson.'

'I'm forgiven?'

'Totally. I'd have you and your runaway mouth no other way. You are priceless.'

'Could I have that in writing for David?'

'My pleasure. Now . . .' He looked around. 'I see Marie has just arrived. I'll get her and the others to listen in, if that's okay?'

'Of course, but just you and Marie in the room, if you don't mind. You guys know the drill — gloves and touch as little as possible. The others can wait where they are, and I'll turn the recording on when you are ready.' Rory held up a hand. 'But first I need to get that poor man down from the gibbet.'

Jackman went over to Marie, who was standing looking around in shocked disbelief.

'And now we are going to hear what all this is about?' she asked.

'Just as soon as Rory has dealt with the deceased.'

Marie pulled out her smartphone. 'I'm asking you not to look, if I just happen to accidentally record what we're going to hear.'

Jackman turned away. 'I didn't hear that.'

They didn't have long to wait.

Jackman and Marie went to the prosecutor's table and looked at the top sheet of paper. It read, "The Crown versus Blake." Beneath it were several typed sheets that appeared to be the prosecution's opening statement, and beneath that, a long witness testimony.

Marie then looked at the papers on the defence's table and let out a small 'oh.'

All the papers were blank, and there were no names under the heading "witnesses for the defence." Jackman shook his head. 'Somewhat biased in the favour of the prosecution, wouldn't you say?'

Rory switched on the recording.

A clear, well-educated voice, obviously that of the "clerk of the court" announced, "All rise. This court is now in session, the Honourable Judge Ashcroft presiding. Your Honour, today's case is the Crown versus Blake."

Marie looked at Jackman and raised her eyebrows.

The "clerk" then asked, "Can you confirm that your name is John Edward Blake?"

There was a scuffling sound but no answer. The clerk repeated the question, and finally a shaky voice mumbled, "Yes."

"John Edward Blake, you are charged that on the Eighth Day of June, 1995, you did wilfully rape and murder Lyndsay Beth Ashcroft. How do you plead? Guilty or not guilty?"

Once again they heard the sounds of a struggle. Jackman could envisage the man in the dock fighting to free himself.

After a while a different voice cried out, "You're mad! I've never killed anyone!"

"Liar!"

The words were screamed, so loud they all jumped. From that moment, Alistair Ashcroft seemed to abandon his carefully-staged courtroom procedure, and instead of calmly presenting his opening statement, unleashed a volley of accusations that Jackman and the others found hard to follow.

As the rant continued, Jackman gradually came to realise that if Ashcroft was telling the truth, his lovely sister-in-law Sarah and her closest friend Suri had made a terrible mistake all those years ago. And what was worse, Brendan Symons really had been innocent.

As Ashcroft's story unfolded, Jackman began to feel something approaching despair. Initially the accused man, John Blake, denied everything or refused to answer the accusations against him. Then, as the minutes ticked by, they could hear him being slowly worn down by Ashcroft's unrelenting pressure. Finally, snivelling and pleading to be set free, he admitted the lot.

Jackman and Marie, and their colleagues gathered in the doorway, listened in shocked silence while the rage in Ashcroft's voice abated. Abruptly, his voice changed to a local accent, and now he was the foreman of the jury, and he was finding the man guilty.

Just as quickly, Ashcroft reassumed his "judicial" tone. They heard the "judge" pass sentence, and the other man screaming and pleading to be released from this madness.

It was hard to listen to. Ashcroft had left the recording running while he sedated the "prisoner" and then forced him up the stairs. The last thing they heard was the sudden creak of the rope as Blake's weight snapped his own neck. Jackman swallowed hard.

The recording ended.

No one spoke, and then they all trooped out into the fresh air. Darkness was falling and he was chilled to the bone. It would be hours before forensics were finished, and right now he needed to go over everything they had heard with his team.

'Back to the station everyone, and Sam and Laura too, if that's okay? We need to talk this through.'

He thought the group looked like mannequins posed in some dark tableau. They stood as if unable to move, clearly shocked to the core by what they had just heard. Then, still silent, they nodded and began to drift away towards their respective vehicles.

'Max?' Jackman called the young detective back. He had noticed Robbie Melton giving a brief worried glance in Max's direction when he had asked them all to return to the station.

'You should get home, Max. I know how worried you are about Rosie. You can catch up in the morning.'

Max took a deep breath. 'No, sir. I'll see this through.'

Jackman stared at him, touched by his loyalty. 'I appreciate your devotion to duty, Detective. But on this occasion, I really think you should go home.'

'No, sir', said Max doggedly. 'As you said earlier, we have to catch this man before he does any more damage. I'll go, but only after your debriefing.'

Jackman watched Max walk back to join Robbie, realising, perhaps for the first time, just how deep the young man's feelings were for Rosie McElderry. Max's divided loyalties were painful to see. Then Laura's words came back to him, reminding him that he should look carefully at the weak points of those around him. There was no doubt as to Max Cohen's Achilles heel.

Where was this all going to end?

CHAPTER TWENTY-EIGHT

As soon as they returned to base, Jackman had Robbie look for the name John Edward Blake on the Police National Computer. Finding nothing, he checked local intelligence and then in desperation, Googled him and checked on social media. He found him there.

'Hey! This guy was one of the Symons family's greatest adversaries! He was adamant that Brendan was guilty, *and* he was interviewed at the time of Lyndsay's death. He lived in the same village and apparently knew her quite well.' Robbie stared at his monitor screen. 'Looks like he ran an opposing campaign group that used to turn up at Sheila Symons's demonstrations and heckle them.'

Jackman frowned. 'If he really was the man who killed Lyndsay, then he was obviously trying to keep the blame pinned firmly on Brendan.'

They had all gathered in the CID room and sat around with cups of coffee and tea, attempting to make sense of what they had heard.

Jackman stared into his coffee. 'The bottom line is that on the night of Lyndsay's murder, there were *three* sets of people in the woods watching her and Brendan. Sarah and Suri, Lyndsay's little brother Alistair, and John Blake. Sarah and her friend didn't lie, they reported exactly what they saw, but they didn't see it all.'

'The only one to see the whole horrible incident was a small, disturbed boy — Alistair Ashcroft,' Marie said quietly.

'Little brother watched Brendan leave his sister in the clearing, and then saw John step out of the trees and approach her. He saw him argue with her, shouting that she wouldn't let him touch her but she let the Symons boy go all the way. Bitterly jealous, he forced himself upon her and when she resisted, he killed her. Possibly killing her was never his aim, maybe he was trying to stop her screaming, but whatever, he lost it and killed her.' Jackman sat back.

'And, Little Al saw the whole thing, and totally traumatised, made the big mistake of telling his father.' Robbie sounded glum.

Laura was swirling her tea around in her mug. 'Did I gather correctly from the recording that Daddy Ashcroft was business partners with John Blake's father?'

Jackman nodded. 'And I think we can safely assume that there was no way Charles Ashcroft was going to have his lucrative business ventures ruined, which is why he sent the boy away before he could tell anyone else.'

'What a heartless bastard,' murmured Max. 'And look at the chaos his decision caused. Twenty-two years later, his demented son is stalking the streets of Saltern, killing anyone who was involved in that cock-up of a trial.'

'Well, he has concluded his vendetta,' Sam added. 'This trial and judgement was certainly his *coup de grace*. The thing is, and I mentioned this earlier, I don't think he'll be able to stop killing now.'

Laura sighed. 'I agree with you. And from his mood swings during that "trial," going from controlled to manic and back again in a matter of seconds, I think he is becoming disorganised.'

Sam nodded vehemently. 'And that is a very nasty supposition indeed. On the one hand, he might get overconfident and hence sloppy, which could help you to catch him, but on the other hand, he'll be volatile and unpredictable, which could make him very dangerous indeed.'

'More dangerous than this?' Marie said.

No one spoke.

'Going back to John Blake,' Robbie rubbed at his chin thoughtfully, 'we should check the whole transcript of the real trial of Brendon Symons. I only read through it briefly, but there were a dozen character witness statements and I don't recall seeing Blake's name.'

'Me neither,' added Max. 'Shall I pull it up, sir?'

Jackman shook his head. 'Not tonight. And since the original verdict was wrong, it won't help us catch this killer. Right now, I want you all to get home. This meeting was just to consolidate our recollections of what we heard. Until we get an official working copy of that recording, it's all we have to go on.' Jackman was careful not to look at Marie, or the smartphone that was in her hand.

'All I keep hearing is the creak of that rope,' Laura said softly. 'I think I'll go on hearing it until the day I die.'

Jackman bitterly regretted having allowed her to be there. If she had nightmares, it would be his fault, and that wasn't what he wished for Laura Archer. 'I'm sorry,' he said helplessly. 'I should *never*—'

'Stop right there.' Her tone was sharp. 'I'm a professional, Jackman. I'll deal with it.'

As everyone finally pulled on their coats and jackets, Jackman's eyes stayed on Laura. One of his vulnerabilities.

* * *

'What time do you call this?'

Max opened his mouth to make excuses, then saw a glint of amusement in Beverley's eyes. Rosie's sister had a powerful personality, and to tell the truth, she scared him a bit.

'Bad night,' he muttered, wanting only to get past her and see Rosie.

'We've been waiting up for you. I thought you were never coming home.'

He stood still. 'Is Rosie worse?'

Bev laughed. 'No, she's a whole lot better.'

'Then . . . ?' Max was tired and confused.

'She wants to talk to you, Max. I'm off to bed. See you in the morning.'

He found Rosie curled up on the sofa, her legs tucked up underneath her, cradling a big mug of hot chocolate.

'Hey, you!' He bent and gave her a kiss. 'Bev says you are feeling a bit better.'

Rosie patted the seat next to her and he flopped down thankfully. She seemed much more like her old self, but he was wary of asking too many questions. Instead he took the mug from her, placed it on the coffee table and took her hand. He squeezed it gently. 'I'm really sorry I'm late, sweetheart. I wanted to be with you, not working.'

'It's alright, Max. I know you have to work.' She squeezed his hand in return. 'And I can guess what's happened, but for once I'm not going to ask. Instead . . .' She turned and looked into his eyes. 'I've found out why this case has upset me so badly.'

She looked so intense that Max wondered if he was ready to hear what she had to say.

'Apparently pregnant women can react to things in a rather over-emotional way.'

He re-ran the sentence several times before it made sense.

'Pregnant? You are . . . ? We are . . . ?'

Rosie smiled tentatively. 'Yes, Max. You're going to be a father.' The smiles faded. 'I just hope the news is—'

'It's the best thing *ever*!' he blurted out. He took hold of her in a tight embrace.

Max came from a big family, and his childhood had been happy. It hadn't been easy, being the youngest of so many, but he'd learned the importance of having a loving support network about you as a kid.

'I couldn't be more delighted, I . . . !' For once in his life, Max Cohen couldn't think of a thing to say.

'I only did the test this morning. It was Beverley who thought of it. I never dreamed . . . I mean, we were so careful.'

'Except once.'

'Oh, yes. You mean that time in the—'

'Yep. But, just once, and this happens?' Max could hardly believe it possible. It would turn their lives upside down, but he didn't mind at all. *His* child! He smiled. It was like a blessing.

'All day I've been wondering how you'd take it. I thought you'd be pleased — I mean, you love kids, and you're so good with them — but it will mean a lot of changes.' She looked down. 'I could never, ever have an a—'

'Don't even say the word. It's not going to happen.' Like the Cheshire Cat, Max's grin stretched from ear to ear. 'You know what, Rosie McElderry? I think it's come at just the right time, don't you?'

* * *

Jackman was exhausted when he got back to Mill Corner. He pulled into his carport, got out and locked the car.

It felt good just to unlock his big, old, wooden door, looking forward to seeing the things he loved. He wanted to escape the madness for a few hours, have some peace for a while.

'Stand perfectly still, DI Jackman.'

Jackman froze.

'Not one move. Understand?'

Jackman took a breath and tried to gather his scattered thoughts. 'I understand.'

'Good.'

Alistair Ashcroft stood in the shadows. Jackman heard a dull metallic click, and knew what it meant. The gun's safety catch was off.

'I don't want to hurt you. I just want to talk.' Ashcroft's tone was calm and reasonable.

'And I just want you in my custody suite,' spat Jackman.

Ashcroft gave a low chuckle. 'I'm sure you do, but it's not going to happen, and you know it.'

Jackman said nothing for a moment. 'Okay, we'll talk.'

Ashcroft stepped onto the porch. The security light lit him up like a spotlight on an actor. He looked vaguely familiar. Yes, it was the man from the CCTV footage, but there was something else too. Jackman knew him from somewhere.

'It doesn't matter who I was, who I became. All you need to know is who I am now, and you know that already.'

'Alistair Ashcroft.'

'Yes. I began life with that name, and then had it taken from me. But now I'm back. That's all that matters.'

'What matters to me is that you drove Sarah, and a lot of other people, to take their own lives. You had no right to do that.' Jackman struggled to keep an even tone.

'I had every right! The law,' he snorted, 'the law failed Lyndsay miserably, and it caused the death of an innocent boy — Brendan Symons. I righted that wrong, Mr Policeman. A wrong that you and your kind couldn't even see, though it was staring you in the face.'

'Then why didn't you tell us? You *saw* what happened, for God's sake! If anyone was to blame, it was you!'

In the silence that followed, Jackman thought he'd gone too far. He clenched his hands and waited for the shot, desperately regretting his words.

'Have you any idea what it's like to be a neglected and abused child, Rowan? No, of course you haven't. You had a mother who adored you. Your father wasn't around much but you had everything you needed, and more. You were privileged. Fortunate. I wasn't. Very nice woman, your mother, by the way. I liked her a lot.'

Jackman took a step toward Ashcroft, unable to prevent himself.

'Think it through, Jackman. Not a single move, remember?'

Jackman closed his eyes for a moment and tried to regain his composure.

'Sensible man. Now relax, and I'll tell you why I never spoke out.'

'I think I already know. You were just a kid, and you'd just witnessed something too horrific for words. Of course you weren't to blame, I shouldn't have said that. But I can never forgive you for what you've done to my nephews.'

'If they are strong, they will survive. After all, I survived.'

Jackman wondered at what cost his survival had come.

'They needed to pay. Everyone who had anything to do with that travesty of justice had to pay.'

'And now they have.'

'Indeed.'

'My God, you've just hanged a man! Don't you feel any remorse at all?'

Alistair laughed. 'Why should I? Did he feel remorse for what he did? No, he didn't. Instead he stood by while an innocent young man went to prison and subsequently died there. He got what he deserved.'

Ignoring this, Jackman decided to chance a question. 'There's something I don't understand. Your sister was dead, and there was nothing that would bring her back. It looks to me as if you are avenging Brendan's death rather than hers.'

'Brendan was the only person who was kind to me. Even Lyndsay was unkind sometimes, although I know she loved me deep down. But she made me promise, swear . . .'

'Promise what, Alistair?'

'Never to speak of what she and Brendan were planning to do. She made me swear.'

As Ashcroft spoke these words, Jackman became aware of a change in his voice. All at once he sounded like a frightened child.

'She said . . . oh, she said terrible things would happen to me. I believed she died because I followed her and spied on her.'

'But you told your father, and you hated him,' Jackman said.

'He *knew.*' Ashcroft's voice trembled. 'He took one look at me and just knew. And he beat me until I told him everything. I even told him they'd been planning on running away and taking me with them. I betrayed her.'

He couldn't be sure, but Jackman thought Alistair Ashcroft was crying. That day, a small boy's hopes and dreams had all been shattered. Not only did he lose his sister, he lost his one chance of gaining a better life.

'Then he sent you away,' Jackman said softly.

'And then he died.' Now Ashcroft sounded almost gleeful. 'And my new life began.' He paused. 'Anyway, Jackman, I just thought it would be nice for us to meet face to face for once. I'm going to leave you now, but we'll meet again, you can be sure of that.'

How could he let him just walk away? But Ashcroft was armed. Jackman felt helpless. 'Who *are* you?'

Ashcroft sighed. 'Work it out. It will come to you as soon as I've gone. But can't you understand? It doesn't matter! How many more times do I have to tell you? I am Alistair Ashcroft, and I'm your worst nightmare.'

* * *

Close by, a motorbike engine roared into life and Ashcroft was gone.

With shaking hands, Jackman let himself into his house. He shut the door and locked it, and then poured himself a brandy. *"Work it out. It will come to you as soon as I've gone."* The words rattled around in his head. Why then? What had he meant? Jackman swallowed a good third of the drink and exhaled loudly.

Ashcroft had told him nothing that he didn't know or couldn't have worked out for himself. His visit had been all about power.

Jackman took another mouthful of the brandy and saw in his mind's eye the tall, slim-hipped figure, clad in black. "It will come to you . . ."

Jackman groaned and the glass almost fell from his fingers. When he uttered those words, Ashcroft's voice had taken on the slightest hint of an accent.

Jackman grabbed his keys and rushed out into the night. He had to get back to the police station. Fast.

* * *

'Annie! Is she in tonight?' he shouted at the officer at the desk.

'Yes, sir, she's probably on the super's floor by now.'

He took the stairs two at a time and found Annie in the conference room, emptying the wastepaper bins.

'Annie?' He looked around for Eric and Stefan. 'On your own tonight?'

'Oh, hello, sir.' She pulled a face. 'And until I get someone new, I could be like it all week.'

'Why?' He already knew the answer but needed Annie to confirm it.

'It's partly my own fault really. Eric has been moved to another location, and Stefan's baby is so sick it needs full-time care. He's left, sir. Put in his notice yesterday. Oh, I will miss him. He was such a nice man, so kind and so reliable.'

And such a good actor, thought Jackman. He thought about Stefan. Tall, slender, his dark hair smoothed back across his head. Those dark almond eyes, and that trace of an accent that intrigued all the women. Alistair Ashcroft had been hiding here in plain sight, working nights with the run of the police station.

'I need to know where he lives, Annie. I've got to talk to him about something.'

'He said he lives in Cartoft Village, sir. I can give you my manager's number. If you ring him in the morning, he'll let you have it.'

Oh very clever. *He* lived in Cartoft, and he knew every person there. Stefan wasn't one of them. He also knew exactly what he would find when he contacted the cleaning company. Stefan would be as clean as a whistle, would have sailed through the vetting process, had excellent references, and be known to be trustworthy and reliable. Of *course* he was clean. Alistair Ashcroft had never stepped outside the law in his life — until he started killing people.

'What is Stefan's surname, Annie?'

'Ash something. Ashton? No, Ashcroft. Stefan Ashcroft. I think he said his father was British and his mother was Polish.'

Richard Stephan Ashcroft. How he must have laughed, seeing his name all over the whiteboards. God, he'd been playing them for fools for months!

Jackman thanked Annie, went down to his office and rang Marie. She was at Gary's, telling him about what he'd been lucky to miss at the old auction house.

'And cadging food, no doubt,' Jackman added dryly.

'Well, you know, while I'm here . . . but why the call, sir?'

He told her about his visitor, and that he now knew who Ashcroft was.

Marie gasped. 'Of course! He has that long oval face that the headmaster talked about. It usually indicates something called Fragile X Syndrome, if I remember rightly. I *knew* I'd seen him somewhere.'

'And he looks like Miles's picture of the Bad Man.'

'Exactly! And the man on the CCTV had thick, wavy, dark hair. Stefan's was always slicked down, giving him a very different appearance.' She was silent for a few seconds. 'Are you alright, Jackman? Hell, you've just had a serial killer stick a gun in your face. That's pretty heavy stuff.'

'I'm fine. I'm just frustrated that there was no way of apprehending him. I had to let him go, and that really hurts. Oh, and he was on a motorcycle by the way. I wished you'd been there. You'd probably have identified it from the engine noise.'

Jackman hung up. His next call was to the super, to keep her up to speed, and let her see that he really was on top of things. They had identified the killer. That should earn him a few brownie points at least.

Finally, he rang Cam Walker.

'The thing that gets me most is that he doesn't care two hoots that we know who he is. He says it doesn't matter, and I'm beginning to see what he means.'

'At least we now have a face to put to the name. His cleaning company will have staff ID photos, and so will we. He'll have needed to have a pass issued by the station before he could come and go.'

'As I said, he doesn't care. He just wanted me to see what we are up against. He believes he is untouchable, but . . .' He thought for a minute. 'Part of the time he sounded like Mr Cool, and then at others, he was like an insecure child. It was creepy, and even though I wanted to tear him limb from limb, I—'

'Couldn't help feeling sorry for him?'

Jackman pondered this. 'I wouldn't go that far. I mean, it's hard to understand how an abusive upbringing could screw up a little boy so badly.'

'And *then* have the extraordinary bad luck to witness his sister being murdered. I hate to state the obvious, but it's hardly surprising he's a mess.'

Jackman yawned. 'I need to get home and get some sleep, Cam.'

'Mightn't it be a good idea to get uniform to go with you, just to check your place out? Ashcroft has got you well and truly in his sights, hasn't he?'

Jackman was silent for a moment, thinking. 'No, he won't be back tonight. He's delivered his message. He just wanted me to see my adversary, my nemesis, close up.'

'You're welcome to stay with us for as long as you want.'

Jackman smiled. Cam Walker was a kind and thoughtful man. 'I'll be fine, Cam, honest. But thanks. I appreciate it.'

'If you're sure?'

'I'm sure. I'll see you tomorrow.'

As he hung up, he wondered if he wasn't being a little too glib, but he knew he was right. For tonight at least, he would be safe.

* * *

Alistair Ashcroft prepared for bed, thinking over his meeting with Jackman. It had gone exactly to plan. He now saw Jackman in a different light, as an adversary, an opponent in a deadly game of chess.

He decided that he quite liked Jackman. He had admired his spirit. Even when looking down the barrel of a gun, he had been prepared to have a go in order to protect someone he loved. And he didn't mince his words. He liked that too.

After his talk to Jackman, he had had a desperate urge to go out to his lonely place on the marsh edge, but instead had come home and taken a long, hot shower.

He looked around him. They wouldn't find him here. Not unless he wanted them to.

But for now he needed a sanctuary. He walked barefoot across the thick pile carpet to his bed and pulled back the covers. He would use the coming night-time hours to plan his next move in detail. He had his target already lined up, and his research was pretty well complete. Now for the timetable. His latest victim's countdown to death.

He settled back against the pillows and smiled.

CHAPTER TWENTY-NINE

Jackman arrived at work early, and found Max already there. He appeared to be a very different Max from the one he'd left the night before.

'Sorry to tackle you so early, sir, but could I have a word before everyone gets in?'

Intrigued, Jackman held open his office door. He could only think that Rosie was very much recovered.

Max sat down. 'Thing is, sir, I expect you were as puzzled as I was about how come Rosie took that last call we had so badly — the one to the Whitman twins murder scene.'

Jackman nodded. 'It was a shock to see her so badly affected, but it does happen. We all have one case that does us in.'

Max wriggled in his seat, apparently unsure how to proceed. 'Well, it wasn't just that. Like, well, we didn't know . . .'

'Max. Get to the point.'

'She's pregnant, sir! We're going to have a baby! *That's* why she was all over the place!'

Jackman's mouth fell open. This wasn't what he'd been expecting. 'I say!'

'Yes, isn't it fantastic?' Max's broadly beaming face said it all.

'Congratulations, Max! I'm getting vibes that this isn't exactly unwelcome news?'

'It wasn't planned, sir, far from it, but now it's happened, I couldn't be happier.'

'That's plain to see.' Jackman smiled warmly at him. 'So what are your plans?'

'The first thing we're going to do is get married, sir, ASAP. We both want that. These killings have really put things into perspective for us. Even without a child, we've decided that we make a good team, so why not make it an official one?' Max gulped. 'I love her to bits, sir.'

'That's a pretty good reason for tying the knot. And after that?'

'We need to think about that, but we've got plenty of time. We both love our jobs, and if we can, we'll both keep working, even if one of us has to stand down for a while. We've both got supportive families, so we'll work out what's best for us all.' He paused, still grinning. 'We just wanted you to know first, sir, before I tell the world.'

'Thank you, Max, I appreciate it.' Jackman suddenly thought of Ashcroft, and was overcome by a feeling of dread. 'But I'm going to make a suggestion, and I hope this doesn't mess up your plans. I think you should keep this news to your very closest friends for a short while.'

'Sir?' His face fell.

'Well, until we know more about Alistair Ashcroft, I really think this is something you should keep very quiet indeed.'

Max frowned, and then the penny dropped. 'Oh hell! I've been so excited that I forgot how he works. He plays on vulnerabilities, doesn't he?'

'Exactly, Max. So you see what I mean?'

'I'll ring Rosie. I'll try not to scare her, but I'll make sure she doesn't do anything silly like stick it on Facebook!'

'Very sensible. And Max? I'm thrilled for you.'

'Thanks, sir.' Max stood up. 'I'll tell the sarge. I guess the others can wait a while, it's very early days. Oh, and

Rosie says that hopefully she'll be back next week. She feels so much better since she heard the news.'

'We'll be very happy to have her back, but she needs the FMO's okay first.'

'She knows that, sir. We'll see how she goes.'

'Max? You do know you're going to have to be a damned good actor over the next few days, don't you? Right now, you look like the cat that got the cream.'

'Well, that won't be quite so easy, but if anyone asks, I guess I'll just say I'm happy that Rosie is feeling much better.'

After Max left, Jackman sat on, worrying about the way things were proceeding. Sam and Laura had both warned him that Ashcroft could change the way he operated, and begin to take and destroy the things people close to him loved. That could be precious items, or precious loved ones. Everyone was vulnerable. Was Max most vulnerable of all?

* * *

Charlie Button was deep in conversation with Robbie. 'What I don't get,' he was saying, 'is why was there no forensic evidence linking John Blake to the murder scene? If he killed Lyndsay, surely there would have been something left behind?'

Robbie shrugged. 'Think about it, mate. It was twenty-two years ago. Plus they had two witnesses who not only testified to seeing Lyndsay and Brendan together, they also saw him leaving the clearing alone.'

Marie was listening in. 'Add to that the fact that Brendan's DNA was all over Lyndsay, and the prosecution would have a very strong case indeed.'

'And from what I've read about the trial, Phillip Seaton QC was hot as mustard, so why look any further?' Robbie added.

'But *we* could now, with all the new techniques,' Charlie persisted.

Marie shook her head. 'Charlie, that case is over. Everyone involved in that whole terrible mess is dead. Except Alistair Ashcroft, who is our priority now, not Lyndsay. It's

Alistair we have to concentrate all our energies into finding.' She looked at Charlie's rather peeved expression. 'One person we *will* tell is Sheila Symons. It wouldn't stand up in court — after all, Blake's taped confession was extracted under duress, but she would be able to rest, knowing that we all believe it to be true.' She smiled at Charlie. 'And who knows? If the family keep pushing, someone might just open up the old inquiry in order to give Brendan a posthumous pardon, but right now, we have a killer to catch. Right?'

Charlie smiled back. 'I know that, Sarge. I just hate injustice in any form.'

'That's why we do what we do, kiddo,' Robbie said.

Gary walked in. 'Sarge? I've just heard from uniform that they went to the address we were given for "Stefan" Ashcroft, and it's a bedsit in a back street of Saltern. All they found was a camp bed, a table and a chair, a phone with answer phone, a kettle and a mini-fridge. It's certainly not been lived in. Ashcroft obviously used it to validate his identity and for mail and to pick up phone messages for "Stefan."'

'And he won't use the place again.' Marie puffed out her cheeks. 'Not that we expected anything else.'

None of them heard Jackman approach. 'Well, he must live somewhere. Is that place also hidden in plain sight? Maybe it's right here in Saltern-le-Fen.'

'Registered to another one of his personas?' asked Robbie.

'He said he was now Alistair Ashcroft again and all the other names were finished with, but was he lying? Anyway, right now it's time for daily orders.'

Jackman gave the gathered officers the details of the scene at the old auction house the night before, and then what had transpired at Mill Corner. Marie listened — or rather watched. She thought Jackman looked worried. Perhaps his run-in with Alistair had shaken him more than he was admitting.

'So, I want you to be fully aware of the kind of man we are dealing with, and on no account should you underestimate him. At the four o'clock meeting I'm going to ask Laura

Archer to give you a brief rundown of how we can expect his behaviour patterns to evolve as the case goes on. But right now . . .' Jackman stooped and picked up a handful of sheets of plain A4 paper and passed them round. 'This might seem odd, but to protect your privacy I'm going to ask each of you to write down a list of names for me. Only Marie, Laura Archer and myself will see these names, and we'll treat them in the strictest confidence. There's no nice way to put this. Ashcroft targets the things and the people we love. I need to know anyone and anything that each one of you holds dear. That includes your beloved granny, your new puppy, your collection of silver teapots, or your secret lover. And, please, don't hide anything! These pages will all be destroyed as soon as we have Ashcroft locked away. I just need to know your vulnerabilities. Understood?'

Looking at each other, everyone took a sheet of paper.

'Do it now. Think carefully about it, and then bring them to my office immediately. And someone must be responsible for making sure anyone who's not present does the same.'

He ended the meeting, and Marie followed him into his office. 'You seem on edge, boss? Is it your late night visitor?'

'It unnerved me alright. At one point I thought I'd pushed him too far. I really believed . . .' He shook his head.

'He had a gun trained on you, sir. Lord, you had every right to shit your pants!'

Jackman gave her a tired smile. 'Didn't get that far, thank goodness. But there was something really disturbing about him. It was the way he changed his mood and his voice. And some of what he said was totally believable. You start to get drawn in, to almost feel some kind of sympathy for him. Then the next moment he says something so callous that you want to rip him to pieces.'

'A bit like the recording from his kangaroo court.' Laura Archer stood in the doorway. 'Sorry. Wasn't eavesdropping, I just wanted to let you finish.'

'Come on in, Laura.'

Jackman smiled at her, and Marie again sensed that tiny sizzle of electricity in the air. She couldn't wait to read Laura's list!

Laura looked immaculate, as she always did, this time in a soft oxblood red leather jacket and slim fit grey plaid pants. Unlike Marie's biker jacket, this one was a simple zip-up bomber with a baseball collar. Marie reckoned it must have set her back close to five hundred quid. Though Laura would look a million dollars in a black bin bag.

'I've asked Laura to work with us for a while, Marie, to try and get a handle on what Alistair's next move might be.'

'Excellent.' Marie smiled at Laura.

Gary arrived, carrying a sheaf of papers. 'The first ones to be handed in, sir. Thought you might like these to be getting on with.' He grinned at Marie. 'And I haven't peeked, honest.'

'Thanks, Gary.' Jackman laid them face down on his desk. 'It feels a little like voyeurism, but we need to do it.' He looked at Laura and Marie. 'We have to assume that because he worked here for so long, he knows a lot of the staff already. As Stefan, he mainly worked nights, but we often do early shifts. He would have had plenty of access to overheard conversations and all sorts of other unofficial information about us.'

'Sam and I talked long into the night about this man,' Laura said, 'And we came to the conclusion that we have absolutely no idea how he is going to evolve. As we said, he's complex. He's still showing signs of the dark triad, and he could be the product of a lethal combination of psychoses. We know how he has functioned before, but we are frightened that he might just step outside the box.'

Marie stared at her. 'And change his MO completely?'

'He has grown more confident with every death, and I think his Crown versus Blake performance will have caused it to escalate further. We're sure he believes that you'll never catch him, unless *he* decides it's time for that to happen.'

'He said as much when he made his house-call last night.' Jackman looked pensive. 'I told him I wanted to see him in my custody suite, and he said he was sure I did, but that wasn't going to happen.'

'But don't forget,' Laura leaned forward. 'You mustn't buy into that. He has an inflated opinion of himself, and he's as liable as anyone to make mistakes.'

'So, down to good old-fashioned police work. Is that what will catch him?' asked Marie.

'It's caught a whole lot of other killers who thought they were untouchable,' said Jackman. 'I'm sure that's what'll stop him in the end.' He picked up the papers and divided them between the three of them. 'Let's see what we have here.'

They studied the papers in silence. As she read, Marie gradually began to feel overwhelmed by the enormity of what they were up against. She put her pages on the desk and shook her head. 'This is impossible! So many vulnerabilities and our little cuckoo in the nest could be aware of all of them.'

'A lot can be discarded,' said Laura calmly. 'If he continues as he has before, he is driven by the manipulation of intense love.' She pointed to the lists. 'He won't be even mildly interested in most of this. He's after intense emotion.' She paused. 'And justice. Sam disagrees with me on this, but I still think he needs a cause of some kind to make what he does acceptable to himself. I think he needs to be the avenging dark angel, the damaged child now grown up and fighting for justice.'

Jackman's gaze slid aside, and Marie caught a glint of something in his eyes. Was that fear? 'Is anything in particular worrying you, boss?'

Jackman took a while to respond. 'You'll need to know, although I've told Max not to mention it to anyone other than his closest family. He and Rosie are expecting a baby.'

Her initial delight vanished in a second. What could be more vulnerable than a new baby?

'But Alistair does *not* know this. It was only confirmed last night, and it has to stay well under wraps. That's why Max hasn't written it down.' He turned to Laura. 'I'm assuming this is exactly the kind of thing you're talking about?'

She nodded.

Gary brought another batch of papers, and Marie really had to concentrate. The news about Max and Rosie had left her with her head full of questions. With an effort, she pushed them aside. 'It's interesting how some people have listed a whole load of people and things, and some are like this one . . .' Marie held up Gary's paper. On it he had simply written, "The Team."

Jackman smiled at her. '*The Team* features heavily in a lot of these. But yours mentions someone called Harvey. Who's Harvey?'

Marie blushed. 'My bike. My Suzuki Hayabusa. I call it Harvey.'

'Alistair Ashcroft rides a bike too, Marie. Maybe it's called Roxanne, or Flossie, or something.' They laughed, grateful for a moment of light relief.

Just as Marie was starting to wonder whether this exercise was any use at all, Gary knocked on the door.

'This is the last of the lists, sir, and Robbie asked me to tell you that we've picked up a very good photo of Stefan from the cleaning company. He's done some work on it so it's now got the same full wavy hair as he had in the CCTV picture. He's circulating it to all forces and also the media.'

'Good work. I suggest we flood the town with them too. Shop windows, bus stops, anywhere you can find. I want everyone in Saltern-le-Fen to know this man's face.'

Gary nodded. 'I'll see to it immediately, sir.'

'Sir?' Marie said. 'I don't think I'm being too helpful here. Could I go and do something else? You and Laura have this exercise pretty well in hand between the two of you.'

'I value your input, Marie, but okay, we'll fill you in when we're done.'

'I was wondering if you'd mind if I went to see Sheila Symons. We know she hasn't much time left, and I'd hate for her to find out about Ashcroft and Blake from somewhere other than us.'

Jackman nodded. 'I did want to go myself, but I can see it's not going to happen. Yes, Marie, you go.'

Marie escaped as fast as she dared, and once outside the office heaved a sigh of relief. She couldn't tell Jackman this, but she was sure the only way they would know what Ashcroft had in mind was *after* he had brought it about.

She didn't phone ahead. Sheila was going nowhere, and there would be someone looking after her, so she pulled on her riding gear and set off for Nettleby Oaks.

Marie loved riding. Today the roads were clear and the weather good, just what she needed to blow away the cobwebs from her overcrowded brain. Riding her bike relaxed her and made her feel alive. Though Harvey wasn't a flesh and blood loved one, she had put him on her list because she would be devastated if she lost her precious bike. She'd already lost one beautiful motorcycle through the actions of a crazed killer, and she had no intention of losing another.

She pulled off her helmet and rang the doorbell. The door opened and she saw a face she hadn't seen before peering suspiciously at her. 'Liam! So you do exist!'

She thrust her warrant card at him. 'A word, if you please, and then I want to talk to your mother.'

'Sod off!'

She jammed her boot in the door and put a hand on his chest, pushing him backwards into the hall. 'It wasn't a polite request, chum. You've been giving us the run-around for days. We can do this here and now, or I get a car to pick you up and we take it into the nick. Your choice.'

Liam threw her a poisonous look, turned and slouched into the lounge.

She had known the minute she saw him that Liam wasn't their killer, but she reckoned he deserved a bit of arm-twisting for his refusal to be interviewed. Leaving her boots in the hall, Marie followed him inside. 'So, what made you decide to go against your mother's wishes and refuse to talk to us? Something to hide, have you? Something you don't want the rest of your family to know about?'

Yvette appeared in the doorway and gave Marie a knowing smile.

'I've got nothing to hide,' Liam growled at her. 'I just think Mum's wrong. Being so ill, she's not thinking straight. Why should we help you?'

'Because we are trying to get to the truth, and we're also trying to find a bloody dangerous psychotic killer. Any help, even yours, would be appreciated.' She narrowed her eyes. 'And your mother's a damned sight cleverer than you'll ever be, sunshine.'

Liam was silent.

She reached into her jacket and pulled out a copy of Alistair Ashcroft's picture. 'Do you recognise this man?'

Liam looked at it and laughed. 'This some kind of windup?'

Marie felt a moment of confusion. Yvette looked over her brother's shoulder and the recognition on her face too was instant.

'That's Alan. He's not in trouble, is he?'

'Sorry? Alan who?' Marie asked.

'He's our counsellor. He's been helping us for, oh, six years or so. He's been amazing.'

This wasn't going the way Marie had expected. Even Liam showed signs of warmth when his sister spoke about this man.

'He listens,' he said. 'I mean, really listens to us. Doesn't give us any flannel either. He's a solid bloke.'

Marie tried to assimilate what she'd just been told. Alistair, as Alan, had been counselling the whole Symons family for over six years? This was massive! Maybe, just maybe, there would be a way to trace his lair. 'How did you come to meet him?'

'He was friends with two of our longer-standing supporters,' Yvette said. 'Christian and Mark. Mark was worried about us, and the strain that the campaign was putting on the family, and he asked Alan to talk to us. We still see him occasionally. He's been a real tower of strength.'

Yvette spoke so warmly of this man, this murderer. It made Marie feel oddly cold inside.

Now Yvette was looking at her, frowning. 'Why are you showing us a picture of him, Sergeant?'

What to tell her? 'We believe he can help us with our enquiries, Yvette. It's imperative we find him.'

'He's missing?' said Liam warily.

'Yes. Have you seen him recently?'

Liam shook his head. 'No, not for weeks.'

'What do you really know about him? And I assume the others you mentioned are Mark Courtney and Christian Ventnor?'

Yvette nodded, and sat down on the sofa next to Liam. 'He had some connection to the church, didn't he, Liam?'

Liam nodded. 'Yes, but he never preached at you. He just seemed to understand what you were going through.'

'I said "church," but he wasn't a minister or anything like that.' Yvette was still frowning. 'It was Mark that told us Alan worked with church aid groups, and he also had something to do with disturbed children in care.'

Marie swallowed. 'Excuse me for a moment, I have to ring this in.' She stood up, hurried into the hall and phoned Jackman. 'Get someone to go and speak to Christian Ventnor, and also Mark Courtney. Tell them to ask about a counsellor they recommended to the Symons family, someone by the name of Alan. I don't have a surname. Jackman, Yvette and the elusive Liam have just fingered the photo of Alistair as this man they know as Alan. He's been infiltrating this house for over six years!'

Marie returned to Yvette and Liam. 'Sorry, about that. I suppose you wouldn't have an address for him, would you?'

'No. He called round here regularly, but we never went to see him,' Yvette said.

'A phone number?'

Yvette shook her head. 'Sorry. We were grateful for the help he offered us, and it was all gratis, so we tried never to bother him in his private time.' Yvette stared at Marie, her eyes wide. 'You seem very anxious to speak to him. There isn't a chance that he is . . . ?' She gasped.

'Let's just say it's a matter of real urgency that we find him.'

254

Liam looked anxiously at Yvette and — to Marie's surprise — took her hand and squeezed it. 'Shit, sis! Looks like we cocked up, opening our hearts to the lovely Alan.' He looked at Marie. 'Or am I wrong?'

'No, Liam, but none of you could have known. This man is one of the best confidence tricksters we've ever come across.' Then the thought struck her. If Alistair was intent on manipulating love, love was in abundance here. Their love for Brendan had kept them going, kept them together for years. Surely one of the Symons family would make a perfect victim. She must mention it to Jackman, and Laura too.

'One last thing before I ask to see your mother. Did Alan look exactly like this when he came here?' She held up the picture again.

'His hair was gelled back in a sleeker style, but other than that, yes, that's Alan.' Yvette looked to Liam and he nodded.

Yvette stood up. 'Why did you come today, Sergeant? I know you said to see Mother, but why?'

Marie smiled gently. 'Your mum doesn't have long, I know, and I have some news for her. It's something we would normally keep strictly to ourselves, but under the circumstances we wanted her to know before it's too late. She deserves to hear it.'

Liam glanced at his sister, and then Marie. 'Can we hear too?'

'Any of the family that are here can listen to what I have to say, but you have to promise to keep it to yourselves until we say otherwise. This *must not* be leaked to the press. That might completely ruin our chances of catching the killer.'

Yvette opened the door, and they climbed the stairs to Sheila's darkened room.

* * *

Jackman went in person to Mark Courtney's house and found him in his home office, typing. Presumably yet more letters regarding Brendan's posthumous pardon.

He showed Courtney the photo of Ashcroft. 'Where did you meet him?'

'At a lecture, I believe. Yes, that's it. When I retired I started work on a paper. I attended some lectures on the subject and he was at one of them. We hit it off immediately and we kept in touch. Interesting man. Had a wide knowledge of psychological theory.'

Now why doesn't that surprise me? thought Jackman. 'And you say he worked as a counsellor?'

'He specialised in depression in teenagers. His main interest was teen suicides. He'd done extensive studies apparently.'

A specialist in suicide. Oh, perfect! 'Did you see any proof of his qualifications? Any diplomas? Anything at all, really?'

'I never went to his home, Inspector. He always came here.'

Jackman began to lose heart. He needed to know where Ashcroft lived. 'And Christian Ventnor knew him too? Is that right?'

'I introduced them. Chris found him fascinating.' He paused. 'By the way, though I never went to Alan's place, I think my sister did.'

Jackman perked up. 'Your sister?'

'Yes. Pip. She and Alan became quite friendly. I'm sure she said she visited him once or twice, for business reasons.'

'What sort of business?' asked Jackman.

'You'd have to ask Pip. I know she became quite fond of him, then he told her he was gay, but he did care for her as a friend. It was all rather sad, but they still remained pretty close.'

'Can you tell me where I can find Pip, please, sir?' Jackman half stood, ready to leave.

'She lives next door. I'll give her a call.' He pulled a mobile from his pocket and phoned his sister. 'Got a mo, Pip? Police are here. They want a word about Alan.' He ended the call. 'On her way.'

Jackman studied him. 'Can I ask, why the continued interest in the Brendan Symons case? It's been years now, but you've become a central part, maybe *the* central part of the campaign. What made you persist with it for so long?'

Mark Courtney stared into space. 'The honest truth? Sheila, that's why.'

'Sheila Symons? You admire her stamina in keeping up the fight?'

'I do, but it's more than that. I'm in love with her. I've always loved her, even way back at school, and I never looked at anyone else. Unfortunately my friend Symons had more charisma, and he won fair lady.' He sighed. 'Now he's dead, and I do the best I can to look out for her. She doesn't know, Inspector, and considering she doesn't have long left, I expect this conversation to remain between us, okay?'

Jackman nodded. One big question answered. Before he could say more, Pip Courtney strode into the room.

'Alan? Is he alright? He's not hurt or anything, is he?'

She was a vivacious redhead. Her voice was rather high pitched, and Jackman found it slightly irritating. 'No. He's, er, missing, and we need to find him as a matter of some urgency. Do you have his address?'

'I did, but he moved about two months ago, and I haven't seen him or heard from him since. I've been quite worried. Now I'm even more so, if you say he's missing.'

'Your brother tells us that you had some business dealings with this . . . gentleman. Isn't it odd that he should move without leaving you a forwarding address?'

'Our business dealings had been finalised,' she said rather haughtily.

'And what kind of business would that be?'

She bit hard on her bottom lip.

'Would you like me to leave you for a moment?' Mark asked his sister. He turned a long-suffering smile on Jackman. 'She's always played her cards close to her chest, my sister. I've learned to keep my nose out.'

'No, Mark. It's over now, so it doesn't matter anymore.' Pip Courtney gave a deep sigh. 'Because of what he was — you know, the way he was . . .'

'Gay?' prompted Jackman.

'Yes. Because of that, his father threw him out and the rest of his family were less than supportive. I really felt for him, poor man. How he must have suffered!'

Jackman kept his expression impassive.

'Anyway,' she coughed, 'he had some properties, and he was anxious that his family shouldn't know about them. He was paranoid that something would happen to him and they would come swooping down like vultures and get hold of his estate.'

Mark was leaning forward, clearly wondering what was coming next.

'We worked out a way to fool them. Alan sold the properties, then, when he found somewhere he liked, he gave me the money and I purchased it. As these were in my name, there was no way the family could touch them. For a small fee, I kept an eye on them, talk to the neighbours and the like. I would say that Alan was renting, he was such a good tenant, and so on.'

'Keeping up appearances,' murmured Jackman. 'And everything was legally documented, should he need to sell or recoup his money?'

'Exactly. It was just a paper transaction. I never had any real claim on his houses.'

'How many were there?'

'Three.'

'He's left them all?'

Pip looked sad. 'He — or rather, we — sold them not long ago. He said he wanted to travel and the properties would just be a burden, even if he let them out.'

Jackman thought for a while. 'You must have used a solicitor for the conveyancing?'

'Yes, Rotherham Keats. They are down one of the back alleys in Saltern town. It's a very small company, but Alan didn't want to use anyone his family might know.'

Jackman scribbled down the name. 'Could you give me Alan's surname, Ms Courtney? I suppose it wasn't Ashcroft, was it?'

She looked mildly surprised. 'Yes, it was.'

'And I'd also like the names and addresses of those three properties please.' Jackman added the information to his notes. 'And you have no idea where he might be staying now?'

'He said he'd be in touch, but . . . Why exactly are you interested in him?' Suddenly she seemed doubtful.

'We need to talk to him urgently about an ongoing case. So if you do hear from him, please say nothing about our talk, but phone me immediately.' He handed her his card. 'Thank you both for your time.'

Outside in his car, Jackman rang Orac direct.

'Jackman? Goodness! Well, there's a first time for everything, I guess. How can I help you, Detective Inspector?'

In his mind's eye, Jackman saw her silvery eyes. 'If I give you two names, three addresses of recently sold properties, and a firm of solicitors, could you work your magic and find out if the man involved, who is really Alistair Ashcroft, has any other dealings with this particular law firm. What I need is a current address.' He gave her the details.

'I'll ring you back when I have answers,' Orac said.

Jackman ended the call, and then contacted Robbie. 'Any luck with seeing Ventnor?'

'Yes, sir, although he knows pretty well nothing about Ashcroft, other than some load of old tosh he's been fed. I reckon Ventnor was a bit enamoured with the enigmatic Ashcroft.'

'Courtney said much the same, although he used the word "spell-bound."'

'Wraps people around his little finger, doesn't he, sir?'

'Sadly, yes. Have you heard from Marie?'

'On her way back, sir. And she says to knock Liam off the list. He's kosher. A right little tosser, but kosher. Her words, not mine.'

Jackman smiled. 'I thought that might be the case, Robbie. Okay, back to base.'

CHAPTER THIRTY

Marie rode back to Saltern feeling that, for once, she had really made a difference to a life. Even if that life was drawing to an end. Several times she had needed to lift her visor to wipe away her tears.

Marie had told Sheila as much as she dared, and she had listened with shining eyes. By the time Marie left her, Sheila Symons looked as if the weight of the world had been lifted from her shoulders.

Yvette hugged Marie as if she had just delivered a cheque for a million pounds. Dale and Liam appeared to be on the verge of tears, and Kenny and Susie looked at each other and smiled in utter relief.

Marie had made sure they understood that the recorded conversation could not be used in court. But she assured them that when this present murder investigation was brought to a close, she would do her best to see that Brendan's case was reopened, using the information they now had, and new forensic techniques. She couldn't make a firm promise, but they had her word that she would try.

* * *

Still smiling, Marie entered the CID room to be met by a sea of grave faces.

'Okay? What have I missed?'

Robbie spoke quietly. 'It's Jackman. He's had to go to his parents' home. His brother James never turned up for a work meeting. He's missing, Marie.'

All her hope and elation faded. Marie looked across to Jackman's office and saw that the door was open. She hurried over and found Laura still staring at all the sheets of paper.

'Is it possible? Could Alistair have targeted James?'

Laura looked up at her. 'Oh yes. In fact *very* possible. It confirms what I was saying earlier about justice.'

Marie sank into Jackman's chair and stared at Laura across the desk. 'Explain.'

'I've been thinking about this man, and his terrible history — all the things he witnessed, and what he has done himself. I've come to the conclusion that he could never hurt a child.'

'Surely, psychopaths lack all empathy, and wouldn't that extend to children too?'

'He's not a textbook case, Marie. He wasn't born with a mental impairment, he's the result of what he suffered, and somewhere inside, there's still that little boy who craved love.'

'But what about the boys' suffering when their mother died?' asked Marie.

'He knows people can overcome that kind of hurt. He did, after all. He might even believe that he is helping them to achieve greater inner strength through suffering and loss.' Laura took a breath. 'What I meant was, he couldn't *physically* injure another child. Which means, if my theory is correct, that Ryan and Miles are relatively safe.'

'But why James? He's been almost a shadow all along. *Jackman* has done more for the children than James.' Marie paused. 'Oh, of course.'

Laura nodded. 'If Alistair is killing with the aim of restoring justice, then James is the perfect candidate. He's never been there for his boys in their hour of need. He puts work before his children. He is therefore guilty of neglect.' She puffed out her cheeks.

'Once again, Alistair is prosecutor, judge, jury and executioner.' Marie groaned. 'But where is he? Where has he taken James?'

'That's the big problem. I don't think James has much time left. We heard that recording. Alistair has a short fuse and his anger is escalating. One wrong word from James, and that would be the end of him.'

Marie sighed. 'Oh, those poor children.'

'And poor Jackman,' Laura said. 'The task of finding this killer is resting squarely on his shoulders.'

'You really like him, don't you?' Marie had blurted this out before she could stop herself.

Laura smiled almost apologetically. ''Fraid so.'

Marie grinned broadly. 'I think that's the best thing I've heard in years.'

Laura looked at her through her eyelashes. 'I'm not treading on your toes, then?'

Marie snorted. 'Me? No way! He's my boss, my friend, and I'd lay down my life for him, but anything more . . . no, Laura. The field is clear.'

Laura shook her head. 'Not exactly. I don't think I'm the only one who cares about him.'

Marie straightened up. 'Excuse me? I can't have this! Something going on I don't know about. Who?'

'Ella Jarvis,' Laura said. 'I was watching her when we went to talk to the boys.'

'Really? Well, all I can say is I happen to be pretty good at people watching myself, and I'm dead certain Jackman feels the same about you. So I'd go for it, if I were you.'

Before Laura could answer, Jackman's desk phone rang.

'DI Jackman's extension, DS Evans here. Can I help you?'

Orac sounded almost excited. 'He asked for a trace on properties purchased by Ashcroft, possibly under another name. I've discovered a small firm of solicitors that he's used, and found out that he has recently taken a long-term lease on a place. The solicitor wouldn't give me any details, other than a rather handy email address for his client. I've accessed his in-box and found several documents regarding the lease. And the rest, as they say, is history. I have the address of the rented property right here.'

Thanking Orac profusely, Marie scribbled down the address. 'Sorry, Laura, we have a possible location for Ashcroft. I've got to get some men out there.'

She ran from the office, calling for Robbie and Max. 'Get uniform! And we might need a firearms unit. We may have just found Ashcroft, and we know he has a gun. So get out there, fast!'

'And you, Sarge?'

'I'll liaise from here. Just keep me in the loop, all the time, okay?'

Next, she ran upstairs to the superintendent, who immediately authorised the use of firearms officers.

'Where is this place?' Ruth asked.

'A small farmhouse, off the road to somewhere called Chapel Rise. I've just Googled it. It's secluded and pretty remote.'

'He'll hear us coming.' Ruth's face formed lines of worry. 'Nowhere to hide out there.'

'I've requested softly, softly. No blue and twos. We can't do any more than that.' Marie looked at the superintendent. 'Should we tell Jackman?'

'Not immediately. He's doing his best to hold his family together. We'll ring when we know whether this place really is Ashcroft's bolthole.'

'*And* whether his brother is there,' added Marie, leaving out the dead or alive part.

Back in the CID room, Laura asked her why she hadn't gone with the others.

Marie paused. 'Because I don't think he's there. I'm sure it's his temporary home, but — don't ask me why — I just think he won't dirty his own backyard.'

Marie's mobile rang — Jackman.

'How are things?' she asked.

'As grim as you'd expect. But I'm coming back shortly. There's very little I can do from here, and there are several officers with the family.'

Marie understood that. 'Okay, we'll see you soon. And drive carefully.'

As she ended the call, she saw Laura's face. 'He's on his way back, and before you ask, he sounds like shit.'

'Was that the boss?' Gary approached, his face drawn with anxiety.

'He'll be back soon. Gary? What's the story about James? What do we actually know?'

'As far as I can gather, James was working from home in the morning, and he left around lunchtime to go for a meeting. At two thirty his secretary phoned to see if there was a problem, as he hadn't arrived. He never did.' Gary pulled a face. 'His phone was switched off, something he never does. Jackman's father drove the route to his office, just to see if he'd broken down or had an accident, but zilch.'

'Did they check Rainham Lodge?' Marie asked.

Gary nodded. 'Jackman got a crew out there straightaway, but he wasn't there.'

'So he's not been missing for long, has he? Ashcroft likes his dramatic settings, as we know. He likes to stage his murder scenes carefully. It isn't his style to capture his victim and then just kill him. He would need his subject to be fully aware of what was happening and what the charges against them were, don't you think?' Marie turned to Laura.

Laura nodded. 'He needs them to be aware of how powerful he is, and to admit to their failures, how they have failed their loved ones. He wants them to admit that his accusations are justified.'

'So James could still be alive?' Gary looked into space, then jumped at the sound of Marie's mobile.

Robbie sounded hyped up. 'It's his place alright, Sarge. But he's not here. The firearms unit went in first, but there

264

was no sign of anything untoward. No one has been held here. It's neat and tidy, nothing out of place. There's no gun either, or a motorcycle, although there are bike tyre tracks outside the property.'

'How about a car?'

'One vehicle, a Nissan, around the back.'

'Okay, Rob, seal it up. I'm going to need every scrap of paperwork, every document, every receipt, every letter, anything to get a handle on where his real home is, or what he's planning. And, Robbie, I want several uniforms there round the clock, just in case he comes back.'

'So you were right.' Laura looked impressed. 'Nice one.'

Marie walked over to a big map of the area pinned to the wall, and looked at the position of Ashcroft's rented farmhouse. It was secluded alright, ten minutes' drive from several main roads. So where was he now? And how had he managed to kidnap James? If indeed that was what had happened. She looked around. 'Laura?'

Laura hurried over.

'Any chance that James has had some kind of "episode?" You know, been overcome with grief, and just taken himself off for a while?'

'Possibly, if it all got too much for him. It does sound like they are under a kind of house arrest at the stables, doesn't it? He might have needed some time out.'

'And turn off your phone? When you have little children and a whole family under threat?' Gary interrupted. 'I doubt it.'

'If he's in turmoil, he might. He wouldn't necessarily be thinking straight,' Laura said.

'We're thinking it's Ashcroft because we are waiting for his next move, but what if James has just cracked?' Marie mused. 'Anyway, we still need to find him, no matter why he disappeared.'

They waited for what seemed like an eternity, unsure of what to do next. Then one of the desk phones rang. Gary answered it.

'Traffic have picked up James's Toyota on a link road to the Lincoln Avenue. It was parked in a layby, undamaged and locked.'

'When was this?' The sound of Jackman's voice made them all turn round.

'A few minutes ago, sir, and the officer reckons it's been there for a while. Cold engine.' Gary put the receiver back.

'CCTV on that stretch?' Jackman barked.

'Only at the town intersection on the main road, and he didn't show up there. If he turned in from one of the side roads there are no cameras for miles.' Gary looked at the scribbled memo. 'However, an attendant in the petrol station close to the layby did notice a Toyota pull up to help another motorist who had broken down. The description fits James.'

'They *must* have CCTV. It's a bloody garage, isn't it?' Jackman sounded edgy.

'Uniform are looking at it now, sir. They'll report in if they find anything.'

'Looks like that's how Ashcroft caught him. The old breakdown trick,' Marie murmured. 'But, sir, we need to fill you in on one development that happened while you were out.' She told him about the rented farmhouse.

Jackman nodded. 'So, we've prevented him from returning to his lair. That's good. But where the hell is he now?'

In the ensuing silence, Gary tactfully went off to make everyone a hot drink.

Jackman went into his office, and Laura followed. Marie was about to join them but thought better of it. It was the worst of times, but she hoped that Jackman and Laura would get a chance for some happiness when all this was over. But what state were any of the Jackman family going to be in when the final curtain came down on this terrible case?

'Sarge?' Gary hurried back into the room. 'Uniform have just confirmed that the man on the garage CCTV, the one that James was assisting, fits the description of Alistair Ashcroft. I'm just going to break it to the boss.'

Marie felt her heart sink. Okay, they had already decided that that was what had happened, but the positive confirmation made it real. She needed to think, and fast! She tried to imagine what she would do if she were Alistair Ashcroft. Where would she take James?

She sank down in her chair and closed her eyes. *If I were Alistair Ashcroft . . .*

* * *

Alistair Ashcroft looked thoughtfully at his victim, his prisoner on remand. The culprit, in custody, pending trial.

Alistair Ashcroft had chosen DI Rowan Jackman to be his adversary and he had found him to be a worthy opponent.

He looked at the brother.

He would never have chosen *this* man for anything. What he was doing to his sons was beneath contempt. He wondered what on earth the dear departed Sarah had seen in him. Ah, Sarah! He smiled to himself. She had been far stronger than he'd expected, and had shown great courage. Few knew it, but she'd suffered from a morbid fear of crowds and high buildings. Ever since they were children, both she and her friend had avoided going to big cities. It had been fitting that they should end their lives in a place that terrified them. He saw again her face when she made her final leap to oblivion. He hoped never to forget it.

James wasn't a pretty sight. He was slumped in a chair, his ties preventing him from sliding off. A trickle of saliva dribbled from the corner of his mouth and made a dark stain on his pale blue shirt. It wouldn't be long before he woke up, and then Alistair could proceed.

He stood up and stretched. Certain of not being discovered, he was in no hurry. He had a few small adjustments to make to the scene, and then the trial would begin.

CHAPTER THIRTY-ONE

What if? Marie's eyes snapped open, she hurriedly pushed back her chair and made for Jackman's office.

'Sir? This might be nothing, but I've had a thought.'

Jackman and Laura looked up expectantly.

'I don't want to send uniform barging in, all guns blazing, but what if Ashcroft has taken James home? To Rainham Lodge?'

Jackman frowned. 'It *is* empty, isn't it? Uniform checked it earlier, and no one was there, but he could have waited for them to leave, then gone inside. You could be right, Marie! And if Ashcroft is holding my brother there, he'll kill him if we race in mob-handed. I want to check this out myself. James's only chance is for me to try to talk to Ashcroft.'

Laura looked horrified. 'You can't reason with a psychopath, Jackman. He plays by his own rules.'

'But I could buy us some time. Marie would be waiting in the wings, and if he is there, we bring in the heavy mob, but under the cover of darkness, on foot and silently.'

'It's too dangerous.' Laura looked ready to throw herself against the door to prevent him leaving.

'We have to go, Laura.' Jackman reached out and Marie noticed him touch her arm gently.

'We will be back. I promise you,' Jackman said.

'Don't make promises you can't keep.' Laura's voice trembled.

'We *will* be back.' The words rang out.

Wishing she felt half as confident, Marie nodded.

Outside the office, Jackman pulled her to one side. 'I know this is not correct procedure, in fact far from it, but I can't risk something happening to James because I've sent an armed squad in there. You know as well as I do, these things don't always go to plan.'

He looked distraught, and Marie felt for him. 'What if I tell Robbie, and get him and an armed unit to tail us at a distance? If he hears from me, then he can send them in, as you said before, softly, softly?' She looked him in the eyes, 'And don't try to keep me out of this, I know the risks, but I happen to agree with you. Let's do it your way.'

'Okay, then talk to Rob and let's get out of here. The more I think about it, the more I think you're right.' Jackman was about to throw her the car keys, but she held up her hand.

'You drive and I'll follow on my bike. You say Ashcroft is a biker, so if he decides to make a run for it, I'll stand a much better chance of keeping him in sight if I'm on two wheels.'

'Good point. You follow me. We'll park up before we get to Water Lane and approach Rainham Lodge on foot, okay?'

She gave him a thumbs up, spoke to Robbie, then hurried to the locker room to get her gear.

* * *

The Landrover pulled over and disappeared into the gloom as the lights went off.

She cut her engine and coasted in behind it. She pushed off her helmet and hung it over the handlebars. Rainham Lodge was a short walk away, over a bridge and then up to the house itself.

'The front of the house is in darkness,' whispered Jackman, 'but I can see a glimmer of light coming from an upstairs window.'

Marie scanned the dark shadowy driveway. 'I can't see a car, can you?'

'No, but he's had plenty of time to hide it. Or he could have brought James here, then taken the car back and returned on his motorcycle. After all, if he kills James, he won't be needing to chauffeur him anywhere afterwards, will he? Then he can make that fast getaway you were talking about. People might notice the make of a car, but very few can identify a motorcycle.' Jackman fished in his pocket. 'Luckily I always carry a spare key, just in case Ella or the boys need me.'

They crept closer, keeping to the damp grass to one side of the gravel drive. They waited outside the front door and listened. Marie could hear nothing, but she was certain they were not alone. She felt a tremor of nervous excitement. Get this right, and Alistair Ashcroft would soon be in custody. Get it wrong . . .

Jackman slipped the key into the lock and turned it.

Still no sound. They eased themselves into the hallway and Jackman closed the door behind them with a faint click. He led the way to the bottom of the stairs. He had been right, there was a dim light coming from the far end of the landing.

'That's the boys' playroom,' Jackman whispered. 'Some of the stairs squeak. Keep to the right hand side.'

They inched their way up the staircase and into the corridor leading to the playroom. Now they could hear voices.

Jackman held out his arm and brought them to a halt. He and Marie stood shoulder to shoulder and listened.

Initially, Marie thought there were three people in the room. Then she realised that two of them were Alistair, his voice changing. One moment he sounded strong and commanding, and the next, feeble and whining. *This is not good*, she thought. Laura had said he could be unravelling. It was as if she were listening to a ventriloquist and his dummy.

Jackman's jaw set firm. 'He's losing it, he could kill James at any moment. Marie, go back outside and call Robbie. Get that squad down here. I'll buy us as much time as I can.'

The last thing Marie wanted to do was leave him with this madman. But they had agreed. She touched his arm, nodded, and slipped back down the corridor.

It seemed to take forever to get downstairs and then outside, where thankfully, her phone had a good signal.

Robbie answered instantly.

'He's here at Rainham Lodge, and he's got James. We need armed back up as arranged, silent approach and the last part on foot. Understand?'

'We're not far away, Marie. Just stay outside and guide us in, okay?' She could hear the tremor in his voice. He was scared for her.

'Sorry, Robbie. I need to be with Jackman.' She ended the call.

Before going back inside, she ran to where she had left her bike, and pushed it to a spot much closer to the house. She wanted Harvey within easy reach. She concealed the motorbike behind a large bushy laurel and then ran back to the front door. With a glance to check it couldn't be seen, she took a deep breath and slipped back into the house.

* * *

Jackman's blood ran cold. His brother's terrified voice was shrill through the closed door. Self-assured, dogmatic and sometimes patronising, James now sounded like a frightened animal.

He had no strategy worked out but Jackman recalled Laura's words. There would be no reasoning with this man.

So what the hell! He burst through the door and came to a halt in a makeshift schoolroom.

His brother cried out, 'Rowan!' A hefty slap across his face made his head slew sideways.

Jackman made out two desks. He had bought them himself, ready for when the boys started doing homework.

A brief glance revealed several chairs, all facing the front of the room, and Alistair had painted a blackboard on the plain wall. On it, in white marker pen, were the words, "I must not neglect my children."

Ashcroft stood on an upturned crate that the boys had used to store toys in. James was tied to a chair within striking distance of Ashcroft, "taking class."

'Leave him alone! Alistair! You have to stop this!'

His unexpected entry had made Ashcroft angry. 'How dare you! This is a private court, and this man is charged with neglecting his children.'

'And I'm his defence.'

Ashcroft gave him a look of unalloyed malice. Then — suddenly — he smiled. 'Ah, I see. In that case, please take a seat.' Ashcroft now seemed amused. 'I have to hand it to you, Inspector. I never thought you'd guess where I'd bring your brother. You are remarkably astute.'

Jackman remained where he was. 'Alistair, please. I'm going to ask you to let my brother go. You can take me instead.'

Out of the corner of his eye, he saw James's eyes widen.

'I mean it. You and me, Alistair. You don't need James. You took away the woman he loved with all his heart. Isn't that enough punishment? *You* made him like this. He loves his sons. He's grieving for his dead wife, and you are to blame, not him.'

'Do the children understand that they are being ignored and left alone at night with only a nanny because Daddy misses Mummy? Do they understand when nightmares claim them, and their father is not there to comfort them because he's working late? How do they feel when he misses their big football match or their presentation at school? They still hurt, Jackman. They still feel it in here!' Ashcroft thumped his chest. 'To be ignored, made to feel like you don't exist, that you are nothing! It's soul-destroying! No man should make his sons suffer like that. You say I don't need James, but I do. Sorry, Jackman, it's your brother that needs to pay, not you.'

The gun was stuck in the waistband of Ashcroft's trousers. With no way of getting hold of it, all Jackman could do was try and talk him down.

'Why do you want to destroy my family?'

Ashcroft laughed. 'What? It was *your* Sarah that destroyed *my* family! This trial is simply to right a wrong. I don't want to hurt your family. I don't care one iota about your family. I'm just here to see justice done.'

'The man who killed Lyndsay was the one who destroyed your family, not Sarah.' Jackman tried to think. *Come on, Jackman, reason isn't going to work.* Maybe he should try to provoke some physical reaction from Ashcroft. He was pretty sure he could get the upper hand in a fight, so long as the gun didn't come into play. Time to up the ante.

'Do you know what I think?'

Ashcroft narrowed his eyes.

'I think you just love hurting, no, *torturing,* and killing people. But you need an excuse, something oh so high and mighty, some worthy cause. Otherwise you'd be just like any other low-life scumbag with half a brain, roaming the streets with a knife in his hand!'

The eyes were mere slits now, and Jackman knew Ashcroft was fighting to control his rage.

'Think what you want. But you're wrong. I am not like anyone you've ever dealt with, Jackman.'

'No, Alistair. You're just another damaged kid whose mind couldn't take it. Just another psychopath to be hunted down and locked away. You're nothing special, Alistair.' He shrugged. 'Sorry.'

Ashcroft clenched and unclenched his hands, his knuckles white. 'You'll regret this, Jackman. I'll make you eat those words.'

He snatched the gun from his waistband, snapped back the safety catch, pointed it at James's head, and . . .

Ashcroft screamed. The sound of the gun echoed around the room.

It took Jackman a moment to realise that Marie had burst into the room and flung a cast-iron frying pan at Ashcroft. It had hit his arm, knocking the gun from his hand, and the shot had gone wild.

Before Jackman could grab him, Ashcroft snatched up the gun and lunged at Marie. Jackman called upon his rugby days, and hurled himself across the room in a flying tackle. His shoulder made contact with Ashcroft, making him stumble, but as he did, Ashcroft caught Marie a punishing blow to the ribs. Jackman heard her groan and go down.

Then the gun swung round towards him again, this time at point blank range.

A second deafening shot rang out, but Marie had managed to jam her boot hard against Ashcroft's calf, dead legging him, and Jackman felt the shot tear into his upper arm.

'Sir! Jackman!' Marie flung herself down alongside him, gasping for air.

'It's okay, it's okay, Just my arm. You saved my li—' He looked around frantically. 'Where is he?'

Marie didn't answer. Instead, she hauled herself up and staggered through the door. 'Phone Robbie!' she yelled back. 'I'm going after Ashcroft.'

* * *

Outside, she heard the roar of an engine and paused to listen. 'Yamaha R6,' she whispered to herself. 'Fast, but it all comes down to who is riding it.' Clasping her bruised ribs she sprinted to where Harvey waited for her. She pulled on her helmet and in seconds was heading for the only way out, over the bridge.

As she banked sharply into the lane, Ashcroft's rear light now in her sights, she saw a stream of fast-moving cars heading towards her. 'The cavalry,' she muttered. 'Too late for this particular race.'

Ashcroft blasted past the police cars, with Marie right on his tail. For a fleeting second, as she flew past, she thought she saw Robbie Melton's ghost-white face. 'Sorry, Robbie,' she murmured.

She knew the road they were on, hopefully better than Ashcroft did. It had a long straight stretch that ran for miles, and then it got tricky as it headed out over the fens. There, the road began to wind in a series of sharp, tight bends. They were scary in daylight. At night, well, if you overcooked a corner on a fast bike, heaven help you.

Ashcroft was riding well, but she detected a slight hesitation when he took the corners. The problem was, where was he going? Should she let him reach his destination, or try to cut short this hair-raising ride? After a mile at high speed, she knew she was the better rider, but how to use it to her advantage? Marie tried to visualise the road. She knew it widened just ahead and then gave way to a gentle bend, followed by a narrow stretch with a wall one side and a dyke the other.

She drew in a breath and closed the gap between them. The Yamaha was handling well, but she knew it was no match for Harvey, so long as she kept a cool head.

Offering up a prayer to her Bill, asking him to keep her safe, she eased down on the accelerator. She tailgated him down the wide stretch of road, then, just as he leaned into the corner, she pulled out and cut in, braking as she did. Her rear wheel nicked his front tyre, and Ashcroft spun out of control.

Marie went into a controlled skid, vaguely aware that his bike was spinning like a top on the tarmac. Then it crashed into the wall.

As it did so, a piece of fairing tore off and flew across the road like a javelin, jamming into Harvey's front forks and sending her beloved bike into a cartwheel.

It happened in slow-motion. Air all around her. Flying . . . then she hit the ground, and skidded on her leathers to where Ashcroft was trying to extricate himself from the wreckage of his bike.

At the same moment, each of them fastened their eyes on the gun lying in the road. They were both injured. Marie

275

wondered who was stronger. What did they call her in the mess room? The Amazon. Damned bloody right!

She knew her leg was bad, but she dragged herself towards the gun, which seemed to shimmer on the asphalt. She saw Ashcroft, too, blood flowing from an arm that hung limp against his side. But he was on his feet. He leaned forward to grab the weapon. Marie summoned her strength and used her good leg to kick it out of reach.

She heard the splash as it landed in the dyke.

Now he was standing over her, his face a mask of pain and rage.

'This isn't over,' he gasped. 'I'll let you live, but only to give Jackman my message. Tell him I'm a patient man, but he would do well to keep looking over his shoulder. One day I'll come for him.'

Ashcroft drew back his foot, and kicked her bruised ribs hard. Just before she lost consciousness, she saw his dark shadow move away. He meant what he said.

He would be back.

EPILOGUE

TWO MONTHS LATER

Robbie looked around his home and liked what he saw. Now he could really call it a home. It had taken Max about ten minutes to tell him what it needed. Then he brought in Rosie to add her thoughts, and in another two weeks the transformation was complete.

The thing he liked best was the far wall of the big open-plan living area, in front of his modern dining table and chairs. Max had hung a painting of a beautiful harbour scene, with high cliffs, a calm sea and colourful boats.

Along with new drapes, bright cushions, and some strategically placed, architecturally dramatic potted plants in striking containers, his minimalistic, sterile "hotel room" had taken on real character.

He glanced at the massive station clock on the kitchen wall, another new acquisition. His friends would be arriving any minute. The team had wanted to celebrate Max and Rosie's recent marriage, but because of what had happened, no one felt it appropriate to go and get hammered down at the local. So he had suggested coming to his apartment for an informal get together.

Robbie took two bottles of champagne from the fridge, and thought back over the last two months. It had been a strange time, full of intense emotion and sadness. Alistair Ashcroft had disappeared into thin air, but he'd cast a dark shadow over all their lives, and Robbie suspected that shadow would never go until Ashcroft was found and incarcerated.

Ashcroft's evil presence had had the effect of bringing to the fore those things that really mattered in their lives, and for the first time in a long while, Robbie had seen things clearly. He now knew that he had put Marie Evans, like Stella North, on a pedestal and worshipped her. Now she was simply a dear friend and colleague. Having realised this, he had been able to move on with his life. He and Ella Jarvis had started dating. In just a short time of getting to know each other, she had confessed to having felt the same way about Jackman. She had been vulnerable, and had looked to Jackman to be her tower of strength, but it had never been love.

Robbie wasn't quite sure if it was love now, but whatever it was, they were happy together. Ella had decided that she would stay on with the children until Rainham Lodge was sold. James had accepted his parents' offer for them to move back into the family home where the boys would have their granny and grandpa, and their new pony, and hopefully a better life. Then Ella would be able to move on, and the direction she had decided to take, was back into forensics, and Rory had welcomed the decision with open arms. Apparently the biggest surprise to her had been the radical change in James Jackman. Hearing his brother offer to take his place at the hands of the killer had caused a profound change in him, and as soon as he was recovered, he took extended leave of absence from the business and became a father again.

Marie and Gary arrived first. She still walked with a limp, but the surgeons had given a good prognosis, and she was already scouring the Internet for a successor for the irreparably damaged Harvey.

'Wow!' she exclaimed. 'Robbie Melton! What a fantastic place!'

Robbie flushed with pride. Stella's "hotel room" was no more.

Marie and Gary were soon followed by Rory and the others, and by the time Robbie had uncovered the buffet food and handed out the drinks, the flat was full of the sound of chattering voices. Robbie stood back for a moment, and watched them. They were all relaxed and enjoying the celebration, but something had changed in them. Their encounter with Ashcroft had left a scar. No one laughed quite as loudly or for as long as they used to, the banter was less animated, smiles faded quicker. Ashcroft moved among them, the uninvited guest who spoiled the feast.

Robbie turned to his boss. 'Jackman, sir? Like to propose a toast?'

Jackman, who had been sitting close to Laura on the couch, stood up and raised his glass. 'First, thank you, Robbie, for allowing us into your beautiful home! And it's come as a bit of a surprise, I must say. We all thought you lived in some bedsit, tucked away down a Saltern backstreet, not this magnificent apartment!'

Everyone laughed. Robbie smiled and nodded at Max and Rosie.

'Now, for the reason why we are all here. We have come to wish our dear friends, Max and Rosie, a wonderful life together, with their little one. May the path you walk together, even if sometimes it's steep or rough, have a wonderful view from the top! To Rosie and Max!'

They all raised their glasses and the room rang with cheers.

When the noise died down, Jackman remained standing. 'If I may,' he looked around, 'I'm not going to spoil this lovely evening that Robbie has kindly arranged, but I can think of no better time, as we are all here together, to tell you something that I feel is very important.'

Robbie frowned. This sounded serious, and for a moment he was scared that Jackman was going to publicly acknowledge the elephant in the room. If anything was going to spoil the celebration, surely it would be that.

'As you all know, if the jungle drums are working as efficiently as usual, Laura and I have been going out together for almost two months.'

'And about bloody time!' Marie called out.

'Hear, hear!' echoed Rory. 'You're far too good-looking to be a bachelor!'

Everyone laughed, and Jackman pulled a face at them.

'The thing is, this should be the happiest of times, but I haven't allowed it to be, and for that, I want to apologise to Laura.' He gently laid his hand on her shoulder. 'And I want to promise her something. In fact, I want to promise you *all* something.'

Robbie watched, and having felt anxious about what his boss might be about to say, now felt a kind of excited anticipation.

'The fact is, I have been eaten up with guilt about the way I handled our last case. I failed to bring an evil man to justice, but even worse than that, I've allowed that failure to blight everything from that moment on. It's been like a cancer eating away, and I've seen the way you have all been caught up in this terrible negativity. But no more.'

There were murmurs of dissent. No one blamed Jackman for what had happened.

'No, listen, please. Tonight I'm going to tell you all that Alistair Ashcroft is no longer going to creep amongst us like a dark unspoken-of wraith. He will no longer poison our minds with his insidious whisperings. Every time we choose to mention him in hushed tones, he wins.' His eyes became hard. 'And that man is *not* going to win! Tonight we put him back into the category where he belongs. He's a twisted and cold-blooded killer, a psychopath that has no place roaming free, and we, my friends, are going to put him away!'

Electricity coursed through the room. Backs straightened and eyes lit up.

'This is my promise. I will not let my feelings, or my guilt, affect any of you again. We're going to become the fully functioning dynamic team we always have been. We're going to be first-class detectives again, and this will give us our lives back. Oh, he hurt us, hell yes. But he won't do it again. We won't sit and wait for our patient killer to decide what happens next . . . *we* go after him, and we take him down.'

It was as if someone had injected something powerful into the room. The apathy that had clung to them seemed to fall away, and a new resolution was born.

Marie raised her glass. 'We are with you, sir! All the way! To Jackman and catching that sick psycho!'

For the second time, a cheer went up.

From that moment, the party started, and Robbie relaxed. With a contented sigh, he sat down next to Ella and took her hand. She smiled at him. 'You did well, kid. This evening was just what we needed.'

Robbie sipped his champagne. There was more than just a marriage to celebrate tonight, there was a new beginning for them all. Okay, Alistair Ashcroft was still out there somewhere, but now, instead of feeling like he was hunting them, the tables had been turned, and once again, they were the hunters.

He raised his glass and gave a silent toast. "We're coming for you, Ashcroft. Just you wait and see."

THE END

In the UK, the Samaritans can be contacted on 116 123. In the US, the National Suicide Prevention Lifeline is 1-800-273-8255. In Australia, the Crisis Support Service Lifeline is 13 11 14. Other international suicide help-lines can be found at www. befrienders.org